# PRIESTESS RISING

## Book Three Of The Priestess Chronicles

## JULIEN DUBROW

Published By Julien DuBrow Ventures

San Francisco, California

Published By Julien DuBrow Ventures: www.JulienDuBrow.com

Book Cover Images by Helena Nelson-Reed: www.fine-art-studios.com

Map by Brenden Hickey: rednecter@hotmail.com

ISBN: 978-1-7352164-2-3

First Printing, 2018
Second Printing, 2020

For my beloved, Martin.

*"The air is filled with the fragrance of Mandrakes*
*And at our doors, rich gifts of every kind,*
*New and old, my love,*
*I have hidden away for you."*

Song of Songs, ca. 3rd c. B.C.E.

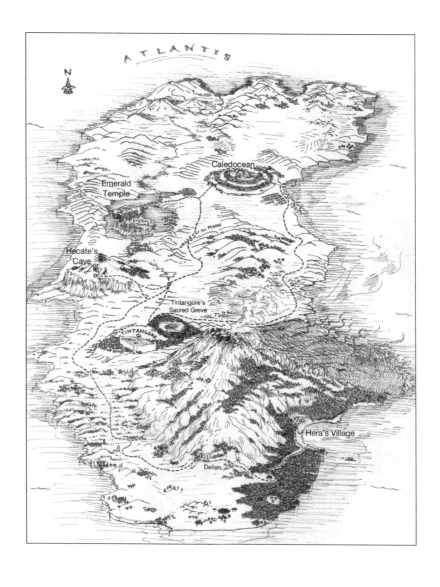

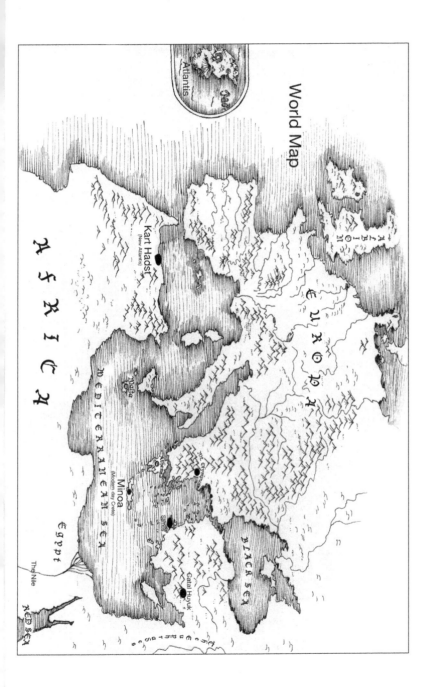

World Map

Atlantis

Kart Hadst
(New Atlantis)

AFRICA

EUROPA

MEDITERRANEAN SEA

Malta

Minoa
(Modern day Crete)

Egypt

The Nile

RED SEA

BLACK SEA

Çatal Hüyük

# HERA SPEAKS

I CAN STILL REMEMBER how it felt to be mortal.

Before I became a Goddess, when I was Hera, High Priestess and Queen, and just a woman, I was part of the cycles of life. I sensed myself caught up, in a perfect forward movement, with all things. I was not afraid, as I am now, of the passage of time for I knew I was part of something eternal that was carrying me along its ascending, spiral path.

I grieve the loss of my mortality, as millennia pass me by, and I become no more than a misunderstood myth. I will press on with my tale for the truth that existed before you gave the divine a gender, before you made Gods and Goddesses cannot be hidden any longer.

I have told you how I awakened to my mystical gift, controlling the element of fire, and how I became High Priestess of the Emerald Temple and married Zeus for the good of Atlantis. After that, I put into motion a political plan to keep those I loved, safe. My daughter, Ilithyia, was raised at the Emerald Temple, under Artemis's guardianship, and I bore Zeus a son, Ares, whom I gave into the care of his father and family. Then, I did my duty, strengthening myself to stand up

1

against the enemies of the Sacred Feminine. The call of my heart, once wild, once fierce, began to elude me as the years became a procession of obligations. And so, we come again to my story.

Now, I will take you into the mystery of the temple and expose the sacred dragon. I will show you the enduring face of the Sacred Feminine, long abandoned, but not forgotten. And in the telling, may the priestess within you remember…

Come, let us begin.

# PART ONE
## THE SPIRAL PATH

# CHAPTER ONE

Danger.

My chest tightened, and I shut my eyes, using my inner sight. I caught a glimpse of a woman's face, amber eyes reflecting a flame and then the sharp flash of a blade in her hand as her lips formed the words, *Dragon's Blood*. I breathed in hard and sharp, as I heard the woman speak my name: *Hera*.

Darkness rushed toward me then, and my body throbbed with fear. Opening my eyes, I shuddered, backing away from the temple door. Beneath my ceremonial robes, Medusa, my faithful serpent, coiled around my arm as if ready to strike at something just beyond me.

Lifting the torch above my head, I spun around, turning back toward the empty sanctuary. I had just finished anointing my daughter, Ilithyia, in preparation for her ordination as a priestess into the Emerald Temple and the room was still filled with the power of the act. The flames from my torch cast their jagged light across the space, and the strong sense of an intruder pressed upon me again. It was an impossible notion, for this chamber was protected from the outside by two other rooms, and their doors could only be opened from within. The only direct way into the sanctuary was through an entrance to the rear, one hidden to all but me and the few priestesses I'd initiated into the secret. Demeter, the eldest and most revered among us, and Athena, who led our warriors, were the only other women on the island who knew the way in. They had both just escorted Ilithyia and her guardian, Artemis, out of the chamber. The door had locked from the inside, behind them.

I turned around, holding the torch above my head. I did not feel the presence of another in the room. The sanctum had not been breached. Taking a deep breath to steady my intuitive senses, I reached for the handle on the door. Again, the violent flood of images accosted me, and I staggered backward. When I was young, I might have thought myself ill or delirious or misreading the mystic vision, but that time had long passed. I was a woman in my full power; I would not see such a thing without reason.

I backed away from the door and crossed the room. At the altar, I reached for the sacred blade, with its double dragons carved into the hilt, and pushed my way through the hidden doors at the rear of the chamber. I spiraled down the long staircase to the tunnels below hurrying through the long, dimly lit passage that would take me back to my chambers. Images of Ilithyia rose in my mind as I went. My daughter had been so radiant and strong during the ordination, yet as I had anointed her, I was keenly aware that I hardly knew her. While I spent most of my time in the capital city of Caledocean, Ilithyia had been raised on this island, by Artemis and my priestesses. I had sent her away to protect her, but now, as I reached the end of the tunnel and rushed up the stairs, a terrible sense of dread and failure overtook me. My body trembled as the intuitive awareness became clear: *Someone has my daughter!* I could feel the truth of it just beneath my skin as if an invisible cord that bound me to Ilithyia was being stretched very thin.

My breath was labored as I wound my way up to the stone door that hid my private chamber. When I emerged, I was in the High Priestess' sanctuary, my place of prayer, back in the main building, on the temple grounds. Women stood guard outside the entrance.

I burst through the doors, into the courtyard, shoving the torch, which trailed a long tail of black smoke, into one of their hands.

"My daughter," I cried as I tore off my ceremonial vestments, dropping them at their feet.

They stepped back in surprise. Erin, the leader, gripped the hilt of her blade.

"Reverence," she said, signaling to the sentries outside the main hall, "What is it? What's happening?"

"There's an intruder!" I cried, my voice shaking with emotion. "She has my daughter. She's taken Ilithyia!"

Erin reached out her hand to steady me as women gathered around us.

"Reverence," she said in a low breath, "Lady, this is impossible. Your daughter is with Athena—"

"No!" I shook my head, looking Erin squarely in the eyes. "I fear that Athena is taken as well."

Erin's eyes narrowed. "Athena? How? Who?" she started, but I shook my head.

"I don't know how, but it's a woman, and she's at the temple. I can… *feel* her." I said, turning toward the hill upon which the sanctuary was built.

7

As I pointed to the gold domed temple, the women around me gasped. There was an unmistakable flame blazing at the entrance for all to see. I breathed in sharply. To light a fire in such a place was sacrilege, a blatant sign of disrespect, and I knew it was aimed at me.

"Athena's up there," I said, "and so is Demeter and Artemis and—"

I could not finish. Every person I cared about was now in the hands of an enemy, I was sure of it. It was someone who knew that the only way to the holy oil of immortality, the Dragon, was through me. The only way to me, of course, was through my daughter and my most beloved priestesses. The gravity of the moment hit me full force, stilling my mind as a quiet fury filled my body, lending me the strength I needed.

Erin snapped orders to a guard sending the woman running for Athena's warriors. She pulled out her blade and turned to me.

"We should wait until they've gathered," she began, but I had already moved past her toward the spiral path to the sanctuary.

Erin and the remaining guards followed close behind as I began to run up the hill pulling up sharply as we heard the sound of footsteps running toward us. Suddenly, Athena appeared, out of breath, and holding her side. Her robes were torn and bloodied, her hair loosened from its bonds. The women pressed in on her to hold her up, but she pushed them away.

"Protect the High Priestess!" she commanded. "Take her back to her rooms!"

"No!" I cried. "Athena, what's happening? Ilithyia, Artemis—"

She shook her head, trying hard to catch her breath.

"Artemis and Demeter are bound together and gagged at the entrance to the sanctuary, but they're unharmed. The assailant doesn't seem to care for unnecessary bloodshed."

"The assailant?"

She looked at me then Erin and grimaced. "There's a woman, dressed in initiates robes, but she's no priestess! She has sharp fighting skills I'll tell you that. She surprised us as we stepped out into the light. I would have taken her down, but, she took Ilithyia," she stopped there bowing her head, shoulders sagging.

"Yes," I said. "She has my daughter."

Athena's head snapped up. Her voice came low and desperate.

"I commanded Ilithyia to run, but she wouldn't go. The girl is as stubborn as you are! She tried to fight! I think she was protecting Artemis, but as soon as Ilithyia moved in the woman took her, and then what could any of us do?"

Athena shook her head slowly.

"The woman had me bind Demeter and Artemis then she made us wait for you to come out of the temple, but when you didn't, she had me light the fire and let me go."

Athena looked at me then, strain in her eyes. "This is my fault! I placed no guard because I thought the isle impenetrable. I've relied on the mists to protect us because only a handful of the most trusted priestesses know how to lift it. She must have come in with the new initiates. I was foolish!"

"No, Athena," I reached out my hand to steady her. "You've kept us safe all these years against too many enemies. Let go of the blame and set your mind to the task at hand. Come, I need you to meet this threat with wisdom. You must lead your warriors to victory this day!"

"Of course, Reverence," she said, her voice low and fierce. "I will take down this woman you can be certain of that!"

Erin handed her a blade, and Athena took firm hold of the hilt as if drawing strength from it. She looked around herself then, taking full stock of the scene, and shouted orders. Her women took up an arrow-like shape, spears in the front, shields at my side, and then she turned back to me.

"We are the finest warriors in Atlantis," she said as if to reassure me. "You must listen to me now, Reverence. This is no place for you. Let my women protect you—"

"There's only *one* intruder," I said.

"As far as we know," she answered. "What if there are others. The protocol is to protect the High Priestess. And this woman is very skilled, and she has—" she stopped there.

"Ilithyia," I stated. "She has my daughter because that is the only way to get to me."

A commotion stirred below us. I turned to see Athena's troops charging up the hill and a full contingent of priestesses, young and old, pressing up behind them. From where we stood on the hill the entrance to the temple was hidden from view, but I knew that was where the woman waited, with my daughter as her captive.

"Reverence," Athena said again, "Go back with my women so that we can protect you. This woman lit the fire to draw you in. She let me go, knowing full well I'd come back with others. She's manipulating us. Please, go with my women!"

I shook my head and moved toward her. "No. Don't ask me again, Athena. I'm the one this woman wants. Without me, we'll never get Ilithyia back alive."

"You don't know that," she snapped.

I put my hand to her cheek and looked her squarely in

the eyes. She was my first teacher, my guardian, and she had pledged her life to protect me.

"I will not abandon my daughter," I said evenly. "Nothing could make me do so."

Athena stared at me intently. I could see the understanding spread across her face.

"Of course," she said, nodding. "Of course, Reverence."

There was a high-pitched scream from above us. The voice rang out from the other side of the temple, and though we were a full field away, I knew whose it was.

I bolted forward through the women that tried to guard me. I felt a prick of terror as the scream fell away into sudden silence, and I ran with the full force of my limbs toward the temple entrance and my daughter. I heard Athena snap orders, and in a moment, spear-armed women were at my side, but I did not stop until I had topped the hill. The fire and the intruder were in full sight.

The woman was tall and thin, wearing one of our long, white robes. Her back was safely stationed against the sacred tree that grew in the center of the courtyard. She held Ilithyia in front of her, a pointed blade at my daughter's throat. The woman smiled when she saw me.

I heard shouting, and Athena's warrior women moved quickly forming a circle to cut off all chance of escape, but this woman had never intended to leave. I moved toward her, but Athena took firm hold of my arm pulling me away from the other's hearing.

"You can't go to her," she said. "She has no other hostage. Ilithyia is her only assured escape—"

"She doesn't want to escape," I said speaking softly. "She knows she cannot leave this island. The thing she wants is here, in the temple. She has come for the Dragon. She intends to use the oil of immortality."

Athena snapped her head toward the temple then back to me. "So, it really is here," she whispered.

I nodded.

"Draconigena!" The woman's voice rose, strong and clear, above the circle of priestesses that surrounded her. "Keeper of the Dragon's Blood, holy oil of immortality, I command entrance to your temple!"

From the corner of my eye, I saw that my priestesses were arriving. They swarmed up the sanctuary stairs to deliver Demeter and Artemis from their bonds. I took a long breath to steady myself.

As I turned to face the intruder, Athena shook her head, but she stepped forward with me. My body quivered with emotion as my eyes fell on my daughter's face. She stared at me with courage; I knew she had not made it easy for her abductor. Ilithyia looked strong-willed, but her body obviously hurt. She favored one leg, and a thin trail of blood ran from a cut beneath her chin.

"Who are you?" I demanded as I stepped out into the center of the circle.

The woman did not hesitate. "I'm Calypso," she said with obvious pride as if it was a name I should remember. "And you know why I'm here."

I looked at my daughter again. Her hands were bound behind her back, and she winced as Calypso wrenched them upwards. I took a step forward, but Calypso was quick to press the blade into Ilithyia's skin drawing blood. I stopped and held up my hands. Ilithyia clenched her jaw against the pain. I had no doubt Calypso was willing to kill her to get what she wanted, and I could see that my daughter knew it too.

I was in an impossible situation. I couldn't give this woman the oil, or even imply that it was indeed here. All the priestesses were now gathered, watching. I, their High Priestess, who had all but abandoned them for the past decade, had now brought the worst kind of trouble to their shores. Even to bring this woman into the temple would be a breach of my vows, but they couldn't expect me to watch her hurt my daughter. I realized that I no longer knew if I had the hearts of my women, or if they would take matters into their own hands and protect their temple.

"You know why I'm here, Hera. Every one of you knows!" Calypso shouted to the crowd. "Take me into the temple. Give me the oil of immortality or lose your High Priestess's heir!"

She took hold of Ilithyia's hair pulling her to her knees. The warriors raised their spears looking to Athena as the priestesses cried out in outrage.

"The Dragon's Blood is a myth!" Athena cried for all to hear. "We cannot give you what does not exist!"

Calypso responded by again pressing the point of her blade into Ilithyia's white skin until blood showed on the tip. Ilithyia bit down hard on her lip but made no sound.

Anger pushed aside my fear and with it welled a wave of heat I had not felt in many years. Athena must have felt it too for she stepped back away from me.

The element of *fire*!

This ability to channel the flame was my mystic gift. It had marked me so many years ago as the Draconigena, keeper of the holy oil, but I couldn't always trust or control it. I hadn't felt it stir inside me for a very long time and to most of these women here, it was as much of a myth as the holy oil itself.

Again, Calypso made her demand, and again she drew my daughter's blood. This time, Ilithyia cried out, and the horror of it helped focus my mind.

I moved my hands instinctually reaching toward the heat that still glowed from the coals of the fire at Calypso's feet. Deep inside, I opened the door to the wild, untamed feelings I had kept at bay for so long. I let the guilt of giving my daughter to the temple and giving my son, Ares, to his father, Zeus, ravage me. I let the pain of all my failed attempts to protect the divine feminine rise up my spine. The fierce energy of bitterness from all the years I had hid my heart away, raged down my arms toward my palms.

My body shook, and the fire gift had me entirely.

I heard Calypso's voice come once more, very shrill and with command, but I could not make out the words. I was lost in the heat. It swelled with desire, wanting to burst through me. I struggled to hold it in knowing I must not let the flame escape me, or it might take my daughter with it. There had to be another way to end this.

And then the thought struck me, *Medusa*!

I called to my serpent with my inner voice. She moved quickly from her place about my shoulders. I felt her slither against my skin emanating reassurance as I visualized what I needed her to do. Before I could finish, I felt her body slide downward, beneath my robe and drop to the ground at my feet, unnoticed.

"Open the temple!" Calypso cried.

I stepped forward toward the tree and the fire that burned at its base letting the snake slither behind me. My look was hard and cold.

"As Athena has said, I cannot give you what we do not have."

I stepped closer and lifted my hands as I called the fire. There was a loud sound, and then violent heat and flame burst outward in a circle around me. Calypso staggered back but kept the blade at Ilithyia's throat. I pushed hard with my mind, and the flames leaped. All eyes were on me.

Medusa moved quickly. She was a small asp, but wise and ancient. Though I could not see her, I felt the unmistakable rise of power as she laid her body against the tree of life, where Calypso now pressed herself flatter to avoid the heat. No one knew how old the tree really was. It was said that when the thirteenth priestess had discovered the Dragon's Blood and realized the horror it could produce by sealing the soul into the body forever, she'd tried to bury it deep in the ground at the base of the tree. But the oil, in its need to touch and transform, had reached out to the roots and given the white blossoms eternal life. Year after year, through all the seasons, the tree of life stood in full bloom, before our sanctuary. Now, as never before, I could feel its immortal strength reaching out to me, and Medusa, the oil's protectors.

"So, you are indeed the Draconigena!" Calypso said. "If that myth is true then the other must be as well! I want the oil! I want the dragon!"

I pushed against the flames with my heart, and they moved closer to Calypso and Ilithyia.

"You have the gift of fire, Hera, but what will you do with it? You can't frighten me this way, for to scorch me you'll have to send your daughter to the flames as well!" Calypso cried.

Ilithyia's eyes were big and round with fear. She stared at me in shock, and I realized with a sickening feeling that she wasn't sure what I would do. I gave her the slightest nod, trying to reassure her. She looked at me intently, then closed her eyes.

*Good*, I thought. *Don't look, my dearest. This isn't over yet.*

I lifted my arms and raised the flames, my own body burning with the effort, but I had no choice for as I did, Calypso's body responded as I had hoped. The instinctual need to escape the flame pressed her so far back against the tree that it took only a moment for Medusa to take her. There was a sharp, black blur of motion as the snake sprang from the first branch toward Calypso's hand. With a loud shriek, Calypso dropped the knife. Her body flailed against the tree as if seared by flame.

I tried to drop the wall of flames, but they only flickered and dimmed, but it was enough for Athena's women to breach the circle and take Calypso.

I watched, held by in the sway of power, as Artemis untied Ilithyia pulling her into a healing embrace. A scent priestess pulled off the vial of oil she wore about her neck, pouring it on Ilithyia's wounds, while healers placed their hands on Ilithyia's head. The other women, healers, and warriors, farmers and craftswomen—all priestesses—stepped forward, toward me, and the remaining circle of flame.

I watched all of this in my drunken heat, surrounded by the fire. I had done my work, distracted my enemy, but now I could not let go of the fire.

I heard someone call my name, and then another. Demeter, High Priestess of the healers, joined the others, directing women to douse the small fire pit by the tree. Athena stamped out the circle of flames with her boots, but still, the heat within me held sway.

*Fools!* I thought. *Stay away from me. I'm a danger to you all!* But I could not speak the words.

The women moved toward me, closing the circle, mere feet from the still smoldering flames. Demeter led them in a chant, something old, but familiar, and I reached out to the words as if they were ropes that I could use to find my way back. Their voices rose like waves, soothing, softening, holding me up, and bringing me back. These women, these *holy* women, touched me with their minds, cooling my heart. We stood like this a long time until my fervor began to subside, my body shaking hard from the burning in my limbs. Tears poured down my cheeks when, finally, I surrendered to their kindness and the fire released me.

All at once there were arms around me while someone poured cool lavender on my head, and then the sacred oil of rose to soothe me. Still, my pain did not subside until I opened my eyes and saw my daughter standing before me, her eyes soft, her arms open, and I heard her voice come sharp and clear.

"Mother, I'm here."

# CHAPTER TWO

I WAITED UNTIL THE SUMMER SOLSTICE to complete Ilithyia's ordination. Though she took her vows in private at the Emerald Temple, her public ordination was held at the Titan palace, in the great city of Caledocean. This was to reassure Atlanteans that their High Priestess's heir was being prepared to take her place. We'd been experiencing small tremors across the island for just over a year, and most Atlanteans now believed in the priestesses' prophecy that foretold of a coming disaster. Many now hoped for a great exodus. Ilithyia's ordination was set in public to quiet people's fears.

The day of the ceremony was unusually warm, and the strong scent of roses filled the women's temple, which was set just outside my wing of the Titan palace. My grandmother, Rhea, tapped her cane on the pedestal by her chair and sent women scurrying to remove some of the vases. Demeter moved to her side, offering her a mug of strongly brewed herbs, but Rhea waved it away impatiently.

I moved toward Demeter and took the cup, frowning apologetically for my grandmother's behavior. When I handed it to Rhea, she muttered something about young people, but laid aside her walking stick and took it in both hands.

"Reverence," Persephone spoke behind me.

I turned. "Yes?"

"The nobles are now seated next to the guild representatives, and all seems to be well. The harpists are entertaining, and the priestesses have taken their places."

I nodded, hoping her next words would be that my daughter had arrived, but she only shook her head.

"What did you expect?" my grandmother said. "You let the girl run off with Artemis before such an important day!"

"Yes, Grandmother, I know. You've said it before."

I looked about the temple. The women from Caledocean had lined the wall of the Temple of the Rose with golden tapestries and filled every altar with flowers and incense, and bowls with baked, red beads, one of our most honored colors. Many of my priestesses had come from the Emerald Temple to share the day, while Zeus had traveled back from his new city of Kart Hadst, across the sea, for the event. He had met me early that morning, sitting on the broad stone steps. I had smiled when I saw him. The years of separation had softened my hard feelings. We were still married in the eyes of the people, so I maintained a cordial correspondence, and he gave me news of our son while I gave him news of our daughter.

The morning sunrise had been purple and gold. In its light, I saw him as the young man I'd met so many years ago. As he moved toward me, his gray beard and the thick lines across his brow revealed the truth: we were both growing older.

He took my hand and kissed it warmly, and I reached out to him in friendship. I was touched that he had come home for this day, for Ilithyia, and I'd kissed him lightly on the cheek to say as much. He beamed at that.

Now, he sat with his father and the Titan contingency in the Megaron, being entertained by our most beautiful singers and dancing troupes, until his newly ordained daughter would be presented.

But our daughter was nowhere to be found.

The event with Calypso had sobered her to the real responsibility and danger of her role as priestess, and as my heir. Though she'd assured me she was alright and her commitment was to the temple, she had become restless and agitated as the day of the reception grew near.

"Your girl is wild!" my grandmother said, breaking my reverie. "What were you thinking letting her run off with that huntress friend of yours?" She shook her head and banged her cane against the floor once again. "It's a good thing Ilithyia comes from our line! The priestess blood will bring her home for this public ordination!"

She said this last with pride and reached out to take my hand. I looked down into her eyes, pale and watery, but very much alive. She was old now but still carried herself with honor. Some people said she'd lived so long because of her contact with the holy oil, and others said that the dragon's blood ran through our veins, but I knew it was dignity that had kept her this strong for so long; dignity, and a life filled with purpose.

"I let her go because I remembered how I felt before my ceremony with Zeus," I replied quietly. "I took those vows out of duty. I was scared and alone. I don't want my daughter to take hers for the same reasons. I thought being alone with Artemis would help her find her confidence again and renew her sense of purpose. Perhaps I was wrong—"

"No," my grandmother interrupted. "Let go of your fears, Hera. Ilithyia will return," she said, with a slight smile on her face.

She dropped my hand, and I nodded but began to pace. I could hear the drummers pounding their rhythms in the courtyard beyond and imagined the throng of people waiting for us. Women came and went, adjusting the altar, and busying themselves with unnecessary things until I wrung my hands with agitation.

"Ili," I whispered, "where are you?"

As if in reply the door behind the altar opened and Persephone appeared signaling me to follow her. I stepped forward quickly but hesitated as I took in the look on her face.

"My daughter?" I said drawing near. "Is she ready?"

Persephone nodded. "Ilithyia is here, Reverence, but, well, I wouldn't exactly say she's ready."

She turned and led me outside. As we emerged into the sunlight, I stopped abruptly. There stood my daughter at Artemis's side, hair disheveled, dirt-spattered face, still garbed in her hunting breeches. Her white skin was burnt and peeling on her nose and cheeks, and she smelled of wet earth and animals.

"Oh, Artemis!" I scolded, throwing my friend a hard look.

She was in no better condition, her brown skin streaked with red clay for the hunt, and there was fresh blood on the sleeves of her tunic. She stood frowning and apologetic, stammering something about a white stag and its doe, but I silenced her with a look and led the way to my bath house. As we stepped out into the courtyard, Athena called forward our guard, but after taking a look at Ilithyia, she shook her head.

"You've done it this time, Ili," she said, but I saw a smile pass between them.

"We must hurry," I commanded, waving Athena away. "Ilithyia must represent us with honor and dignity," yet even as I said it, I took a step back from the dust wafting off of them.

I was already in full regalia, my scarlet cape and emerald medallion in place, and so I directed with a firm hand, but from a distance. I bade Artemis and Ilithyia be stripped down and scrubbed, with no time taken to heat the first pails of water. My daughter's body prickled with the cold as the women emptied the first jug over her shoulders. Artemis held her breath and closed her eyes as the first splash touched her skin, but she said nothing, cooperating as best she could.

"And then the stag appeared from nowhere, and Artemis called out to it with her mind, and you should have seen it, Mother!" Ilithyia exclaimed as the next pail of cold water was being filled. "The stag pawed the ground and bowed its head," she gasped as the cold water was sponged down her back. "It was remarkable Mother, something that only happens in dreams." She gulped hard as more water cascaded over her face. "We *had* to track it!"

One woman scrubbed at the earth beneath her fingers, while another unwound what was left of her long, black braid. I couldn't let them wash her hair, as there was no time for it to dry. I sent for sweet oils to try and hide the days spent in the open wild.

"Artemis was incredible with the beast like they had a bond, a way of speaking between them!" Ilithyia went on as my women rubbed her dry and anointed her with frankincense and myrrh. "I've never seen anything like it, Mother, I wish you'd been there!"

Though I shook my head with irritation, I was secretly relieved to see Ilithyia's vibrancy had returned. She held up her arms as the women rubbed the oils into her skin.

"We tracked him for two days," she said, her eyes wide, "And then finally we found him in the canyon..."

We had hundreds of people in place waiting for her to appear, but she was lost in her tale.

I glared again at Artemis.

"Ili," Artemis said, and then again, stronger, to get my daughter's attention. "Your mother can hear the tale later, by the hearth. Now pay attention, this is an important time."

"I know!" Ilithyia retorted, and then looked at me as if waking from a dream.

My women pulled the gown I'd chosen for her from its place and moved toward her. She looked from the gown to me, and her face grew solemn.

"I'm sorry, Mother," she said in a quiet voice, stepping dutifully into the linen skirt.

The women pulled the gown on and then led her out of the bathhouse and into my room where they could finish her hair. Artemis pulled on the fresh dress I'd chosen for her. We stood alone together, eyeing each other, and then I moved toward her and took hold of her waist.

"Turn around so I can fasten you in," I said.

She did as I bid her, lifting her hair, its thick, silver strands falling in ringlets about the nape of her neck. I began to pull the eyelets over the pearls.

"You wanted me to raise her free," Artemis said into the air.

"I know I did," I answered curtly.

She turned when I was done, and I took her in, long hair splaying about her face and shoulders in a silver shroud of wild beauty. I couldn't help but smile.

"Mother."

Artemis and I both turned to see Ilithyia standing in the sharp curve of the doorframe, her face fresh, her thin, black gown accentuating the fullness of her strong body. Her hair was pulled up high, and a small crown of orange flowers lay lightly atop her head. At her side, she wore the thin, curved *athame,* its hilt bearing the dragons entwined.

Tenderness tightened my throat. I reached for Artemis's hand in silence, and she squeezed mine warmly in return.

"I couldn't have raised her without you, Artemis," I said. "Thank you."

The ceremony was brief, and the rituals extravagant, more for show than meaning; a full contingency of dynastic priests observed. Now more then ever, I knew I must safeguard the Emerald Temple's rites and initiations from those that sought power over us.

Afterwards, representatives of Atlantis's dynasties laid lavish gifts at Ilithyia's feet, in the temple's name. I'd kept her sequestered and safe from the politics of her station for nineteen years, but I couldn't protect her any longer. I hung back and let her receive the nobles that clamored for her attention. Zeus stepped to her side and began managing the populace about her. *Good*, I thought. *Let her father use his power and position as commander of Atlantis's fighting force to lend prestige to Ilithyia's introductions.*

Demeter and Persephone were also at Ilithyia's side, so I moved away from the crowd toward the verandah thinking to address the women I'd been told had gathered outside to do us honor. Once outside I caught my breath at the scene before me. Hundreds and hundreds of women were spread out across the fields of our estate, circling the temple and the labyrinth beyond. They were dancing and singing, some beating drums and others chanting. They had used the wide, marble stairs that stretched out beneath me as an altar for their offerings. I stepped forward and reached down, brushing my fingers lightly over the full breasts and round belly of a small, carved statue that someone had laid there. It was one of our most honored symbols, the feminine face of the invisible force. I glanced at me realizing there were many of them, hundreds, lining the steps and spreading out like a fan at the bottom. Some were carved out of wood and shaped from clay, while others were made of precious stones.

I lifted the small statue from its place and stood, cradling it in my palm. It had two round heads with loving, feminine features, representing two women emerging from one shared source. This signified the dual poles of the feminine in nature. It spoke of sowing and reaping, day and night, earth and moon. It spoke to feminine relationships, to sisterhoods and priestesses and on this day, at this moment, it spoke to me of the relationship between mother and daughter. Deep emotions moved through me. I looked out across the field at the women gathered there, lifted the precious symbol between my palms, and bowed to them.

Someone saw me and cried out, and others turned, and soon they had taken up the old chant, the blessed words of love, and courage and community. I could feel the power rising as they linked, one heart to another, and opened themselves to the invisible current that united us all.

I bowed again, and took up the song with them, my body swaying gently, my limbs longing to rush down the stairs and join them. But I could not do such a thing. I'd been gone from the Megaron too long. Reluctantly, I lifted my hand and bent my fingers in the gesture of blessing, and returned to the reception inside.

I presided at the feast after the ceremony, pleased at the welcome my daughter received from Atlantis's notable families. With Zeus's help, she seemed to have met everyone in the room with charm and grace much like her father. Once my duties were concluded, I removed myself to a seat at the side of the room where I could watch Ilithyia's interactions with her guests from a distance. Already the representatives of Atlantis's dynasties and priesthood vied for her attention knowing she would one day wield enormous power as High Priestess.

As I sat down, I caught a glimpse of my son, Ares, as he stepped away from his father's side and headed toward me through the crowd. I raised my hand slightly to welcome him, but he disappeared for a moment, behind the couples that danced in the center of the room.

Music played, and singers filled the hall with their rich, warm sounds. People danced both inside and out. My eyes fell upon Artemis who was, as always, surrounded by adoring women. Her hand rested gently on the curve of her current lover's hip. The woman was older and very soft, with warm, laughing eyes. I could see why Artemis had kept her as a consort for so long.

I sighed. There had been a time when I'd have given anything to be chosen by Artemis. Watching her now, I knew my longing for her would never leave me.

On the verandah, Demeter and Persephone led the priestesses in their service to those who waited for blessings and healing at the celebration that roared on outside. I was grateful they had taken the service for me on this day. I was tired, and a subtle melancholy rested in my heart.

The stiff sound of military boots rose sharply beside me. I turned around to see my son.

"Ares." I stood and held out my arms to him, and he pecked me on the cheek cordially.

His body was stiff, and his long, narrow face was boyish and brooding. He had his father's light skin, and blue eyes, but his lips were full like mine. He wore his hair long, like Zeus, and was trying to grow a beard, but the hair on his face was still thin. I thought he would be handsome if he'd smile more.

"My sister seems happy," Ares said, looking back at the crowd that thronged Ilithyia. "And Father is well pleased with the attention."

I put my hand on his shoulder, noting that he'd grown. He was a full head taller than me now, and I had to look up at him as I spoke.

"How go things in Kart Hadst? Your father tells me you've done him honor in battle."

He shook his head and didn't look at me as he spoke, his eyes still hard on his sister.

"Does he? I wouldn't know, he never says such things to me." His voice was flat. "There are no such affairs for warriors," he continued nodding at the gathering. "No one throws gifts at your feet. You have only what you fight for."

"And take," I said, but regretted it immediately.

He turned to me. "You don't approve of Father's campaign."

"I don't approve of taking other people's land and fighting battles that can be avoided," I answered. "We've had years to build a place of our own and to continue the resettlement efforts. Why must we take what another has already built?"

The music grew louder as the singers rounded the room and neared the open doorway where we stood. People laughed. A group of young women passed by and curtseyed lightly to me. They held hands and smiled as they eyed Ares before joining the dancers. His form was crisp and hard beside me, and he looked striking dressed in black, as all the Titans did. They had taken the color of the priestess to represent their house, some years ago, but it still made me uneasy to see so many of them draped in the potent feminine color of night.

"Father speaks of you often," Ares said.

"Hmm?"

"Even though we are an ocean away, he refers to you as his queen and takes no other woman publicly."

I was startled by the comment. "Love changes forms, Ares, but does not die."

He nodded as if he'd expected the answer. I tried to sense what he was getting at, but Zeus stepped up beside him. He smiled broadly and patted Ares hard on the back, then reached out a hand to me.

"They expect a dance," he said, kissing my hand lightly. He lingered for a moment, and I could smell the wine on his breath.

Before I could refuse, he pulled me to him and moved me out onto the verandah in time to the music. I laughed despite myself. He danced us back toward the room and into the crowd, round and round, until people moved aside, clapping and shouting encouragement. My hair fell loose about my face. When we whirled to a stop, I looked up to see Ilithyia staring at us in frank surprise. I searched the room for Ares, but could not find him.

Zeus placed my hand on his arm guiding me through the Megaron and out into the hall. We slipped past the other rooms of feasting and into his wing of the palace. He signaled our guard to hang back.

"There's something I want to show you," he said crisply, moving toward a big sitting room at the end of the hall.

We entered and stopped. In the center, the furniture had been moved away, and two large, sprawling tables were set out with a magnificent raised map set upon them. I'd seen small ones before, engineers making clay models of a house or a bridge, but this was on a scale I had never imagined. Zeus spread his arms out wide.

"I give you the city of Kart Hadst," he said. His eyes flashed. "Come, let me show you."

We moved to the table, the edge of which was blue sea. Zeus pointed to concentric circles carved into the coast that were smaller than, but similar to, the ones of Caledocean's great port.

"We have a thriving trade with the Islanders up here," he pointed at small pieces of land sticking up out of the blue. "Here, this one is Minoa, where your priestesses have met with my brother, Poseidon, to build your first temple."

I leaned closer in amazement. I could see the small port built off the half-moon of sandy beach that looked out onto the bay. A set of stairs was carved into the stone cliffs that led to long bluffs and open fields. There was even a thick blue and white strip painted across the length to represent the small river, which ran down from the mountain. Zeus showed me where the temple was being built and described the town growing up around it. He placed his hand on mine warmly as he described all the luxuries he had sent from Kart Hadst and the low lands of the great river valley that was his new territory. I knew better than to say anything against his gifts; it would do no good.

Bringing my attention back to his city, he pointed out the green hill region about it and the vast desert that lay beyond.

A significant watershed was constructed of wood alongside one great hill. He pointed to it excitedly.

"We've secured fresh water, Hera," he said. "This makes the city self-sufficient, and ready for new inhabitants."

"How many do you have?"

"We are five thousand without my army. They are housed here, and here, and here."

He moved around the corner of the table, opposite me, showing me the forts, built in a realistic manner, on three sides of the city. The fourth side faced the sea. We had no need of such protection in Atlantis, why should we need it there? The thought of it chilled me.

"How big is your army now?"

He didn't hesitate. "We are ten thousand to the man."

I gasped. Zeus, thinking I was impressed, smiled with delight. The last reports I'd seen had estimated his troops at half that, and the city at one-third this size. Aphrodite had been sent as the priestesses' representative as she seemed to get along with most of the ruling party. As much as I hated to watch her use her sexuality to gain favor, I couldn't ignore the fact that the men in power responded favorably to her. So when she'd requested the position, I gave it to her. Having her go gave me the added benefit of being free of her condescension. But now I regretted it. She'd reported numbers much smaller than what Zeus shared with me now.

"I'll have even greater numbers soon," Zeus continued. "Poseidon put into port with most of his fleet just before we left."

He snatched up my hands in his and looked down at me with such warmth, I thought for a moment he would lean down and kiss me. I stiffened.

"Poseidon intends to follow us and will be here in the next few days. And Hera," he took a step closer. "He will bring a large number of ships, close to fifty, and we'll finally begin your full evacuation plan."

I raised my brows and opened my mouth to speak, but hesitated, careful of what I would say. So many questions were still left unanswered. I was reeling at the vast discrepancies between his words, this map, and the numbers my people had been telling me. Because of the earth's tremors over the past year, the great council had finally begun to discuss the possibility of relocation efforts, but nothing had been decided on and the word 'evacuation' hadn't been used. I wondered at Zeus's confidence. Even if we could begin, fifty ships would hardly make evacuation possible for our people. We were numbered beyond the thousands.

"Zeus," I began, but there was a commotion outside the door, and as we turned, a crowd stepped through the threshold.

Hades, Zeus's other, older brother, led the group, slowing only for a moment as his eyes met mine.

We were not friends.

Hades had never forgiven me for demanding his removal from the Titan palace and had crossed me at every turn. The years had been kind to him. He was a tall, imposing man who had grown more handsome with age. As time went by he had garnered more power and prestige for the temple of light, which he led. His role as Lucifer, the light bearer, was as honored as my role of High Priestess.

Hades moved past me, ushering in his father, Kronos, and their guests, beckoning them toward the table. Ilithyia and my grandmother entered with several members of the council who were known to favor the Titan dynasty. Zeus and I stepped back as Hades went over the map just as Zeus had done, but focused more on the city's size and scope, building materials, and layout.

Ilithyia moved up to his right and peered beyond the city, pointing to the Isle of Minoa where an imperial looking temple had been placed.

"Ah, an island for the priestesses," Hades explained, his guests moving closer to see it.

"But Mother," Ilithyia turned to me sharply, her voice alert. "There is no land bridge and no lake. How shall we—" but she stopped herself short, remembering the company she was in.

"Protect yourselves and your mysteries?" Hades said, in a thin, unpleasant tone. "Here, niece," he pointed to several fake ships that stood on the board next to the island on all sides. "You will need no more protection than our fleet will offer."

There was an uncomfortable silence, until Zeus cleared his throat, and put a large hand on our daughter's shoulder.

"You will have your mother's intuition. You will raise the mist, Ilithyia," he said softly.

I turned to him, surprised. It was the last thing I expected him to say. I searched his eyes, but they were soft and genuine.

"Yes," I echoed, "we will raise the mist about us as we always have."

I didn't mention that we had already chosen another island, much smaller and farther away, where a secret temple was being carved out, deep inside hidden caves. It would be a small place, and priestesses would be able to travel there from any point in the Aegean on the solstices. We would keep our sacred objects there. Meanwhile, we would play our part and allow the Titans to "banish" us, in effect, by setting us apart from their city and their people.

In the past few years the dynasties, led by Hades, had made a brilliant political move, by joining together. They'd gone from twelve separate houses with individual agendas to three, and the Titans controlled the most significant share of people and resources. I had no doubt who would run Kart Hadst.

Hades went on with his tour of the structured map.

"Here we have your estates," he said pointing to the green painted hills that overlooked the city. "They're being built as we speak. We've brought in help from the tribes to hurry the process now that our need is more—" he hesitated, avoiding my gaze, "needful."

Ilithyia shook her head. "But, Uncle, shouldn't we spend those resources building a quantity of smaller homes for more people?"

Hades's lips curled. "In time, Niece. All in good time. First, we must create the resources to feed and clothe them." He pointed to the large villas set high up on the hill above the new city, and the vast fields they lorded over.

"But this is inefficient," Ilithyia went on despite my attempt to get her attention and silence her. "We've got thousands to relocate, and we need to build organized settlements much like the Emerald Temple is run. That way people can provide for themselves and not be dependent on the city and its resources—" she stopped there. I realized the real purpose of Hades's plan was dawning on her. He *wanted* the new settlers dependent on him, and his dynasty. The entire city was designed around this premise.

Hades waved her words away as if they were mosquitoes in the room.

"As the Titans promised the council, the city itself is well planned and will hold twice the number we have here in Caledocean. There will be no need of extraneous villages draining our vital resources." He turned to the map and pointed to the massive building at the center of the new city. His eyes glinted with pleasure. "Everything will be centralized. Our plan is in motion. There's no going back now."

He looked at me then, and his stare was cold. "The priestesses will be the only ones with the need to take care of themselves."

I could feel him gloating. Years ago he'd won over the council with his promises of rich new estates and supremacy in the new city. As Zeus had expanded their territories and garnered more resources, Hades had positioned the Titans as the council's saviors assuring everyone Atlantis's calamity was still far in the future. I had no doubt he knew this wasn't true. For all his pomp and need for control, he was still the Lucifer and must be able to read the signs. What would befall the thousands he had not cared enough to evacuate years ago? I shuddered at the truth. Hades had never even considered them.

Hades was speaking again, but I only caught his last words.

"—Poseidon shall arrive shortly to escort us there in person."

So, it had all been planned and prepared and neatly delivered by the Titans.

Ilithyia clapped her hands together and turned to Zeus at the mention of Poseidon. She'd never met her uncle, Poseidon; none of us had. He was more of a legend, the explorer that had sailed the Aegean and beyond. He'd discovered the great isle, Albion, with its myths of blue painted warriors and white cliffs. Rather than a real tenant of the Titan clan, Poseidon was one of Atlantis's great heroes, a fact that Zeus and Hades often tried to ignore.

"Will he bring us news of the tribes, Father?" Ilythia asked Zeus.

"I'm sure he will. He's seen the world, and I'm sure he's collected more than a few intriguing stories to share."

Kronos, Zeus's father, pounded the table and smiled broadly at the news, obvious pride on his face.

"We'll prepare a reception," I began, "We will honor him—"

Hades gave a short, crisp laugh.

"That won't be necessary," his voice rang across the table with authority. "The Titans have planned his welcome, I assure you, Lady. Your presence will not be required."

# CHAPTER THREE

THAT NIGHT I SLEPT POORLY.

An old and familiar dream came upon me like a fury. A wind-whipped about me in violent gusts. I'd dreamt it many times in the past, but it had been years since I'd been swept up so entirely in the old images and feelings.

As always I was on a great ship at sail on an azure sea, and there was a man in the mist standing close by my side. In all the years since I'd taken the *Heiros Gamos* vows and made the sacred marriage with Zeus, I'd been haunted by the intuitive sense of this man from my dream. No matter if the impression of him receded for months at a time, he would always return, his dark blue eyes piercing the gray that engulfed them.

I'd long ago stopped struggling to make out the meaning of this dream, and had surrendered to it. When I'd taken my second initiation and ordination as High Priestess of the Emerald Temple, I'd been welcomed by the mystical dreamers, priestesses who could stay awake in the Dreamtime. They invited me to link with them and seek guidance for the temple through the wisdom of our shared dream. In this

time I'd learned the difference between a personal dream—
one that came from the seed of my ancestors still within my
flesh—and the dream of wisdom, which was alive and meant
to guide my life, or the life of the priestesses as a whole. I
assumed by now that this dream of the sea, the ship, and the
man, was but a haunted memory loosed in my consciousness
from times past. Though it often left me feeling melancholy,
I usually paid it little attention.

But this night it came to me differently. It had the
full-blooded feeling of embodiment that marked a premo-
nition. After the first few vague images, I moved toward the
dream intent on waking up wholly within it.

I stood on the deck of a ship that swayed dangerously
to and fro, in a furious sea. The sail was down, and the mast
cracked in two. Men pulled at the oars with all their strength.
The drum that should have been guiding the paddlers was
silent, and the men cried out as we crested a wave and rushed
down the other side.

The dream came into full focus and became vivid and real.

I felt myself thrown forward, lurching against the rail.
When I hit, a sharp pain wracked my side. I gasped; I had
never dreamed with such lucidity.

I reached for something to grasp. Surreal, golden light
poured from behind dark storm clouds in the distance, but
above us the sky was black. Rain pelted me as I was tossed
with the ship back toward the midpoint, gripping tight to
anything I could latch onto. I made out the prow of the ship
where the man usually stood in my dream and made my way
in between swells toward it. I climbed the small ladder to the
upper deck but found it deserted.

Lightning flashed in the sky above us, and for a moment
the outlines of the oarsmen and the crew huddled helplessly

in the aft of the ship, became evident. Suddenly, there was a shout, and the men turned in my direction as if they could see me. Then the light was gone, and the rain obscured my view. I reached the very front of the ship, where the figurehead was still secure, and grasped on tight as we crested another wave. I looked down to see that I was wearing my loose, black sleeping gown which stuck wetly to my body from the cold sheets of rain that beat down upon me. I could hear more shouting toward the stern of the ship and turned again, just as lightning flashed a second time. There he was, on the far deck directly across from me, his body thrust full force into the steering oar. His eyes were on me. The men about him were pointing at me, some crying out *Draconigena!* But there was another loud clap in the sky above us followed by long slicing bolts farther away. The pennants tore free in a gust of wind and then the light was gone altogether.

I fell to my knees with another roll of a wave before I thought to call on the elements and try to calm the sea. My mind fought me, trying to make sense. This was just a dream, no need to call the invisible forces, it said, but I knew it was more. For a shocking moment, I realized that I was here because I had been summoned. I recalled my grandmother's words: "The current of life is invisible but real. It makes up our bodies and our consciousness. When you rest AS this current, you are the creative force itself with all the power of transformation at your call." I thought I'd understood her meaning at the time, but now, in this dream state, I felt myself not as flesh but as the current itself! This is what she'd meant.

Lightning creased the sky again, and I looked up, feeling the current within it. I reached out with my mind, uniting with it. I chanted the holy words to the fire, water, earth, and air. I lifted my hands to the sky as the ship rode up the face of another swell and then clung to the rail as we fell over the other side. Again and again, I called out, shutting my eyes to find some peace in the face of the gale, and projecting this calm current onto all that was storming about me. Soon, the ship steadied, the waves tossed more lightly than before, and the thunder overhead became a distant growl as if moving on. I opened my eyes to see ships strewn before me as far as I could see. Sailors clung to the sides, and some were lashed to the masts and rails. The rain still streaked down, but it was gentler now, and I could feel the relief in the sea itself. I turned to make out my ship and crew and looked into the eyes of the man I felt staring intently at my form as if he would hold me up with his gaze. Then the scene slipped away from me.

I tried to make out his face before I was gone, but the only thing that remained was the vague impression of the deep blue eyes revealing themselves for an instant. I recognized the life current within them as my own.

I spoke to no one of the dream but carried it quietly in my breast as the next few days passed. Everyone on the estate seemed distracted, talking about Poseidon's return and the Titan gala that was being prepared for him. Caledocean hoisted its flags, preparing a hero's welcome. Zeus led hunting parties far afield to bring back wild boar, deer, and fowl in great quantities to feed the fleet that would soon descend. The extra stores of grain were released from the Titan granaries. Already nobles from neighboring dynasties vied for the honor of preparing the entertainment and festivities that would follow the ships' arrivals.

I didn't take part in such affairs but kept close to the temple, leading the daily services for the women that came faithfully to our door, distributing the herbs and healing balms we gave away to those who had little or nothing to trade. I'd turned Ilithyia's tutoring over to Persephone. My daughter spent her days learning the obligations of her political life. In the evenings when she dined with Artemis and me, she shared her day. To my surprise and relief, she took to her new role. She was sharp of mind and wit as well as fierce in her body. She did well in her weapons training with Athena; where I knew little of such things, Ilithyia was a dedicated student. Athena, in turn, had moved a large contingency of her warriors to our palace and temple in Caledocean where they actively recruited women into their service. I understood her need with the tide of the Titans rising against us, but the sight of a woman's armory built beside the stable weighed heavy on my heart.

My only solace was my horse, Pegasus. He'd been given the run of the lower pastures the year before, but I liked to go out each evening with a handful of grain, to be with him and feel him press his old, familiar body against me. He had sired many other beautiful stallions, and the one I rode now for formal events bore his name, but it was always my original Pegasus that I turned to when my sense of freedom was at stake.

On this day, I bridled him and threw a red blanket from the stable across his back. I was not young anymore, but I could still take hold of his mane and pull myself up, and it filled me with strength and a sense of autonomy. He bobbed his head happily as I turned him toward the open fence and headed up to the temple, and the road beyond. My guards and I were now familiar friends, and they dropped back knowingly as I pushed Pegasus into a trot past the palace to the main gate. I was fleeing my duties of the day, but something inside urged me to do it. Pegasus picked up his pace, and I sensed that he felt it too.

When we moved past the gates and into the city, people waved, and shouted, calling out my name in respect. I nodded as I went, but pulled my scarlet cape about me as if it were a shield of privacy.

The road that led from the Titan estate wound down the hill toward the marketplace, which sat along the banks of the central canal. Reed boats floated up and down Caledocean's channels carrying goods from one part of the city to the next, while larger, wooden vessels docked in the great harbor closer to the sea. Craving the familiar scent of salt air from my childhood, I made my way through the crowded streets, people moving aside pleasantly for Pegasus's massive, but familiar figure. When we reached the open road, I pressed Pegasus into a canter, and we sped across the long bridges that stretched themselves like wings across the canals. The day was crisp, and my cheeks were cold, but the open space and speed excited me.

When I crossed the second bridge and heard the ram's horn sound two sharp blasts from the harbor ahead, I smiled in anticipation. Looking out to sea, I beheld a procession of ships moving into the bay. Even from a distance, I could make out the carved figure of a horse's head on the prow of the lead ship. I knew this must be Poseidon's ship, but the actual size of the vessel was overwhelming. A visceral memory of the dream surged through me, and I urged Pegasus toward the harbor to see the ships more clearly.

As I reached the streets that led to the vast concentric circles of calm waterways, in which ships docked, I was cut off by a throng of people. The sound of the ram's horn came again, loud and sharp, signaling the fleet's arrival. Even with Pegasus to part the crowd I could see that I would only be in the way if I approached the pier. Zeus and the other Titans would not appreciate the added commotion my presence would bring. My guard moved in closer to me, trying to assuage the people that pressed against my knees, reaching out to me for a blessing.

Ahead of me, the first large ship glided magically toward the dock, and people cheered. Men on the ship tossed ropes to outstretched hands.

I turned Pegasus around and headed back a few paces toward a stretch of green that led up a narrow path to the hill I used to sit upon with Zeus as he surveyed his growing city. Pegasus knew the way and dug his hooves in confidently as he pulled me toward freedom from the crowd with their dust and noise.

The path wound around the backside of the small hill and for a few minutes, I was out of sight of the boats. Turning around I realized I'd also lost my guard. I laughed at the thought that after all these years I'd finally have a moment outdoors truly alone. I knew the women would be frantic to find me, but I pushed it to the back of my consciousness, longing to partake of this temporary liberty.

I could hear the roar of applause and loud shouts of approval from below as we breached the lip of the hill. From atop the green, I looked down at the crowd, which now filled the wharf, and saw that each of the ships in the approaching fleet was steered by oarsmen. They pulled in time to a loud drumbeat that echoed off the water above the voices of the onlookers. I watched for several minutes, entertained by the commotion below until I noticed the ships themselves. They were a disheveled bunch and maybe half as many as Zeus had told me he was expecting. Up close, the ships were more impressive than I'd imagined, each boasting double masts and long quarterdecks, which ran across the stern of each. Big holes shone through the planks, and I could see that there were separate rooms inside and furniture as well. Several of the ships only flew one sail, and none had a banner raised except the lead ship, which was now safely tied down and surrounded by people.

Two more vessels docked safely, and I watched as men piled off into the arms and cheers of the crowd. I counted as many as fifty men that left one ship, and several horses followed. Each craft was equipped with a massive bulwark fitted across its prow to protect it from big waves, but on the next vessels to dock I saw that these were split in two, left dangling.

An image from my dream passed before my eyes, as Pegasus paced anxiously.

While so many of the crews de-boarded their ships, mingling on the harbor decks with visible relief and revelry, I turned my attention back to the lead ship, which had been the first to come in, and was now docked closest to the hill. I could see down onto its long deck, and hear the distinct orders shouted out by its commander. Scrutinizing the man, I was surprised to see how different he looked and behaved compared to the other Titans. He was not all what I had expected of the elder brother. He was a small, thin man with a balding head and white beard. His voice was gruff and sharp as he paced the prow of the ship calling orders to a man that sat aloft on the mast, waving flags to the other ships—a clever way to send messages between them. Although the fellow often faced my direction, he was consumed with the details of his station and didn't detect my prying presence. I watched undisturbed as younger men in deep blue tunics ran his orders to the other ships on foot. There, sailors conferred together and then ran messages back. Each time they returned, the commander ducked inside the cabin at the rear and then re-emerged with fresh dispatches. It was a mesmerizing display of order in the chaos that surrounded them.

The sun was high in the sky now, and most of the crowd had moved away some distance from the ships, spilling onto the sandy beach that lined the shore below, when the ram's horn sounded again, but this time it was a long and low piercing cry, announcing the arrival of the heads of state. From my vantage point on the hill, I was shielded from their sight as they looked forward, beholding the magnificent ships. I remained where I was, watching the scene with a sense of heightened excitement growing inside me, my melancholy forgotten.

Two processions arrived with all the dignity and pomp I'd come to expect of such occasions—women were brought along in gilded litters while men rode warhorses in full dress, and chariots scattered the crowd before them with their reckless drivers. I scowled at their carelessness and drew in my breath as children narrowly escaped the pounding hooves and wheels.

Amongst the flowing robes and sparkling jewels that flashed in the sun, three men stepped forward at the foot of the main ship. I recognized them at once. The tall, gray head in the center belonged to Kronos. He balanced himself with an outstretched arm on Hades's shoulder as he walked up the plank that led to the mid-deck of the ship. They all wore their finest robes and long black capes. Hades carried the brilliant bejeweled staff of the Titan High Priest, the Lucifer's wand. As they disappeared into the belly of the vessel the man I'd thought to be Poseidon, moved toward the aft deck and rapped on the door of the cabin. To my surprise, a tall figure stepped out into the sun. I glimpsed his dark head and noted the thin beard on his face, but then the light played in my eyes, and he moved, becoming a rustling blue cape. He reached out his hands to Kronos as the Titan clan stepped onto the deck before him, and the elder man embraced him warmly.

So, *this* was Poseidon.

As the understanding took hold, I felt a strange sensation move through my breast, a surge, as if a wave was pulling me out to sea. To my surprise, Poseidon released his father abruptly, and before moving to his brothers he hesitated, looking beyond them and the crowd toward me. He stared for a long moment so that Kronos, Hades, and Zeus all turned at once to see what he was taken with.

Pegasus, who had been chewing on the grass beneath us, lifted his head. He struck the ground with his hoof and gave a soft sound as if it had been too long since he'd had admiring eyes upon him. I wished then I hadn't stayed visible as I realized how the scene must have looked. While I should have been with the others, or at Zeus's side to welcome Poseidon, and his commanders, here I was looking down at everyone from atop my bold, white stallion, the scarlet cape of my station waving in the wind behind me.

Uncertain what to do next I tried to steady Pegasus with the silent voice, but my eyes still lingered on Poseidon.

He stepped forward on the deck, still staring up at me, and the others followed him. The dignitaries below and the on-looking assemblage turned to follow his gaze. As everyone stared up at me, the noise and entertainment quieted.

Despite my command to settle down, Pegasus paced heroically, enjoying the stage. Hades reached out and touched his elder brother's shoulder, leaning in close as if to say something, but before he could speak, Poseidon crossed his arms over his chest and dipped his head in deference to me.

Hades stepped back in surprise. Then Poseidon turned to his men shouting out in an untamed voice that sent a chill across my skin.

"Look!" he cried, pointing toward me. "The High Priestess of the Emerald Temple blesses our return to Atlantis."

A cheer rose up from around the ships as Poseidon faced me again, and this time, he knelt on one knee, as was the custom of respect. His commander immediately followed, dropping down with a slow and graceful movement. Then, in a long, sweeping wave, his crew and the mingling crowd lowered themselves in the same manner.

Kronos and his other sons hesitated, while Hades looked up at me in disbelief. Then, finding themselves the only ones standing in a sea of men, they too knelt down before me.

For a moment I felt the old heat of pride fill my breast at the show of such sacred trust for a way of life I'd struggled to protect. With the rise of the Titans' power over the council and the people, the old ways were slipping away. I was failing. As if he knew my struggle, Poseidon remained on his knee, and would not rise until I lifted my hand in the air and pressed my fingers into the sign of peace and blessing above them. I stared one last time at Poseidon, letting the dignity of his gesture move inside me, and then I turned Pegasus around and urged him back to the temple.

# CHAPTER FOUR

I DIDN'T NEED TO SEE the color of Poseidon's eyes to know that they were blue. Blue like the indigo streak that paints itself between dusk and night. And I didn't need to meet him in person to know he was the man from my dream.

When I returned to the estate, I let Pegasus run free in the pasture and hurried to my rooms waving away the excited faces of the priestesses, and the breathless objections of my guards. When Athena approached me with her scowl and re-criminations for losing my guard, I waved her away, turning my back and shutting the door tight behind me. Beyond it, I heard their hushed voices and my guards' rapid explanations. I retreated further into my room and bolted the inner door, resting heavily on it when it was done. I shut my eyes.

"Hera."

I jumped, turning to see Artemis sitting on the stool beside the fire.

"I see you want to be alone," she said, rising and moving toward the door.

My body tingled with exhilaration at the portents of the day. I felt as though I was awakening from a long sleep, moving away from the quiet, subdued place I had resigned my life to. Now, a warm heat ran through me.

"No," I said, "please, don't go."

She stopped and smiled, reaching out her palm. My hand shook as I placed it in her grasp. Pulling me to the chair beside hers she poured me a goblet of sweet wine. I drank it too quickly and held it out to be refilled. She didn't say anything but filled the cup again. I swallowed, feeling ease move over me. Artemis waited patiently, watching until I was able to speak.

"I've had a dream," I began and then I told it, as I'd seen it in the beginning, so many years ago when we were young. I remembered the first time the dream had come to me, when I had thought the man in the dream symbolized my union with Zeus, and then all the times after, year after year. I explained the true dream of a few nights past and Poseidon's reaction upon seeing me on the hill. I reached out for another glass of wine, but Artemis waved me away.

"You've had enough, Hera," she said gently, grinning. Her eyes were soft, and something moved behind them. "The day is still young, and you'll have to meet with them," she hesitated, "with *him* tonight. You must stay clear headed."

I nodded. Of course, she was right, but my nerves were still on edge. I looked gratefully into her eyes for she was the only one who would speak to me this way.

I got up, unhooked my cloak, and dropped it on the bed to pace around the room. Then I stopped and buried my head in my hands.

"All these years!" I cried. "I took the *Heiros Gamos* vows with Zeus. I fulfilled my destiny!"

"Perhaps," she said.

I paced again, annoyed with Artemis's calm and unhelpful contemplation.

"But what does it mean?" I said. "Artemis?"

She took my hands to stop my pacing. I raised my head and looked into her eyes pleadingly.

"I think you know what it means, Hera."

My stomach lurched. I laid my head on her shoulder, and she wrapped her arms around me.

"You'll meet him tonight, and we shall see," she said.

I nodded and sighed. "You're right. The answers will reveal themselves in time."

She smiled then, her face lighting up with thin, joyous lines.

"I have other news too," she said. "I've had news that Apollo has come home with the fleet! He's been with Poseidon all these years. He's become the Master healer to Poseidon's fleet."

I pulled back sharply with surprise. We'd lost word of Apollo's whereabouts once he'd sailed to Kart Hadst a decade past. Shaking my head in wonder, I hugged Artemis again, and she squeezed me, happily. She'd been close with her twin all through our childhood, and I knew the years apart had weighed heavy on her heart.

"Artemis, that's wonderful!" I said. Then after a moment's pause, "And remarkable as well. What a coincidence that Apollo, of the many healers, sent abroad, should become Poseidon's."

"I agree," she answered. "There's no denying something is afoot. Something bigger is at play here, and perhaps you'll find out more tonight."

"Yes," I said. "And now that Apollo's here you must join us at the feast." When she shook her head in protest, for such affairs were not to her liking, I insisted. "It will be the earliest chance you'll have to see him. He deserves that, Artemis."

She sighed and let me take her to my dressing room where I picked a dark, green gown for her and a thick gold belt to tighten about her slim waist. She grimaced but dressed as I bade her, even letting me place an ornate feather necklace about her neck. I was delighted to scent her hair and lay flowers in it. I couldn't rouge her cheeks or paint her eyes with kohl; her beauty was much more simple and sincere. She endured my grooming letting me slip out of my thoughts, my worries, and my role as High Priestess. For a short time, we were girls again.

The feast was held at Kronos's home, which was set behind a long wall, deep in the city. The central building was shaped like a horseshoe, curving about lush gardens and pools with flowing water. It was strategically located between the great council buildings, Caledocean's political center, and the Titans' Temple of Light. It wasn't a long way to travel, and the night was warm. The chariots moved easily through the streets with Athena and my guard clearing the way before us. When we arrived, I linked arms with Artemis. Together we walked up the broad stairs and into the Megaron, and whatever destiny it held.

I'd been to Kronos's events before and braced myself for the inevitably formal introductions we'd undertake before the real festivities began. Artemis stood stiffly by my side as I exchanged the usual insincere pleasantries that such occasions required of me. I'd grown accustomed to this political charade long ago, for most of the guests at Titan events were not friends of the priestesses. Artemis was blatantly inept at such trivial discourse, but I kept her close at my side. Her jaw was set in an unwelcoming frown until we made our way into the main room and her eyes fell on her brother. Apollo moved toward us quickly, his arms outstretched, and I let Artemis go as he swept her up. He held her to his chest for a long moment and when he let her go their eyes glistened. Artemis took up his hand and turned to me, pulling him close.

"Reverence," Apollo said to me, bowing his head deeply, but when he rose, I saw the sly smile of his youth flicker across his face. He shook his head. "I should've known our little Hera would become nothing less than the High Priestess of the Emerald Temple!"

I smiled at this and kissed his cheeks warmly.

"Welcome home," I said grateful that time had not changed his warm presence.

There was an audible step behind him, and Apollo moved aside as Zeus came toward us, his two brothers close behind him. I took a sharp breath, bracing myself. I was already nervous enough to meet this strange man I'd been dreaming of for so many years, but to meet him with Zeus by my side filled me with unreasonable anxiety.

Zeus reached out to me easily, kissing my cheeks. "Hera," he boomed, "Let me introduce my brother, Poseidon."

As Zeus stepped aside my eyes fell on Poseidon's strong, poised face. He stared at me for a long moment before he took a slow step forward. Then he dipped his head in deference.

"Reverence," he said, in a voice both intelligent and warm. "You honor us with your presence."

I opened my mouth to speak but found myself gazing into his eyes, which looked back with undeniable familiarity. I was unnerved standing so close to a man who'd been an ephemeral figure in my dreams for so long. No words came to me. I stood there dumbly, staring.

I felt Zeus shuffle uncomfortably at my side, and then his hand was about my waist, pressing me slightly, but my eyes were fixed on Poseidon's, and I fell into them as a drop of rain falls into the sea.

"It is we who are honored to have you back from the world, brother," Zeus said finally.

He put his arm around me then, and I looked up realizing he was staring at me with concern. They all were. Hades's look was intent, and a crooked smile curled forward on his pursed lips. I took another sharp breath steadying myself, nodding vigorously, but my voice was quiet when I spoke.

"Yes," I said softly, "the honor is ours."

Apollo said something I didn't hear, and Zeus laughed as Artemis slipped her hand into my mine, squeezing it gently.

"You'll excuse us, Lords," she said in her calm, but confident tone, pulling me toward the verandah. "Apollo, will you join us?"

The Titans nodded as I gratefully followed Artemis outside. We sat down together on a plush sofa by a fountain. The sound of the water and the fresh air soothed me.

"Thank you," I whispered to my friend.

She tightened her grip for a moment then let me go, an affectionate smile on her face.

Apollo pulled up a chair opposite us as people milled about with food and drink, swaying to the merry music that others danced to inside.

"I've missed you both!" he said leaning forward in his chair. "More than I can say. I've spent half a lifetime traveling the world. But seeing you both now… I feel as if all that was just a dream, and that I've always been here with you, somehow."

Artemis nodded, smiling deeply. "We'll have our time alone," she said, glancing about the festive room. "But you can trust that our bond is still strong. I've dreamt of you many times over the years, dearest. I've seen you living with the tribes, in the low lands by a great river, and on a mountain as well, covered with snow."

Apollo's face lightened as he nodded. Deep lines of age and sun were emblazoned across his brow.

"Now you must tell us of your travels," I commanded playfully, resting back on the couch. Artemis pulled up her legs beneath her gown so that she sat cat-like beside me. "Tell us of your adventures, Apollo. "

He leaned back in his chair and raised his hand. A young woman came to his side setting figs, soft cheese, and wine on the little table before us. Apollo poured himself a full goblet and then took up the stem in his long fingers, moving his wrist about in gentle circles. He inhaled the wine before pressing the red spice to his lips. When he'd drunk deeply, he began.

"I met Poseidon at Kart Hadst while serving as the personal physician to the magistrate. That city is foul," he hesitated and looked about us before he continued, "It was corrupt in its politics, and policies with the tribes when I arrived. I was loath to stay there. So, when I'd heard that the fleet needed healers to sign on, I was relieved to take a new position. Looking back, I now know it was the hand of providence that made me do it, for to meet Poseidon and serve him all these years, has been the greatest honor of my life."

He looked across the room at the steady flow of dignitaries surrounding Poseidon and laughed out loud.

"Nothing could be further from my Master's comfort than to be here, surrounded by such pomp and splendor," he said.

"What do you mean?" I asked, following his gaze, letting my eyes rest on Poseidon's stiff and formal profile.

"I mean the commander's not like them, and he's got no love for politics. When I first met him, one of his ship commanders had fallen terribly ill. The poor man had suffered for days before I was assigned to the fleet. When I arrived on the dock, I was surprised to find that the man had been taken to the Great White Horse, that's what they call Poseidon's ship, and Poseidon himself sat by his bedside."

Several women, who had noticed Apollo when we had all sat down, now lingered nearby. As Apollo continued with his tale, they took up chairs beside our table listening in. Apollo grinned at them warmly as they approached and Artemis, and I tried to suppress our smiles. Apollo was as handsome and captivating as ever.

"Poseidon's not an ordinary Lord," he went on, "I think in his heart he's part priest. I've never met a leader like him. He sat by that man's side all through the night, until the fever broke."

He paused there. One of the women had refilled his goblet while he had spoken and he sipped his wine slowly, his gaze resting on the fountain as he recalled the scene.

"Have you ever heard of an Atlantian leader doing such a thing?" he mused. "As you see, Poseidon's no ordinary man," he continued, coming back to himself. "He's as much at home speaking to the sea as he is directing his men. I was honored when he asked me to serve him."

Leaning deeper into the couch, I let my head rest on Artemis's shoulder, closing my eyes. I could feel the strong connection and love between her and Apollo and relaxed into the softness of it.

Apollo went on, and I listened, dropping into the images that his stories evoked, his warmhearted tone so sincere and memorable. When we were children, growing up together on the Eastern shore, there had been many long nights of story-telling, on the beach, by a fire. That old, safe feeling of being with my friends seemed to rise and hold me as Apollo told his tale of two great rivers called the Tigris and Euphrates, where the people called themselves the Sag-Giga. I listened as he told stories of love and war, sharing his immense pleasure and respect for their science.

"They even have their own form of writing, and they've invented wheels like ours," he said with obvious delight. "The great river floods and fills the valley, irrigating their crops," he went on, but as he spoke, I began to drift with the images his words conjured.

I tried to listen, but the timbre of his voice lulled me deeper into the current beneath his words, deeper, and deeper, until I fell into the realm of true Sight.

I could feel my body trembling, somewhere far away, as I slipped into trance. A strong current seemed to lift me from my chair, as the overwhelming barrage of sights, and sounds, emanating from the people in the room, washed over me. And then there was silence and a vision formed in front of me.

I saw Athena on a horse at my right, and Artemis to my left, each with sword in hand. I could almost feel the crisp air against my face as we rode hard toward the rise of an estate in the distance. A sound carried on the wind that I soon recognized as the ram's horn. It was sharp, and short sounding three times—the call to battle. We sped over the rise of a hill pulling our horses sharply to a halt. The steeds whinnied, steam rising from their nostrils.

Down below us, in the valley, troops gathered. Hundreds, no, thousands of men and women were all turned toward the figure on the ridge below us where a young woman clad in armor sounded the horn again. Three sharp blows. A war cry rose like thunder, and I leaned forward over the horse's neck to make out the woman's face.

*Ilithyia?*

The scene blurred sharply. A thick blackness enveloped me, and the earth began to tremble. I heard people screaming and a loud crack. There was a flash of light, and then I saw it, a terrifying wave of water rushing toward us. Looking down I saw the stone floor about me shatter and rip apart. I cried out as I began to fall into space.

Suddenly, I felt Artemis's hand tight on my wrist and her calm voice.

"Reverence," she said, and then again, "Hera, Hera."

The sounds of the Titan party came back into focus. I could hear people's voices scraping painfully against my mind. I struggled to understand what was happening, and when I opened my eyes, the small group of people around Apollo stared at me. Several women called for the attendant, and Apollo moved to my side.

"You were in vision," Apollo's voice cut through the sound, and I felt his soft touch on my other wrist.

"You cried out Ilithyia's name, and then you seemed to fall forward," Artemis said, concern clear in her eyes.

Apollo's hand was warm, and I could feel him pulling me back through my pulse, and the sound about me diminished its effect on my nerves. I opened my eyes wider trying to take in the features of his face. He was a healer to be sure. All the brashness of youth had softened, and his eyes were kind and wise.

I shook my head forcing a smile.

"It sometimes happens, when I'm exhausted or feel safe."

"Feel safe?" Apollo said glancing at his sister.

Artemis grimaced, taking my hand. "We are not always amongst friends here, Apollo," she said.

Artemis squeezed my hand. "We should get you back to the palace," she said.

"Yes," I said weakly.

I reached out wrapping my arms around Apollo's neck and kissed his cheek to honor him before the group.

"I've missed you," I said in a near whisper.

I could see the acknowledgment in his look. The women and the few men that had been sitting about us rose as I did, making way for me to pass. Their looks revealed that they had all known I was in a vision. Nothing like this had come upon me unbidden in years, and I was surprised at how vulnerable I felt. Artemis and Apollo walked me through the throng in the room, gesturing my withdrawal. The music stopped as was the custom and I turned to give my blessing, but Hades stepped close to my side.

"You've had a vision, Lady?" he shouted, pushing Apollo aside and taking firm hold of my arm.

I shuddered. Touching my person was a gesture of intimacy that I didn't welcome from him. It was something people would notice. I struggled to think if I should shake him off publicly, but my mind was still soft, floating on the surface of what I'd seen. Artemis had tightened her grip on my other side and stood protectively close to me.

"And at such a public place, and time, surely, Lady, you'll share with us what you saw?"

People had stopped dancing and were looking at us now. I struggled to think and act with wisdom. I was not a party trick to be used to entertain Hades's guests, but the images were still soft and close.

"The High Priestess should retire, now," Artemis said,

letting go of my arm so that I could raise my hand in blessing.

"You can't leave us yet," Hades insisted, speaking more to the crowded room than to me. "Come, tell us what you've seen!"

The pictures of the flood still shimmered before my eyes. I should have held my tongue, seeing the trap, but my eyes were flooded again with the images, and the words came from my lips as if being pulled from me.

"There was a wall of water," I said. "And the earth was shaking."

A dull murmur rose about me. I felt Zeus and Athena begin to move across the room toward me.

"It was strong, and I was… *afraid*. The quake lasted too long, and the floor opened up into a wide black space, and I fell!"

The sound of my voice rose, echoing through the hall.

There was movement around me as Athena pushed her way between me, and Hades laying a firm, but gentle hand on my shoulder.

"Reverence," she said stopping me from saying any more.

The images dissipated, like fluttering wings, and I came back to the room with the piercing realization that I'd blundered. I could sense Hades's pleasure. Heat rose in my cheeks.

"Ah, of course, we should have known!" Hades spoke loudly. "The never-ending story of destruction. It amazes me, Lady, that every time the nobility of our land gathers, *some* priestess has a dire vision to share!"

People's faces relaxed, and some smiled, nodding. Soft laughter rose about us.

"You're the one who asked her to share it," Artemis half growled rounding on Hades and the crowd.

It was very unlike her, and I could see the strain on her faces. I held up my hand.

"It's alright, really," I said with as much force as I could muster.

I was tired, but I pulled myself up, looking fixedly into Hades's eyes. My voice cracked with emotion as I spoke.

"The only wonder to me, Lucifer, is that so many warnings can be given, and still so few in power heed them." I smiled tightly turning to the assembly before he could reply. "I will not bore the Titan dynasty, or its noble allies any further with my dreams, or visions. This is a celebration!"

I turned toward Zeus who stood beside Athena, and I saw that Poseidon had stepped up with him. Both men were frowning. I reached out a hand toward Poseidon and continued.

"Our hero has returned to us. Let us rejoice!"

Apollo applauded, and the crowd took it up. Despite Hades irreverent look, I kept the forced smile on my lips. All eyes were on Poseidon now, as he took his place beside me, pushing Hades farther to one side. Poseidon smiled warmly, holding up his hands.

"It is good to be home," his voice filled the room. "My men and I are honored to be back with our people, on our sacred shores for whatever time we may have left here!"

Athena glanced at me sideways. Never, in all the years at the capital had any Titan given public credence to our warnings.

"Let me be clear, Reverence," he continued, turning toward me. "Not all the Titans shall turn away from the wisdom of the High Priestess's visions. There are those of us that know the fate of our people lies in your hands."

I could feel Hades burning. He stepped forward, his thin mouth pursed, strong lines of anger furrowed over his brow, but Zeus laid a heavy hand on his shoulder.

*So, the brothers are not all of one mind.*

I nodded in gratitude as Poseidon looked down at me, and then began to raise my hand to give the blessing, and depart, but Poseidon reached out, taking my palm in his. A shock moved through me. In quick, elegant gesture, he knelt down before me pressing his lips to the emerald ring that bound me to my station as High Priestess. It was an ancient tradition, the highest sign of respect in which a warrior avowed loyalty. Male or female mattered not, to kiss the ring was to declare one's devotion.

There were gasps and exclamations throughout the gathering. Zeus took a step backward, his face drawn in surprise, and I felt Hades's eyes burning into us.

When Poseidon rose to his feet, he spoke with the strong voice of a man used to command.

"You have my pledge, Reverence, and the loyalty of my men, and our ships. It is our honor to serve the Emerald Temple and the command of the High Priestess."

I stared into Poseidon's eyes. The deep blue pools I looked into were filled with strong feeling and strength.

"I thank you," I said quietly.

Turning back to the assembly I gave the sign of my blessing. In a moment, Athena led my guard, which surrounded me like a ship, moving me toward the heavy double doors. The crowd stepped aside, bowing in deference as I went.

As I walked away, I could feel Poseidon's gaze upon me, like a ray of sunlight, warming me. When I reached the landing, I hesitated, turning back. There he stood, radiating a dignified grace as he watched me go. He looked at me over the crowded room and smiled.

# CHAPTER FIVE

THE WEEKS PASSED SLOWLY, and I saw little of Poseidon. His father gave him a room in his estate, but I heard that he usually stayed on his ship with his men. Through Ares and Zeus, who came to me in the evenings to take their supper, I learned that only half of Poseidon's ships were now docked in our harbors. The rest were severely damaged and left to limp home behind them. A small force of fresh ships from an allied dynasty had set off with supplies to guide them.

"It will be several full turns of the moon before the ships are ready to return to Kart Hadst, but when we go, I'll have a ship set aside for your priestesses," Zeus told me one night as my attendant served him more ale.

We sat outside, dining on the wide verandah that overlooked the round temple, the stables and the healing rooms beyond. Far below I could make out the dim outline of the encircled harbors and the sea. The sun was low in the sky before us, and we watched in silence as the orange flame dipped below the horizon, and the clouds that splayed out above it caught fire.

Ares stabbed at another piece of lamb and reached for the wine flask, breaking our reverie. He took a long swallow from his cup and then raised his eyes to his father.

"Does Uncle Hades know Mother will have an entire ship to fill?" he asked.

Zeus's face dropped, and he hesitated. He glanced at me, and I could see that he had regretted mentioning it in front of our son. I reached out and rested my hand on Ares's shoulder, squeezing it gently.

"It would be best if Hades didn't know until the day of departure draws closer," I said. "You and your father are helping us build our temple in Kart Hadst by giving me one of your own ships."

Ares turned to look at me. He paused a moment and then nodded thoughtfully. "I understand, Mother," he said. "But why won't the council allow you the use of the fleet?"

I threw up my hands. "A good question, my son," I said. "Why indeed? And why have they forbidden others from building ships and organizing their own evacuations?"

Ares stopped eating and looked into my eyes in earnest. "Because there are many ways to fight a war," he said.

I was surprised by his answer and turned to Zeus who had put down his knife and was staring at his son.

"The council is using all of you in different ways to assure a new order of things. They keep Father fighting the tribes so he'll be too busy to help initiate new settlements. They keep Poseidon well funded so his ships are far afield and cannot help to bring people who cling to the old ways to their new city. And most importantly, they keep the priestesses from gaining a foothold at Kart Hadst."

Zeus whistled, and pushed his chair back from the table. He rose to his feet and paced to the edge of the verandah, shaking his head. I leaned closer to Ares with keen interest.

"And why would the council do these things?" I asked.

Ares's eyes were on his father, and I could see he didn't want to displease him. He waited until Zeus turned to us again.

"Go on," Zeus urged, but I could hear the note of doubt in his voice. "Answer your mother's question."

I saw a dark shadow fall over my son's face, and I realized how much his father's approval meant to him. When we were alone, he talked easier and was likely to accept my tenderness, but around Zeus, he became wary and stiff. Ares had a keen mind, and the words he spoke now were nothing new to me, but from the look on Zeus's face, the thought hadn't occurred to him.

"Well?" Zeus commanded. "Exactly why would the council use us in such a way?"

Ares swallowed hard. His lips had gone dry. He put down his fork, pushed his chair away from the table and stood as if called to salute.

"It seems to me," Ares said carefully, "that the council is at war with the past."

I smiled. *Well done, my son,* I thought. I turned to Zeus, but the look on his face was hard.

"It's treason to speak this way!" Zeus said. "And from my own son!"

I'd never seen him so quick to flare, but realized by Ares's reaction that this was nothing new for him. I rose to my feet and stepped away from the table, trying to collect my thoughts.

Zeus brushed by me and struck Ares across the face.

"Zeus!" Ares fell to the ground. I rushed to his side as his father moved toward him again, but I threw my body between them and hissed at Zeus. "Have you gone mad?"

There was movement from inside the Megaron, and my guards clashed through the doors with swords already drawn. Zeus rounded on them. He lifted the chair by his side and flung it at the first one, reaching for his own sword to take on the second. I gripped Ares's arm tightly and commanded them to stop, but Zeus swung hard. The woman raised her blade and met his metal defensively. The other woman had dodged the chair and circled behind him. I froze for a moment, disbelieving until I realized my guard would even fight the king in service of my protection.

"Stop this!" I called out again.

The first woman wavered, keeping her blade in a defensive posture as she moved her body between Zeus and me. Ares wiped the blood that trickled from the corner of his mouth with the back of his hand and struggled to his feet. His voice rang out to Zeus to stop his attack on the other woman. Zeus used the advantage of his strength to back her into the corner. Ares called out to his father again, and this time he slowed his attack and then leveled his sword and stopped. He was breathing heavily, his face red with rage. He backed away from us all toward the railing of the verandah. When his eyes caught mine he seemed surprised to see me, so lost had he been in his fight.

"Hera?" he said, and then again stronger, "Hera?"

I shook my head, trying to control my own anger.

"Zeus, calm yourself," I said. "It's only my guard and your own son!"

I felt Ares's hand on my shoulder, and he pushed me gently behind him. It was a brave thing to do.

"No, Mother," he said. "It's my fault, Father's right." He moved slowly toward Zeus. "I didn't think before I spoke," he continued. "I'm sorry, Father."

He dipped his head as if ashamed. I stood aghast, watching the scene, which I now understood was one my son had gone through many times before. Zeus shook his head and put up his weapon. He moved toward Ares briskly and reached out a hand.

"A warrior doesn't question his orders," Zeus said.

"No, Father."

The two faced each other stiffly and locked hands over each other's wrists in the warrior's bond. Zeus dismissed him. Ares turned formally and nodded in my direction than left the room. My guard stood at attention, one on either side, but I asked them to retreat. They moved away as far as the entrance but kept me in their sights. A wave of embarrassment ran through me. I stared at Zeus, clenching my fists. He moved uncomfortably toward the table and took his seat. I took a deep breath.

"The boy's got to learn," Zeus said. "His ideas are outlandish and unwelcome."

"Unwelcome to whom?" I said.

He grimaced. Clapping his hands together for our attendant he barked at her to take away his plate and bring fresh honeyed cakes and more ale. I paced for a few minutes, struggling to control my rage.

When the woman left us, I took my seat beside him and stared out to sea as he picked at his food, until finally he pushed it away and sighed heavily.

"I'm sorry," he said. "I shouldn't have reacted that way. It's just that to hear such things from my own son—"

"You told him to speak."

"I know."

"And it was an intelligent observation."

"Yes, but Hera," he looked at me pleadingly now, his brows furrowed. "If it's true—"

He threw up his hands and leaned forward

"I've been fighting for more than ten years to secure more land on the continent and expand Kart Hadst. I've never questioned why the council has supported me, but if what the boy says is true..." his voice trailed off. He sat staring at me, his brow furrowed and his eyes ablaze with insight. "Why hasn't the council bidden me take my warriors further east to set up new colonies? Knowing a catastrophe is at hand why haven't they recalled Poseidon's fleet to begin an evacuation?"

I shook my head. The answer was obvious, but I could see it was important that Zeus answer this himself. He reached for his ale and sighed, his shoulders relaxing. His look softened, and he sat back in his chair. When he spoke, his tone was soft.

"Hera, I fear that when the time comes, the council will leave the elders behind on Atlantis."

I knew this would undoubtedly be so, but I pressed him further.

"Why?"

"They don't want anyone or anything that will teach the new generation the old ways. Ares is right. That's the true war we're fighting, isn't it?"

I nodded.

Pain apparent on his face as if I'd struck him. "And my warriors, my army—we *are* being used."

I said nothing; there was nothing more to say. The wind blew hard through the palms and somewhere in the distance hounds bayed. Zeus turned away from me then and looked out to the horizon.

"You must speak to Ares," I said gently.

"He's a warrior," Zeus said stiffly. "A warrior follows orders—"

"Yes," I interjected, "a warrior follows orders, but Ares will not just be a warrior, Zeus."

He turned to me with surprise as if the idea had never occurred to him.

"A warrior must follow orders without question," I continued, "this is true. But a leader—" I said it softly, giving the word an air of courage and honor. "A *leader* must question everything and everyone. His orders will be followed."

I could see him trying the idea of it on, finding fault in his own leadership. It soured his expression, but he didn't reject it. I pressed him further.

"Our son will be a great leader, Zeus. He only needs you to show him the way."

He liked that. A smile pulled at the corners of his mouth, and his thin lips quivered. He turned and looked back out to sea, but I could feel that something had changed in the air about us.

"I'll talk to the boy," he said, his usual confidence returning to his tone.

The sky was now growing dark, and my ladies removed the last remnants of the meal. A small man came to fill the oil lamps and light them. As I rose to withdraw, Zeus reached for my hand. His face seemed young, and I could sense a question behind his gaze.

"I should have done this a long time ago," he said, his hand shaking slightly as he dropped to one knee and pulled my hand to his lips. He kissed the ring on my second finger as Poseidon had done and a cold chill swept over me. "I will not let them vanquish you, Hera, or cast you aside."

The words were intensely personal, and I could see his sincerity in his gaze, but I knew Zeus didn't understand the meaning of the gesture. He wanted me. The surety of his desire crackled over my skin, and I had to steady my hand so that I did not pull away. He would not let them leave me behind because he required me. I'd long ago come to understand that Zeus's need could look like loyalty and even love. I wished I could trust his oath, but I knew better. I gave him the acknowledgment he needed, and when he rose, I moved into his arms and kissed his cheeks. It would have to be enough.

I returned to my room and walked the floor anxiously. If Zeus swung the full force of his army in the service of the Emerald Temple… but I stopped myself. No, he wouldn't do that. He was trying to be loyal to *me*. He sought to please *me* as Ares had sought to please him. I realized with exasperation that I should've reached out to this loyalty a long time ago. Now, it was too late.

I slipped on my cloak and stepped into the garden. The moon was already high above me and almost round, a dim mustard hue. *The temple.*

The words filled my mind and senses. Yes. I should take myself to the temple where the ancient power pulsed so readily. I could walk the labyrinth to calm my mind and touch the wisdom I desperately needed to guide me now.

I moved quickly through the halls and down the road toward the small hill and plateau of the temple. Signaling my guard to stay behind, I walked the long, spiraled path of the labyrinth, which calmed my mind and soothed my nerves. As I neared its center, I chanted, sinking further into the current of my true self, formless awareness and my all-knowing wisdom. When I was at peace, I walked back through the spiral, the song in my breast rising to my lips reverberating through the potent darkness about me.

My hips swayed easily as I took the last steps, which led to the temple stairs. I mounted each one slowly, the night moving inside of my body, filling me with her grace. When I reached the temple doors, I stopped abruptly. There was a tall figure standing in the shadows, but I sensed no ill intent.

"Who's there?" I commanded.

The figure moved immediately stepping into the light of the moon. It was a man. He stepped forward and pulled down the hood of his cloak.

"Forgive me, Reverence," he said.

I stared up into his blue eyes and forgot why I had come.

"I didn't mean to spy on you," Poseidon continued. "I came to see the temple, and when I saw you in the labyrinth, I did not want to disturb you."

"But why are you here?" I said, still staring.

He smiled then, and his face softened, making him look much younger.

"This was my mother's temple when I was a boy. She used to bring me here each morning and together we'd sit and pray."

"Your mother?"

I tried to come back to myself, but the power of vision was now close at hand. Images leaped before my eyes, and I saw the young boy kneeling with his mother in this place.

"It must have been beautiful," I said, "We've tried to bring it back. You should see it in the daylight."

He shook his head and looked at me quizzically.

"But you've made it a place only for women, now," he said.

The words stung me, though they were true. I'd ordered the temple closed to men as the priests of the other temples in the city had ordered their doors closed to women. It had made sense at the time, but now, I saw the injustice of my action.

"Times have changed," he said as if sensing my regret. "There's no place in the city for the women's mysteries anymore. I would have done the same."

I reached my hand out toward the darkness and the land.

"The night is a temple," I said. "The moon is High Priestess."

"And the day is a temple," he continued, "and the sun a High Priest?"

"It could be so," I said.

I turned and moved toward the door, pulling it open, signaling him to follow me. He took a few steps and was at my side. A strong, golden glow filled the room from the lamps lit on the altar in the center. I handed him a torch from the wall and beckoned him to light the flame so he could better see the space. As he did so, I saw images in the orange flames. I saw him seated on a horse, and I was behind him, my arms wrapped around his waist. I was laughing, happily.

"Reverence," he said tentatively. "Lady?"

I shook my head, turning away. Moving toward the altar, I pulled cedar and rosemary from one of the baskets there and sprinkled them over the flame. A hiss and snap filled my ears, and then the wonderful aroma permeated me, steadying my vision. I stayed there by the altar as he circled the large room, holding the flame up to the walls to see the images that had been painted there. I had commissioned scenes of women's rites and rituals; symbols of the mind that had set itself free and realized unity with all things. As he stared at them intently, reading into their meaning, I realized that he was the first man that had been allowed inside to see them. For a moment I felt a dim sense of betrayal, but I shook it off. I knew better. These scenes were not for the eyes of beings that held themselves separate, or better than, or in competition. These were images meant to inspire the true Self in which male and female were one. He knew this. And he did them honor.

The time passed slowly, but each moment felt a treasure in his quiet presence. I had a sudden desire to reach out and touch him, and when he'd finished and returned to the altar, my lips burned at the thought of brushing them against his. I took a breath and busied myself with spreading more cedar over the fire. When I looked up, he was staring at me intently.

"Thank you," he said.

My lips quivered. A shadow fell across half his face as the torch flickered and began to die down.

"There's one other thing," he continued.

He took a step closer.

"When my ships passed through the great pillars of the continent we were taken by a storm," he began. "It was unlike any we'd encountered, and I was sure we would not survive its wrath. Even though I called to the elements as my mother had taught me, a trick that had won us our lives before, I couldn't calm the seas. But then," he paused. I knew my eyes had grown wide and I was struggling to keep my composure. "A woman was standing on my foredeck, and she raised herself up as only a priestess could, and she talked to the storm, and it heeded her command."

"I had thought it a dream at first," I whispered.

He nodded. I wanted to tell him then of the other dreams, the ones I'd had of him all these years, but I couldn't find the words or the courage.

"I wasn't the only one to see the apparition," he went on solemnly. "My men know what happened, and it will not take long for them to understand it was you. Rumors are already afoot. I bring this to you, Lady, because I see that the council is set so firmly against you, and the priestesses, and is moved by my brother Hades—."

I frowned. "And when Hades realizes I have so much loyalty in the fleet, he will act swiftly against me. I thank you for the warning, Poseidon," I said.

He nodded, his face grim.

We stood staring at each other. When it seemed he would say no more I began to turn, but then I heard his voice, very quiet, and for the first time unsure.

"I wonder," he said, "why you came to us that day?" He paused as I turned back toward him. "I wonder," he said so quietly that I had to lean forward to hear him, "why you came to me?"

*He is Zeus's brother,* I thought, trying to steady myself against the desire to move toward him.

I was now so close I could smell the mint on his breath, and the rose oil faint on his skin. I struggled to keep my composure, to maintain my dignity as High Priestess, even as I longed to deny the protocol of my station.

"I go where the current takes me," I said.

He nodded. The torch sputtered and hissed, and he held it away from me.

"I should go," he said.

"Yes, it's late."

Neither of us moved.

There was a sound in the room beyond the far wall. I turned sharply realizing the priestess who kept the temple was coming to tend the oil lamps that would burn through the night. When I turned back around Poseidon had moved to the door. Placing the torch back on the wall he dipped his head gently in my direction as he disappeared into the night.

# CHAPTER SIX

IN THE SEASON IT TOOK for the fleet to be made ready again for the sea, Ares became a man.

It was late summer, and the winds were changing their course. The ships would have to leave soon, for it was well known that once the winter set in, the great pillars, guardians of the Aegean Sea, would be impassable until spring. The sailors had enjoyed their reunions at home but when the wind changed, so did their moods, and I could see the change in their pace as they hurried to make the last repairs.

I now spent my mornings at the temple, preparing women for the voyage, and teaching newly made priestesses the rituals I wished for them to keep there. I worked in the afternoons at the harbor until late in the day. I'd heard some say that I was over dedicated to the success of the Emerald Temple in Kart Hadst, but staying busy was the only way I could keep away from Zeus's elder brother. After the night in the temple, Poseidon had thankfully remained at his father's house, and I took great pains to avoid him.

Though the weather was turning, I still wore a short tunic when I worked at the harbor and took part in the organization of the ship that Zeus had set aside for the temple. By now, the council was well aware of what he'd done, but couldn't cross him for they had no hold on his fleet. Zeus's consortium of ships was small compared to the massive fleet of big-hulled ships that Poseidon controlled, but it was enough to shuttle a half legion of his men from port to port. He had brought six vessels with him and over three hundred men. The ship he'd set aside for me was lightly manned and had a deep bulkhead in which I was able to take sacred items safely to their new port.

I'd named Persephone, who was now a high priestess in her own right, as ambassador of the journey. She would take the new priestesses to Kart Hadst and try to make sense of what was going on there. I knew Aphrodite, who ruled in my place at the temple there, would not welcome her intrusion, but the two had trained together for many years, and I hoped their common past might help them now. Thirty young priestesses would go with her, along with a small honor guard that Athena and I had hand-picked, of eight well-trained temple warriors whose loyalty would never come into question.

Several hundred families had been chosen to make the journey on Poseidon's fleet, and they were busy each day at the docks as well. I watched them carefully noting they all seemed to have been chosen from Caledocean itself, and most were quite young. There were many more children than I'd expected, but then, this would fit into Hades's plans perfectly; the council would be seen as embarking on our expansion efforts while taking only those who were used to their ways.

I thought of my mother, then. She had left us, years ago, on a small ship of my father's design, intending to see his homeland in the East. It had been a difficult goodbye for I knew I wouldn't see them again. Mother had held me in her arms a very long time, and when she was done, she whispered, "The time is coming Hera. Save as many as you can." She pressed her lips to my forehead. The place on my brow still tingled when I thought of her.

Now, as I stood beside my own vessel overseeing its detachment of women and the supplies we sought to store, I recalled her words and felt the chill of failure creep over my skin. *One ship.* It was not enough, and it was difficult to pretend I was grateful for it.

Zeus waved to me from his horse where he rode with a small detachment of his men to oversee the camp they'd struck in the flatlands outside the city. I shielded my eyes with one hand and waved back with the other. We'd grown closer on this visit. He and Ares joined me at supper regularly. I'd noticed a change in Zeus's countenance toward our son and Ares bloomed under his father's lighter hand.

As I waved at Zeus, another hand appeared in the air, and I recognized Ares at his side. The Titans had taken to wearing the priestess's colors, years ago, and the troupe was all clad in black. Ares had added a long cloak like his father's with the lightning bolt insignia sewed in gold along its hem, and it made him look taller in the saddle. He veered off from his father and trotted in my direction, dismounting at the dock. I moved to him and held out my arms. He no longer stiffened when I required a hug. He smiled at me, which was a rare thing, and his eyes lit up when he did. He had grown another half foot this season. He was now as tall as his father.

"How go the preparations?" he asked.

I turned to the boat with its high stack of crates and barrels still sitting awkwardly on the deck.

"It will only be another few days," I answered, "and the priestess ship will be ready to sail."

"Good."

He turned to the west and pointed out to sea. An arrowhead of pelicans, their wings stretched wide, glided to the north.

"The birds are nesting," Ares continued. "We don't have much time now. Father says the winds are changing."

"We will be ready in time," I assured him, as I turned and reached for Pegasus.

Ares passed a sharp eye over him as I mounted and then took his place on his own steed.

"Mother, you can have your choice of any horse," he began, but I gave him a hard look, and he held up his hand, laughing. "I know, I know. There is not another horse like Pegasus!"

He accompanied me up the long slope to the road and then to my surprise, instead of turning off to join his father, he nudged his mount closer to me and kept pace as I turned back toward the estate.

"I imagine the priestesses are pleased to be making a stronger stand in Kart Hadst," Ares said mildly.

I'd never known my son to make idle chat and was surprised.

"We are," I answered. "It will be good to have someone I trust at the temple there so I might know what's going on!"

"Yes, I've met your emissary, Aphrodite, and aside from her social skills I can't imagine how you'd meant her to lead the effort there!"

I shook my head. "It was a mistake," I admitted. "One that you and your father will now help me rectify."

Ares smiled at that.

"I want to help the priestesses," he said. "I've been learning more about what you face, and it's not right, it's not fair."

I turned to him. His jaw was set and his brow furrowed.

"There's a young woman," he went on, "an initiate in the Emerald Temple," but here he hesitated and looked off into the horizon abruptly.

"And she's your friend," I questioned gently.

"Oh, she's more than that, Mother," he said quickly. "I love her."

A cool breeze moved over us, and I pulled my cloak closer about me taking a moment to sense his sincerity. His look was softer now, his full lips smiling.

"Who is she?"

His eyes flashed as he said her name.

"Aria," he said warmly. "She's the daughter of Asterion, a well-liked priest at the temple of light. Uncle Hades says he's a smart man who'll join us in Kart Hadst soon, but she's being trained to come to the temple, Mother. She wishes to serve you."

Ah. I glanced sideways at him, knowing now where this conversation was going.

"If you meet her, Mother, you'll see how wonderful she is. She's already passed her tests with Athena." He stopped there, but I sensed there was more. He wanted something but was having a difficult time asking.

"So, you love her," I said trying to make it easier for him. "And I'm sure that means you'd like her to come with you to Kart Hadst."

He nodded, "Yes, yes that's really it, mother. You see, all that's left is her final pledge and your acceptance and then she could take her training in Kart Hadst."

I was quiet for a long time as the horses passed through the busy market and up the familiar hill to the estate. Ares didn't press me. We both knew he was not telling me a story but asking a question. He was able to hold his own desire in check to give me time to consider. Thinking back to when I was his age, filled with desire and love, I didn't blame him for the asking.

When we'd passed the noise of the market and the tanners sheds at the base of the hill, I spoke.

"I can't interfere with the process a woman must go through to become a priestess," I said.

"And she wouldn't want you to, Mother," Ares said hastily. "It's only that I thought things might be done more quickly, and if she is found worthy—"

"And if she's not?"

He was silent, his lips pursed as if he was strategizing.

"She must still pass Demeter's tests, and that will take three full nights. I cannot hurry what must be done. And if she passes and still wishes to join the temple, then she must face me."

He turned uncomfortably in the saddle at that, his eyes gone thin and alert like a bird's.

"If Demeter finds her worthy, surely—"

"No, Ares. I do not choose a priestess. In the end, it's the great current which tells me who is meant for the priestess' life. I cannot say what the right action is."

We rode on in silence until we mounted the hill and the horses picked up speed as they neared the stable. When we dismounted and pulled the light saddles from the horses' backs, Ares took hold of Pegasus's halter.

"I'll brush him down, Mother," he said solemnly.

The smile was gone from his face, and I felt the consternation in his strong limbs. I nodded, patted Pegasus warmly on the neck, and then nuzzled him. He nibbled on my hair and cheek until I laughed. Turning, I saw Ares staring at me with soft eyes.

An awkward feeling rose up within me until it became a defined sense of guilt. This is what I'd never been able to give my son, this warm, playful love that endured imperfection. He'd never known this kind of love with his father, and even in this short time with me, I could see he would have thrived under such attention.

I dropped my hand from Pegasus and turned to Ares.

"I can't assure you the outcome, but Demeter is here for the ship launching, and I will bid her give the girl her tests now, rather than waiting until the spring."

His eyes locked on mine. He didn't smile, but nodded and turned back to his horse with the brush in his hand.

"Thank you, Mother," he said over his shoulder. "We will both be grateful to you."

I regretted the promise almost as soon as I'd made it. The next few days were hectic and hurried and filled with diplomatic demands. Demeter had said nothing when I'd asked her to oversee the arrangements to take Aria into the temple here, at Caledocean, but I could see the strain on her face.

I relayed Aria's progress to Ares as it came. He had retreated into himself since our talk and now sat rigidly at the supper table, night after night, barely eating.

Zeus looked at me across the food and tilted his head slightly in Ares's direction, but I shook him off. The girl was excelling, and yet I grew miserable at the thought of what my son would think if, at the final interview, the great current did not give permission to make her one of our own.

When Ares left the room, Zeus and I exhaled loudly, then caught each other's eyes and laughed.

"I think he's really in love," Zeus said sourly. "Fine time, when I need him to see to the men!"

"Oh Zeus," I chided, "You of all people, to say such a thing."

He smiled at that. "It's true," he said. "I wasn't much older than him when I fell in love with you."

His eyes burned into me, and he wasn't laughing anymore. He reached his hand across the table with the palm open to me. Slowly, I set my own on top of his.

"I've been thinking," he said in a low voice, then. "About what you said about the difference between warriors and leaders."

I listened intently.

"It seems to me that Kart Hadst isn't the only land fit for Atlanteans to settle. I have a desire to see some of these other places my brother has mapped for possible settlements in the land they call Macedonia. There's one to the north of Kart Hadst. It has a great mountain they've named Olympus, after our own Olympia, and Poseidon tells me the land is fertile from the foothills to the sea. The tribes there are still nomadic, and the land is not settled. When we leave, I plan to set your ship in my brother's care and then go on to Olympus with my men. We'll winter there and return to Kart Hadst in the spring."

My mouth fell open. Was he actually going to break from the council?

"No one will oppose me, Hera," he said squeezing my hand. "I have firm control of the army. They are loyal to my captains and me. I've thought it through. This is what a good leader should do."

I nodded but didn't trust myself to speak. He leaned forward and lifted my hand to his lips, slowly, softly.

"I have always hoped—" he began.

I reached out my other hand, placing my fingers beside his cheek. "No, Zeus, don't say it. I cannot give you what you want. We both know it." I paused to let the truth rest about us. "But this thing that you speak of, this new settlement … You will have my full support. This, we can do together."

I moved closer to him and took both his hands in mine. "Perhaps this is our true destiny together, Zeus? Perhaps now—"

But he pulled away sharply. He nodded and made a sound of assent, but he'd retreated behind his eyes. This was not what he wanted to hear.

He pushed his chair away from the table and gave me a rigid tilt of his head and then turned and left the room.

The next morning I received the call that Aria had passed her third night of Demeter's mysteries. She had been taken to the healers' court where she rested now, awaiting a final audience with me in the temple. Ares hovered at the door of my chamber when I came out, and to my surprise, Hades and Kronos were at his side. They followed close behind as I strode out toward the temple. When I pointed to the building Aria was housed in, Ares trotted off with the first smile I'd seen on his face in days. Hades and Kronos waited until he was out of earshot and then came to the point.

"There are some things we thought you should know," Kronos began. His body was still tall but slightly hunched, his hair long and white. He leaned heavily on his son's arm as we followed the path Ares had taken.

"The girl comes from a very prominent family," Hades said. "Her father, Asterion, has been a good friend to the

Titans. We owe him a debt of gratitude for his work in Kart Hadst."

I nodded but kept quiet as we neared the healer's complex outside the temple.

"He will make a fine representative in the new city," Kronos said. "And should his daughter join him, Ares could make a powerful union."

I stopped for a moment, and the men slowed, turning back to face me.

"What sort of union do you think a priestess of the Emerald Temple could make with a layman? Certainly not one of your new marriage rituals."

Hades stepped forward his chin raised slightly so that he appeared to be looking down his nose at me. "And why not?" he said. "You married Zeus, didn't you?"

"No," I countered, "I took the Heiros Gamos vows. We made the sacred marriage for the good of Atlantis. A priestess might take a consort or one day have a mate, but the kind of union you speak of is a marriage, a contract that gives a man ownership of a woman and her children. Such a thing would never attract a woman of the temple."

"But who knows?" Kronos sputtered shuffling toward me. "She may not even finish her training once she's in Kart Hadst and sees the life Ares might give her!"

The old man stared at me expectantly oblivious to the insult he'd just cast upon the devotion and dedication of the priestess' calling. I sighed.

"I assure you I'd like nothing more than to grant my son his desire, but it isn't my decision alone. I cannot yet speak for the great current that knows the right action of all things."

Hades scowled openly. I was taken aback for although we differed in our politics, I had thought that surely one who ruled the Temple of Light and carried the title of Lucifer must have some access to the life current. But then, if he had, the Temple of Light would not have become so corrupt since his rise to power.

Kronos twisted his mouth into an ugly expression and turned away from me as Hades did. The two men started off toward the healers' chambers. I watched them go, lifting their hands to the man who waited anxiously at the chamber doors. He was, no doubt, Aria's father. I watched him shake hands with Hades and Kronos, and then the three men disappeared inside.

My breath was audible with relief when they were gone. Still, a low level of agitation pressed at my limbs, and a light humming sound rang in my head. *It's just frustration,* I said to myself. Moving quickly up the temple steps, I entered the inner sanctum, and sat down at the altar. I anointed myself, pulling out the emerald medallion that lay warm against my skin. I touched it lightly to my brow to bring my focus to that place that could see beyond the visible outline of things, deeper into their essence. The chant of Peace rose to my lips and reverberated in my chest. Still, my mind was pulled by the strange sensation that swam throughout my limbs.

*Calm yourself,* I insisted silently. *The current and I are one.*

A long time passed. Smoke rose from the altar. My senses stilled and numbed, and quiet filled me. The power of the place always brought on my visions with startling ease. I wasn't surprised when images leaped before my closed eyes.

I could see the boats in the harbor, peaceful, lulling, ready to sail, and then a wave reached up from beyond the banks stretching its white fingers forward against the stone harbor walls.

I stopped chanting, opening my eyes slightly, confused by the scene. As I looked at the altar, each holy item became infused with light, just as it should be. I knew my physical eyes were no longer seeing the objects themselves and that I'd dropped deep into the truth of things. I saw the objects as they really were, as particles of light.

I shut my eyes again. The current turned to light, and I saw my body then, nothing more than a radiant sun itself, and all the objects about me, the walls, the roof, the floor itself, as vibrant light.

*Good.*

I pictured the girl, and called to the life current that knew Aria's destiny. *Show me,* I asked. *What is the right path for her to take?* There was a strange pulling sensation again on my legs, and the light about my inner vision flickered and began to fade. For a brief moment, I saw the young woman, her form only a dim outline as light blazed from every limb. She seemed to smile at me, a radiant blessing in my vision, and then suddenly, everything was black. I sucked in my breath sharply, unprepared for the change, and struggled to reconnect with the firmament of my form. A wave of nausea rose up inside me. The aching in my legs grew and the blackness enveloped me. Suddenly, a new image struck me: the earth shook and the girl fell. There was a sharp snap and then the light around her figure dimmed. She turned to me, still smiling, still made of light, but I could see she was broken in two. Even as her form began to lose its human shape, becoming an even more radiant light, I struggled to turn back from the vision. As I tried to raise the chant again in my mind a quick flash shattered my inner vision and the image of the ships slipped in again with an enormous wave, a wall of water rushing toward me...

"Ah!" I cried out, suddenly overwhelmed. I foolishly opened my eyes. For a moment I was blinded by the light of the lamps, but then I moved into action, scooping up the pillow from the floor beside me and dousing the flames. I cried out the names of my priestesses as I struggled to my feet, though I was lost in the vision of light. As two women threw open the door to the anteroom and stood frozen at the sight of me, I stared blankly at them, their forms still merged in light, their names inconsequential as I perceived us all as only One, with no distinction. I shook my head hard, trying to regain my sense of self, of individuality, to do what must be done.

"Ring the bell," I said at last.

One girl looked at me oddly, the light about her still smiling. The other one was older, a woman, and I pointed to her and repeated it with as much force as I could muster. Both just stood there staring, until I realized they couldn't understand what I was saying. I began to panic. The Wave... the wave is coming! I thought frantically. There was a sudden movement in the door, and a third figure stood behind the women. The light of her body blinded me, and I had to turn away, but then I heard her voice.

"Hera!" she cried out, and then again, "What is it? What have you seen?"

There was movement all about me, and then they were rushing toward me, their hands made of light, their voices turning to light as the sound moved forward from their lips. Cool hands pressed themselves upon my forehead, and someone bathed my face with water. A voice began to chant and then I could feel my legs, separate and strong. They were the light still, but now they had taken form as well, and suddenly I came back to myself. As the voice continued to chant a name formed in my mind to identify it. Demeter. When I opened my eyes, I could see them again, and I pulled away.

"The bell," I gasped, "Ring the bell!"

The women looked to Demeter. She pointed to the older one and commanded her to go. She turned to me swiftly.

"What did you see?"

I was still too shaken.

"Douse the fires." My voice was weak. "And get everyone else outside. Ring the bell!"

Demeter didn't hesitate. She took hold of my arm and pulled me with her toward the door shouting sharp orders to the women that now gathered about us. There was commotion all around me as I came back to myself, my feet moving again.

I looked out into the labyrinth where dozens of people already gathered and then glanced up to the lookout above the temple. The bell still hadn't rung.

An image of the girl, Aria, flashed through my mind. I had been looking at her life path when the vision had met me. Somehow the two were entwined. I moved away from Demeter and pointed to the bell. She nodded and ran to see why it wasn't ringing. Then, I rushed down the steps toward the healer's chamber. As I pushed open the doors to the courtyard, I realized that the place was mostly empty for I'd ordered every able hand down to the dock to help in the final preparations of our ship. I moved quickly from room to room throwing open the doors and sent the few girls I found running toward the labyrinth. Beyond the courtyard stood the main chamber where two of our strongest women tended Aria her after her long nights. When I threw open the door, I was startled to see Hades and Kronos standing with Ares at the girl's bedside, which lay in the center of the room.

Persephone, the healer priestess, stood at her side, anointing her with holy oil. The man I took to be her father stood by Hades' side.

As I entered, breathless, they all turned toward me, and the girl smiled…

There was no time to warn them. The floor moved and cracked and the earth rose up and took us all into her black belly. I was thrown forward, violently, my arms about my head as I hit the hard stone floor. For a moment I looked up at the ceiling which now gaped open. Sunlight poured through where wooden beams and limestone slats were supposed to be. The men bellowed, and I heard the girl scream as the roof began to fall. Another jolt came, stronger then before, and the floor gave way. There was no time to think or respond. My body lurched forward, and I slid downward, across the thin, stone slab, into the dark.

# CHAPTER SEVEN

I LAY IN THE DARKNESS for a long time before I realized my eyes were open.

Voices mingled with the blackness.

"We're going to die," said a voice that was cracked and deep. "Find her Hades, take the oil!" It was Kronos, and he was pleading.

"Quiet, Father." Hades's voice rose from somewhere to my left. "She isn't carrying the oil on her person."

"But their line lives longer than any other, Hades; you know that," Kronos's voice was desperate. He coughed hard. "There, you see, I'm dying! Find her Hades; see if she wears the oil!"

My head swam. Slowly, and as quietly as I could, I moved my hands and arms, feeling about my form, which was completely lost in the darkness. Everything hurt but nothing seemed broken, inside, or out. Pain stabbed at my temples as I strained to see.

"She no longer keeps the snake with her, Father, and I assure you, the oil about her neck is not the holy oil. Be quiet now; we have to find Ares."

My stomach lurched at the mention of his name. Now the vision came back to me—Ares bent over his love and the men standing in the background watching, pleased, as if a transaction was taking place.

"Who's there?" Hades's voice rang out.

"Hera," I answered numbly.

I moved my toes and heels gently, checking my legs for damage. I could feel a wet patch creasing the inside of my right leg, and a slight stinging sensation there, but the leg moved as it should. Pushing myself up, on one hand, I reached out trying to feel about me. My head seemed unconstrained. There was more motion ahead of me and a groan and then Ares's voice mumbling, "Mother? It's all darkness. Am I dead?"

There was a slight whimper in the direction of Kronos's voice, but I spoke out clearly.

"No, my son. There's been an earthquake and we…fell."

"How many of us survived?" Hades's voice moved toward Ares.

"Call out your names," I commanded

"Ares, Hades, Kronos, Persephone…" and then, after a short silence the girl's quiet voice, "Aria." Rough footsteps scrambled toward the voice. I knew it was my son.

"No!" I commanded. "Stay where you are, all of you. I will give us light and then we may see what must be done." I felt my son's anxiety, but as Asterion's voice was unaccounted for, I knew the scene might be grim. "Hold strong; I will make the light. Prepare yourselves. We may see difficult things."

Reaching for the hem of my tunic I tore a long strip of linen jaggedly from its edge and held out my hand. My fingers shook. It had been a long time since I'd called to the element, but a weak fire came quickly to my summons, and the cloth caught flame. It was the best I could do. I was still shaken. The fire leaped over objects on the floor before me while I surveyed my immediate scene.

Kronos gasped as the flame spilled in his direction. I caught a glimpse of his crumpled form, his skin gray and covered with dust. Hades was crouched beside him. His face was grim, and aside from a gash across his cheek, his body seemed intact. The fire reflected its light against a large pillar slanted halfway between them and the rest of the room. I looked up, but there was only darkness above me.

"Light more," Kronos urged. "Give us more light!"

I shook my head. "We must be careful with the fire," I said evenly, collecting my wits. "We could suffocate from the smoke or catch ourselves on fire."

I reached for a piece of wood I'd found splintered off from some furniture, tore another piece of linen, and wrapped the cloth about it. The other one was sputtering out. I lit the small torch in it before calling the fire away from the fragments that still burned. Carefully, I stood and lifted the torch above my head.

The ceiling, if there was a ceiling, lay far overhead. The light of the torch couldn't show me its height. Somewhere above us, there must have been a draft of air because the smoke rose upward without filling the room about me. That was good at least. I said so to the others then pulled the torch down toward the pillar, stepping gingerly around it.

Ares sat cross-legged as I'd taught him once long ago, in a position of prayer and calm. A long gash cut clean through his tunic, but the blood had already turned brown and was not flowing.

"Are you alright?" I asked him as I moved close and

kneeled by his side. He looked into my eyes earnestly and with great relief.

"I think so," he said, "But—"

I watched his gaze move to the place Aria had been. The table was there, and Persephone sat erect at its side, her hands already taking the girl's pulses. Aria looked up at me then, her skin covered with the gray dust so that her blue eyes seemed the only thing alive.

"Reverence," she said weakly. "It's an honor."

I blanched at the deference in her voice knowing I'd failed her. Ignoring Kronos's whine behind me I moved forward at once, reaching out to take Aria's hand, but then I stopped. The light jerked in my hand sending shadows across her ashen face. Persephone caught my eye and shook her head slightly, nodding at the column that had clearly crushed the girl's legs, and at the wound in her side that was slick with blood. A thick piece of limestone had pierced her belly. It was a shocking sight and I had to call every bit of courage in order to keep my composure. She clutched her chest in terrible pain. It showed in her eyes. Glancing back at Ares, I realized he'd seen the reality of the situation. He clutched his chest as if wounded there and bit his lip, drawing blood. Somewhere behind us I heard Hades pull Kronos to his feet and the older man hobbled toward us.

"Why she's—"

"Silence, father!" Hades snapped as they looked down on Aria.

I asked for her father, but Hades shook his head and pointed to the corner. Persephone placed a hand on Aria's head, but the girl winced and cried out. This brought Ares back to himself. He moved to Aria's side and took hold of her hand.

"I'm here," he whispered, but his voice carried in the eerie chamber. "I'm with you, my love."

I turned to Hades and handed him the torch. It was burning low, but I called to the flame, and it leaped again in his hand. I signaled Kronos to sit and gave him a hard stare that said I expected his full cooperation. He nodded as if I'd spoken. I searched about quickly for more wood, found it, and made another torch, which I gave to Persephone.

"Stay together," I said. "Hades and I will see if we can find a way out, or to get help. Keep making sound so that we can hear you."

Kronos looked desperately toward his son, but Hades laid a reassuring hand on his shoulder. He leaned down and whispered something in his father's ear and patted the old man on the back.

"Ares," I said sharply. "Keep hold of your grandfather as well."

Ares looked up and nodded absently. Hades laid a hand on my shoulder, and for the first time, I didn't mind. He pointed to the back of the chamber where an exit used to be. We stepped over rubble that sent up waves of dust. We covered our mouths with our cloaks as we moved. The chamber was cold, and the exit was not where it should have been. In fact, the wall that we had expected to find, seemed to lay in rubble all about us and another expanse of room lay behind it. We climbed over the wreckage, Hades picking up another torch on the way. This one must have been on the wall of the room for it was freshly painted with pitch. When he lit it, far more smoke rose upward than from the small ones I'd called the fire too. I made a note of it again. When we came over the rubble and then passed beyond the barrier of what should have been the wall, we stopped and held up our torches together.

I gasped.

We stood in an underground chamber; its walls were hewn in stone. Engraved on the floor was the unmistakable outline of a labyrinth. Bronze statues stood at the four corners, and at its center was a plinth of gold. Hades moved a step closer and pointed his flame at the plinth, but my eyes turned to the carved stone walls, and the holes set deep inside of them. I'd seen a place like this before, and I knew what lived inside those holes. I pulled Hades back sharply.

"We must not enter here," I said quietly.

He turned toward me to protest, but when he caught the look on my face, he stopped. He studied me for a moment and then nodded.

"I think this must have been built beneath the labyrinth outside the temple. This is the true source of its power. This," I pointed to the carved out spiral, and then to the holes in the stone, "and what lives here."

I moved away slowly, not turning my back on the room, and Hades did the same. When we reached the other side of the wall of rubble, perspiration clung wet and cold against my skin.

"I think we've fallen through to the older temple that was once built here," I said. Hades nodded. "It must be very deep underground, and perhaps the ceiling of the healers' court has fallen on top. I think we have to assume that no one will know to look for us here."

Again Hades nodded. "But there is air," he said. "Aside from the dust that chokes us, I can sense that there is fresh air. If we can find out where it's coming from we can follow it."

"Yes."

"And we have gifts to keep ourselves alive," he finished.

He didn't look at the vial of oil I wore at my neck, but he didn't have to.

"Persephone and I are healers," I offered, "and I have the gift of fire and vision."

I waited. He stared at me for another long moment until soft moans rose over the column that stood between the others and ourselves.

"I have only my mind to offer," he said.

I glared at him and spread my hands out wide, pointing out the desperation of the situation.

"You are the Lucifer! You can see the dead," I chided. "You can see the moment their consciousness becomes aware that it's light, that it's one with all things. You're the light bearer himself and can help each of us cross—"

"After death, there is nothing," he said.

"What?"

"I've sought after the invisible as you say, but I've never found it. No current, no light," he spat these last words. "Death comes with pain and then there is nothing."

Hades's face was cold and expressionless, but I could see the fear in his eye. I had stumbled onto his secret, which could be dangerous especially in such circumstances. I cooled my temper.

"As the light-bearer, you should be able to reach out to the light that is beyond our seeing and call to it in its various forms. From your light to my light."

He shook his head.

"Those are not the skills required of the Lucifer in this age," he said steadily. "I am a visionary, an architect of a new generation."

He stared at me and didn't drop his gaze, even as the moans of discomfort rose from behind us. Again, I tried to calm my astonishment. In the past, the Lucifer was the most powerful of us all, intricately connected to the whole. Hades should have been able to reach out from a unified state and touch the minds of others.

"Can you call to anyone silently?" I asked. "Anyone outside that may sense your need?"

He shook his head and wiped his sleeve across his brow firmly. "I don't believe in such things," he snarled. "They're stories to bring the ignorant to your temple, but such fantasies will do us no good here."

I shut my eyes and took a breath to steady myself. Reaching out with my inner sense I scanned the room for other life, but the only thing I felt was something very old and potent emanating from the labyrinth on the other side of the crumbling wall. When I opened my eyes, I could see that Hades had felt it too. He had lifted his head and turned toward the chamber, his body rigid.

"We must take action," I said. "Before—" I hesitated and thought better of evoking it with words.

I directed Hades to search one side of the chamber for an exit, and I turned to search the other. Time passed slowly, and I could hear Hades's movements and his occasional calls for help to others who might lie on the other side of a wall, or above us. As I searched my side of the room, I listened to the crunch of his boots as they moved heavily through the rubble, and Aria's death sighs. At some point, Ares crooned a low chant I'd taught him as a boy. I ached to go to his side but continued my necessary search. A clear sense of danger had now risen in my chest. It was obvious to me that we'd dropped into a circular chamber intended to house those that served the labyrinth. When this chamber had been closed, the people had known the guardians set in the room beyond would not need tending. I knew the ancients had kept to the practice of burying their place of power. This chamber was sealed. Also, the presence that loomed in the labyrinth had moved. I could sense it watching us and waiting.

When I'd circled half the room and met Hades beneath a sagging beam, I shook my head. The flame of his torch had dimmed, and I saw that he had picked up several more as he'd made his way around. He lit a new one and handed it to me. Mine was about to sputter out, so I dropped it on the damp floor. Hades stomped out the last of its light.

"The chamber is sealed," he said.

I nodded. As I held the bright new torch high above me, we both stared into the endless darkness above us. We could see no roof or slab, but the smoke rose steadily. I called out several times and my voice echoed.

"The roof of the healer's chamber was made of limestone," I said.

"And you think that has come down to bury us alive," he finished.

I said nothing. Ares's song grew louder. Persephone stood now, turned in our direction. She had built up a small flame on the floor beside them. Kronos leaned against the back of a limestone slab, his eyes closed as if he drifted in sleep. She'd laid her cloak over him.

Persephone waved Hades and me over. We moved carefully across the room to where Aria lay gasping for small breaths on the pallet. Ares's cloak was laid over her body, and he held tight to one of her hands. Clean wet streaks cut through the dust on his cheeks.

"It's time," Persephone said softly.

I nodded and moved to the girl's side, handing over my torch to Persephone. She moved to Hades's side. I took up the girl's other hand. Her eyes seemed alert still, and they darted in my direction. Her breath came in small, swift gasps but her gaze was steady. First I moved my thumb lightly up my brow to make the mark of my inner eye, and then I gently reached out to Aria. I stared into her eyes and marked the same space above her brow.

"Aria, priestess of the Emerald Temple," I said softly. The girl blinked hard and a smile came to her lips. I felt Ares's eyes on me, but I didn't take my steady gaze from Aria. "The pain will soon be over. This body will release your consciousness, and you shall perceive the Truth. You are the creator itself, as well as the creation. There is nothing to fear."

Her face softened, and she held my gaze. I could still feel fear in the room and realized it came from Ares. I reached my other hand out to him.

"Calm yourself," I commanded. "She is more sensitive now than ever and can feel your fear. Grieve if you must, but do not be afraid."

Ares's face contorted in confusion. He looked to Hades and then back to me, and I realized something had passed between them. Suddenly, I understood that Hades had instilled fear of death in my son. I shook my head as if someone had spoken.

"No," I said sharply, poignantly, "there is nothing to fear in death. There is no ending here, only freedom, Ares." He was staring at me now, and Aria moved her hand in mine as if to squeeze it. I went on. "We must look to the essence," I said, "to that which is beyond our thoughts and our bodily form. The priestess and the priest call it the great current only because we, as healers, use this imagery to merge ourselves with it. But it is beyond an image or gender; it is the essence from which all form arises."

Tears showed in the girl's eyes. I knew she already experienced in part what I said. Emotion rose within my breast, and I felt tears moisten my own cheeks as I looked beyond Aria's form, which could now barely contain her; her consciousness merged with all that was.

"You are wisdom itself," I whispered as her eyes fluttered. "You are the current from which all life arises."

Her body twitched lightly, and she took her last gulp of air. Ares made a sound of grief, and his head sagged.

"There is nothing to fear," I said again into the rich, living space that surrounded us. I could sense Aria's warmth settle over my son. Her glowing grace brushed his cheek as her light gave us all strength. Persephone moved back to my side, moving her hands gently over Aria's eyes. She closed them and pulled Ares's cloak up over the blank face. I let several minutes pass as Ares clung to her hand, pressing it against his chest. Kronos dozed quietly beside us. Persephone had come to stand beside Hades who, for the first time, looked shaken. She reached out her hand to him, and he took it. As I watched the way he looked at her and the sudden relief in his eyes as she took his hand in her own, I wondered, for the first time, if he might not truly love her.

I looked about me at the dismal scene and stopped my mind from wandering. In silence, I reached out to the current and called strength into my heart.

When Ares softened and let go of Aria's lifeless hand, I rose to my feet and helped him stand. His legs shook beneath him as he stood.

"She's free," I said to him.

He was deeply grieved, and fear still lingered in his eyes. "But how do you know, Mother, for certain?"

I looked around at the dark shadows of the wreckage

we'd fallen into, and I thought of the desperate reality of our situation. Death was only days away for all of us if we couldn't find a way out. I didn't want Ares going to that death unprepared. I turned back to my son.

"The reason that priests and priestesses spend their lives doing sacred practices is to open all their senses so they might perceive beyond what their physical eyes see. I know that death is not an ending because I've traveled to the place that exists beyond death. I can perceive form as well as the essence that gives the form life." I said this as much to Hades as to my son. "We are all born with the skill, but most never take the time to hone it. Once you've experienced it for yourself, it is impossible to believe that only physical form exists."

Hades stepped closer then. "It is an easy thing to say," he said, "from one who proposes to have touched this invisible essence and perceived it. But how do we know what you say is true? How do we know there is power in what you perceive?"

Power. That was the most important value in everything Hades considered. Persephone turned to him with an exasperated look on her face. I could see that she had spoken to him of this before.

"It is proved by our ability to heal," she said smoothly. "Priestesses can touch the current, but priests do it as well. Look at the temple of healers. There are hundreds of men—"

"But you didn't heal Aria," Hades interrupted, looking down at the form beneath the cloak.

We all followed his gaze despite ourselves, and I felt the fresh wave of grief rise in Ares.

Persephone let go of Hades's hand and spoke earnestly. "The essence has its own wisdom, Hades; you know that. It knows better then we do when Aria's time had come. She was beyond saving. Everyone must die."

Hades's tall, dark form moved away from the light of the torch as she spoke. He'd put his own down in the small fire on the ground, which made him look like a shadow moving in the periphery about us. Suddenly, I felt a stark chill run across my skin, and Hades stopped his movement abruptly. Something had moved in the darkness beyond us, and he'd felt it as well. He stepped back into the circle of light and looked at me intently. No one else seemed to have felt the presence. I wondered how he could sense it and still not understand how he did so. The presence moved into the chamber and circled the room, staying close to the outer wall and wreckage. I knew we were running out of time. I turned to my son.

"I will prove it to you then," I said boldly.

Ares stared at me. I signaled Persephone to move the fire away from the dead and bade everyone huddle around it, letting Kronos sleep on. It would be easier without his fear to block me. I moved with false confidence, for I felt weak. I knew that what I was about to try was possible. I'd seen it done, but had little experience with it myself. The true Lucifer should have been able to accomplish such a thing with ease, but I was certain we couldn't count on Hades.

I had Ares collect some more wood from the broken chairs and bade him keep the small fire going. No matter what happened, I knew we didn't have to worry about the fire now, for a greater danger was close at hand.

I sat across from Persephone who was already chanting words of power under her breath.

"Everything we see, everything we are, has arisen from pure space," I said easily hoping that Ares would accept my words with the surety I spoke them. "Imagine that this space is the ocean, and each wave rising from its surface, a human form."

Ares pulled his knees to his chest and crossed his arms over them. He nodded.

"It is clear that we are trapped here in this place. Hades and I can't find a way out. We must reach out to the mind of another, to the essence, and guide it to us. Do you understand?"

My son nodded.

"Imagine that you are the wave, Ares," I said, closing my eyes. "And you're the sea as well. You exist as both. You are formlessness, and you are form."

Persephone strengthened the chant. It was lulling and hypnotic to settle our minds. Beside me, I felt Hades relax into the tune, and the ancient, magic sounds. I thought of Artemis then, knowing she would be most likely to hear my call, but she was days away at the Emerald Temple. Athena might sense me, but she was no doubt involved in command, and she often got mired in protocol rather than staying close to the fluid movement of the life current. She was unlikely to hear my call.

*Poseidon.*

The memory of the dream and the very real encounter on the high sea moved through my mind, and before I could consciously choose, his image fixed itself in my inner vision. I said his name out loud to the group.

"I want you all to picture Poseidon," I said. "See him, call to him, and envision the healer's chamber as it was before the quake."

I didn't stop to question how this would sound, or what questions it might evoke in those around me, for to call Poseidon instead of Zeus must certainly have seemed strange. Instead, I moved forward as the current bid me. The vision of him came easily to my inner eye.

I saw Poseidon knee deep in water, standing by his ships at the harbor. The entire lower dock to which the ships were tied was under water, and he stood above it by three feet. Several ships had loosened from their moorings and others had been dashed against the harbor walls. One lay on its side, entirely aground. Men swarmed like mice over the scene. Some people were being pulled from the water, while others had tied ropes about their waists to steady themselves and were struggling to pull horses from the decks of ships as the vessels moved wildly beneath them.

*Poseidon.*

I called his name. I reached out with the full sense of my body standing beside him, and put my hands on his shoulders. I stepped in front of him as he looked out to the ship before him, calling out orders and waving his hands. Men rushed to do his bidding, and a horse was plunged into the sea from a stranded ship. He called out orders to his men as they guided it safely to shore.

*Poseidon!*

I slid my hands about his neck and turned my head up, pressing my lip to his cheek and chin as I'd longed to do so many times since I'd seen him that night in the temple. I heard sounds about me, men's voices calling over the rush and roar of waves slapping the limestone seawall.

*Reverence?*

His voice drowned out the distant roar of the sea. I struggled to keep hold of the vision, to establish a vivid cord of life force and a connection between us. Somewhere in the background I could hear Persephone's voice and feel Ares beside me, but I let them go and reached out again, aware that my desire for Poseidon was the strongest current I could take.

The image of him on the dock flashed strong before me again, and this time I pressed myself to him, arching up on my toes to press my lips against his mouth. A strong tide leaped through me.

*Poseidon, hear me...*

He spun about on the dock, his feet sloshing through the water as he moved toward the road and called his horse to him. Then he shouted out a name and Athena moved to his side.

"The High Priestess?" she said.

*Yes!* I thought, *Good!*

I sent Poseidon the image of the healer's court, the floor caving in and our falling through. I pulled him to me as the images began to fade, drawing an invisible river from his form to mine, letting it spill through what must be the wreckage of the healer's court, turning into a waterfall of love.

Time passed oddly as if I was in a dream. I felt the ancient thing that watched us in the rocks move closer, slithering, but the life current was strong in me now, and I sent it images of peace. Soon, a sweetness rose between us, and I could feel its benevolent heart press against its protective instinct. It stopped moving toward us.

I floated then, in the current and as the current, dimly aware of my body sagging and strong hands laying me down. I was lovely and weightless, returning to Poseidon, as he took to his steed with Athena close at his side. There was a flurry of movement as they rode through the packed streets, dismounting to push their way through the crowds that had gathered outside the buildings, many of which had toppled to rubble.

*Poseidon!* I called out to him again as I reached for his face and pressed my lips to his furrowed brow. *Find me! Save my son!*

I felt my ethereal form pull him to me, my body soft as sand, urging his wave to break over me.

*Poseidon!*

There was a long lull in which I drifted without form or image, desire itself becoming the ground of being. My light shone like a sun, and I knew I could not be contained in this tomb.

When fatigue came over me, my body collapsing somewhere at the center of my light, I felt the warmth of another sun lend me its strength. It was my son.

"I believe you, Mother," Ares's voice filled my senses. "I'm not afraid."

I laughed, maybe out loud, and a thousand suns burst forth from my joy. There was sound somewhere above me, and then voices. The slinking presence that watched from the hewn stone withdrew to the labyrinth bidding me farewell. I slid with it for a while, cold, but bright, my belly on the sacred earth, until I heard my son's voice again.

"Mother," he said, "Mother, come back."

I opened my eyes. Ares stood before me, shining. He reached down and touched my skin. I cried out at the shock of it. There was light shining above his head—sunlight flooding the chamber through a hole above us. A long rope hauled Kronos through the air on a makeshift swing. I laughed again, and the giddy, faraway apparition of my body moved closer. Persephone pressed a hand to my head and then I saw Hades lifted on the swing above me. I shut my eyes and strayed back toward the chasm of light.

More sound and movement followed and then Poseidon's voice was in my ear, sweet, soft, and warm like honey.

"Hera," he said. "Hera."

I had never heard him speak my name aloud, and it

thrilled me. My eyelids fluttered, and I was lost in the light that caught the deep blue of his eyes. I felt his arm slip around my shoulder and waist as he lifted me to his chest. I smiled and closed my eyes at the heavy sensation of being pulled from formless light, back into form. I laid my head against his chest, resting in the care of the man I loved.

# CHAPTER EIGHT

I OPENED MY EYES to find Zeus hovering over me, his face filled with strain. I reached out my hand to touch his cheek, not sure if he was real. He said my name, and I tried to move, to answer him, but my voice caught in my throat. Persephone moved to my side and pressed a rough wooden cup to my lips. I tasted the bitter herb that we used to calm sacred visions. I shut my eyes but struggled to speak.

"Rest now, Hera," Zeus said, his voice filled with tension. "The children are safe. Ilithyia and Demeter led the Emerald Temple, tending the southern villages that were hit, and we have Caledocean's victims tended to as well."

I relaxed, feeling his rough palm take up my hand. There were more words, soft, kind sounds, but the darkness overtook me.

When I awoke again, I was alone. I pushed myself up on my elbow and saw that I was lying on the ground on a bed of straw, a thick deerskin beneath me and woolen blankets on top. A cock crowed in the distance, and I looked about me to find that I was inside a tent. It was sparsely furnished, with only a wooden stool and a chest, which I recognized as my own. The thin flap that hung over the door had been pulled aside, and through the gap, I saw another tent set up just outside. The sounds of people stirring were all about me. A fire crackled somewhere nearby, and a child's voice called out for its mother.

I pushed the blanket away and sat up stiffly. Every part of my body ached, and as I ran my eyes over my skin, I realized that someone had bathed me by hand, for I bore no trace of the dirt and dust from the entombment. I wore a fresh white tunic that was too big. As I surveyed my legs, I saw a thin, clean bandage about my shin. That must have been where I'd felt the blood after I'd fallen. My arms were scraped and bruised, and when I stood, a dull ache throbbed inside my hip. I moved gingerly to the stool by the chest that held my personal treasures. I pulled back the lid and reached for the belt that Artemis had given me, to make the tunic cling to my body. Then I pulled on the doeskin boots Father had made for me so many years ago. There was Mother's old gray cloak, and I clutched it to me for a moment before wrapping it around my shoulders. Then I pulled out my family blade—with the dragons entwined on the hilt and the leather sheath—and tied it to my good ankle. I closed the lid.

Someone had set out bread and more of the bitter herb tea, and I took both and then limped to the door. When I stepped outside, the soft pink of the morning sky welcomed me like an old friend.

The tent was set upon the hill that overlooked the harbor and the shore. There were dozens of more tents set up about mine bearing the banners of several houses. The Titans' flag flew on the tent beside me, and Zeus's thunderbolt was sewn on silk outside another. I turned to see the double dragons, one red and one green, flying above my door.

Slowly, I moved toward the gentle slope of the hill and looked down at the harbor and the field that stretched out before the mouth of the city. I shuddered at the scene.

There were thousands of campsites, some with tents, and others with only fires to mark them. The legions had obviously been called upon to create the city overnight. The sites were set up in long, neat rows. The red flags marking the latrines on the ends were clearly visible. Horses grazed loose on a remote plateau, and on every side of the makeshift village soldier's banners flew in the wind as if to protect the people within.

*Or keep them there,* I thought.

The harbor was a shocking site. At least half of Poseidon's ships, the big bulked vessels, were badly damaged. They had been moored closest to the first sea wall. Some lay dashed, their timber afloat in the long channels that still lapped out to sea. The water was as high as the western docks. Goods from the laden ships now floated around the circular channels, some coming in toward the waiting hands of men eager to fish them out before they escaped to sea. At the far end of the dock, closest inland, the ships seemed unscathed. They were Zeus's and a group of his men in black tunics tended them. I was relieved to see this, knowing that now, the need to flee our shores would be evident to all. Zeus would be able to sail as soon as the tide turned.

I strained to make out the figures on the shore. Athena directed a large group of women and men in their efforts to secure horses in a makeshift pen just outside the harbor. Priestesses were clearly outlined against the dawn, helping women and children into a large, white tent that must have been a healer's den. A figure on horseback rode at the head of a group of men, circling the large encampment; even from here I could read exhaustion in his body. It was Zeus, and Ares was by his side. Still, my eyes pressed forward, searching.

"Hera."

I jumped, losing my balance, and winced as I pressed down on my leg to steady myself. Large hands reached out and caught me. I looked up. Warm blue eyes stared down into mine. I flushed.

"I'm sorry," Poseidon said, "I didn't mean to startle you."

I smiled up at him and shook my head.

"No, I'm glad to see you," I said with more pleasure in my tone than I should have shown.

His mouth opened as if to reply, but then he stopped, and let me go.

The wind was blowing cold off the water, and his hair waved behind him with his cloak, which he pulled about himself. I studied his face for a long moment, slowly taking him in. The wide forehead and dark brows gave way to a chiseled nose and full cheeks, giving him a dignified look. His lips were uneven, the bottom one rounded and full. His chin was stubble, but I could make out the thin cleft that set him apart from his brothers.

He stood very still as I stared, and then I reached out my hand touching his cheek to make sure he was real. He did not move letting my palm linger on his cheek until I realized my mistake. I was still fragile, my mind soft and undefended. Pulling back my hand I flushed.

"You're still coming back into form," he said gently. "It's alright. Everything will seem real in time."

He turned back to the scene below us, and I followed.

"Three thousand at last count are homeless," he said, looking back out at the scene. "Zeus and Athena have acted boldly and brought them here, thinking it safer than behind the city's crumbling walls."

"Three thousand!" I exclaimed, but my voice was weak. "What parts of the city have fallen?"

"Your estate and the lower west side that leads to the harbor. All is lost there, and many people are dead." He pointed to what used to be the city wall in the distance. A thin line of smoke rose steadily from behind the rubble. "They've already made pyres to burn the dead."

Pulling my cloak closer about me against the biting wind, I asked questions, my voice scratching against my throat at first, then warming up as I went on. He told me the council chambers, and the rest of the city fared quite well, and reports coming in from the north told of little damage. Pointing toward his ships, he confirmed that he would not be sailing to Kart Hadst. He'd have to wait until spring and even then, only if the ships could be repaired and re-supplied.

"The council has already declared that Zeus will leave as soon as the channels are cleared and the tide has changed. I'm sure it will be no surprise to you, but the dynastic rulers have decided to go with him."

I scowled openly at this last comment, but Poseidon said nothing. We continued to stand side by side, the silence between us comfortable and familiar. I glanced at him again and wondered how much of my true desire he had glimpsed in my invisible call to him.

"Poseidon," I didn't have to say his name, but I'd been longing to hear it pass my lips since I'd opened my eyes.

He turned.

"Is it you I have to thank for our rescue?"

He didn't reply right away but stared at me thoughtfully. Then, as if he'd made a decision, he stepped forward so that he stood very close.

"Lady," he said.

"Call me Hera."

His face creased with pleasure. "Hera," he began again. "I've seen your image in flashes of my dreams much of my life."

My pulse quickened.

"Then came the vision on the ship, the storm, I told you about that," he continued. "But yesterday was different. I didn't see your form; I...*felt* you. When I steadied myself and listened, I heard your voice, calling my name."

I was delighted by his bluntness. I wanted to speak but didn't know what to say.

There were loud shouts from the harbor below, and we both turned in time to see Zeus thunder onto the main road that overlooked his ships. His entourage pulled their horses up sharp behind him, Ares on one side, Ajax on the other. Zeus slid to the ground, his arms outstretched to his men on the dock who struggled in their labor. Ares stood quietly beside the men, overshadowed by his father's presence. Ajax cursed at someone who'd dropped the lead to the horses and was now scrambling to reclaim them. Zeus seemed not to notice either of them as he moved to the group who stood below him. I knew that he gave them strength through his very presence.

*Poseidon and Zeus...they are so different,* I thought. I'd seen Poseidon with his men and noted how calm and steady he was. He projected a sense of separateness even when surrounded by people, but this didn't detract from his strength. He was not a man to offer compliments where none were earned, and this reflected in the service of his men. This was not true with Zeus. I looked at the men now, scrambling about to please him. It was clear they feared his displeasure as much as they sought his blessing.

Below, Athena walked up the makeshift steps they'd cut into the hillside, as the real stairs were still covered in water. Zeus reached out a hand and pulled her to the top. I delighted to see them working together, and my feelings seemed to leap out of my breast like rays of light.

Suddenly, Zeus and Athena both turned, as if they'd felt me, and stared up the hill at Poseidon and me. A strange, awkward moment arose, and I felt an odd sense of shame wash over me as if I was doing something wrong, but then Zeus held up his arm, boyish delight on his face as he waved to me. I remembered his worried look as I'd first opened my eyes. I wondered now how long ago that had been and how long he'd stayed by my side when the entire world was pulling at him. I lifted my hand above my head and waved back, giving him a warm smile.

Poseidon did not move. His body was poised, calm and detached, but I felt him watching me. Zeus turned back to his men, but Athena's stare lingered in my direction for a moment longer, before she turned back to her work.

I pulled my cloak tighter around my shoulders turning back to Poseidon.

He stared at me intently, and then said in a low voice, "You love Zeus."

I was startled by the statement.

"Yes, I suppose I do," I answered. "But not as a lover. That ended many years ago after the birth of our son. He's the father of my children, king to my queen."

"You've made the *Heiros Gamos* with him." Again, it was a statement. "But I wonder, Lady, that you didn't send your intuitive call to *him* when you were in need. As you say, he is the father of your children, one of whom was trapped with you in the fall. There are those who will wonder that I received your message instead of Zeus."

I stiffened, knowing he was right.

"In fact," Poseidon continued, "It is something I have been pondering ever since."

The wind had died down and people now moved freely around the tents. I was suddenly aware that we were not alone, and people were staring. A woman stood at a large cauldron that hung over a deep fire pit, and two boys poured pails of water into it. I caught her eyeing us as she scooped in handfuls of grain. Two girls peered around the corner of a tent, giggling in our direction. A sense of apprehension swept over me. As if he understood my tension, Poseidon fidgeted on his feet and took a step away. He nodded in deference.

"I must join my men," he said softly.

I wanted to take hold of him as I had done in the vision, to reach out and slip my hands about his face and feel my lips on his. I wanted to feel him holding me again, pressing me to the warmth and safety of his chest, but I only nodded agreement.

"Of course," I said. "And I should see to the priestesses."

We stood there staring at each other. Again he dropped his head and turned to go. He took several steps away before I called out his name, my tone slicing through the air. He stopped, but stood a moment with his back to me, before turning to face me again. When he did, I recognized the ancient knowing and desire in his eyes and my body flooded with longing.

"Lady," he said again, bowing low.

He turned and walked away down the hill into the city of tents. I stayed there watching him go. He walked with quiet grace, and as he went, I felt a part of myself go with him.

# CHAPTER NINE

HIGH ON A HILL in the midlands of Atlantis stood the ancient Titan fort called Tintangore. I'd been taken into the estate's belly for my first initiation on the way to the Emerald Temple; it was a place I'd thought never to return.

I sat at a table set outside on the hill, surveying the growing city of tents and fires, listening to the final count of refugees that came to us from the city. It was now clear to all of us that we would not be able to rebuild before winter. The priests from the main temples had gathered with us and said they would open their doors to take in as many as they could, but that would still leave nearly a thousand people without a home or food for the winter. Kronos rose and addressed us with an alternate plan.

"I have been readying Tintangore as a country estate. We've brought life back to the town with our rebuilding efforts, and there is a new wing the priestesses and healers of the Emerald Temple could take as their own."

"The priestesses?" I interjected. "I had thought to send them back—"

"They will be needed," Hades said.

There was assent from around the room. Zeus, who sat by my side, his bulky frame resting back in his chair, leaned forward and spread out his hands to the sea of people below us.

"They must have a leader," he said emphatically. "Hades must remain in Caledocean with the council, and I will take to my ships by the new moon. Tintangore is a good place to go. It's surrounded by woodland, so it will be easier to build housing quickly with timber rather than stone."

He had obviously already spoken to his father about this and given it thought. He nodded across the table toward Poseidon.

"You won't be able to tend those ships until spring," he said. "If you and your men take charge of building at Tintangore, and the High Priestess takes charge of their relocation and healing, it will be an easier winter for all."

I felt something tug on the invisible thread wrapped around my heart. Did Zeus just suggest that I spend the winter with Poseidon?

As Poseidon nodded assent to the plan, others about the table turned to me. I looked into their tired eyes and worn faces. It had been a long week for all of us, and the apparent reality that Atlantis did indeed face inevitable change was now sinking into the minds of those that hadn't wanted to believe it. As my eyes traveled across the table, they came to settle on Poseidon. He stared back at me evenly, but I could feel the intensity of his gaze. My skin tingled.

I nodded my consent and gave the command to make ready for the journey.

Zeus and his men, all well practiced at making camp and traveling light led our caravan of travelers. We journeyed slowly, some on horseback, but mostly on foot, carrying only what we needed for the trip. There were over a thousand refugees that had elected to go with us across the limestone coast to the inland road that would take us to Tintangore. We traveled the old dusty path that kept the sea to our left, the scent of brine rising in the air all through the first day. On our right side, a warren of jagged, white hills of stone rose steeply.

On the second day, our long, straggling line of travelers snaked its way about the base of the canyon where hammers hewed loudly into rocks from the quarries in the center. People were tired, and Zeus grew restless as we often stopped for the children to rest.

In the afternoon of the sixth day, we entered a valley suffused with green. The sky created a round, bowl-like feeling overhead. As we came into the village that sat at the foot of the hill upon which Tintangore loomed like a giant box of stone, I was relieved to see that what Kronos had said was true; the market ran down two streets, and there were several taverns and an inn. The buildings in town were sturdy, made of brick and square hewn rock. Those made with timber and mud were scattered along the outskirts. The runners that had been sent ahead had already prepared the townspeople for our arrival, and the main camp was set up by the stream running alongside the base of the hill. The scent of meat roasting in pits was a welcome delight. Zeus's men moved with orderly skill directing the camp to be set, and we labored until dusk creating a village of tents. It was good to feel a part of something so essential, and I felt more hopeful then I had in a very long time.

When my tent was set, and our people started to settle in, Zeus came to my side and led me away from the site. We walked up the hill toward Tintangore and passed beneath the stone arch where a tremendous wooden gate, covered with a thin plate of metal, gaped open on a square courtyard. A stable was set to the left and a cookhouse of stone far to the right. The main building was massive and square, with two stories and four tall towers, one set at each corner. Before it, a modern portico with marble columns stood solidly, with a wide courtyard and garden placed before it. The old and the new clashed severely, but Zeus pointed out the benefit.

"The old castle of Tintangore has withstood every siege in the times of the priestly wars," he said. "The thick wall that surrounds us makes repelling attacks a far easier matter, as the attackers must take the hill and then the wall, which has never been done."

"But why in this age of expansion would your father put so much trouble into rebuilding such a place, Zeus?"

He shrugged. "Kronos grows sentimental. He spent many of his boyhood years here. Until now I don't suspect he believed we would ever really evacuate Atlantis. Either way, it is a good thing for us that he has. Look."

He took me up the stairs to the portico and into the castle itself. There were already black-uniformed men standing at attention by the gate, but they stood aside without asking a question as we stepped through. Once inside, I was able to take in the true vastness of the place. The center of the square was open to the sky. All of the rooms had wooden doors that opened out into this central courtyard, half of which was still flooded with light from the sun. The garden needed tending, but benches and tables were placed all about the space.

"You can house a fair number of your women on the first floor," Zeus said, waving his hand across the courtyard in a generous gesture. "And your room will be upstairs, beside mine."

He took my hand and drew me toward the staircase, and we ascended to the second level stepping into a large apartment.

I caught my breath at the luxury of the space. It was large, larger then the rooms I'd taken at our own estate. It had two hearths, one across the room by the bed, which was slightly blocked by a mural screen of silk making it a room of its own. The second hearth was large and stood across from a wide door that was thrown open to the large verandah. I strode outside to behold a view of the entire valley. I could see the village below and the road leading to the estate. I shook my head at the extravagance of it. The verandah wrapped itself around to join with that of other rooms as well. Stepping back into the room I let my eyes linger on the finery strewn about the place—the mosaic of blue and gold tile set into the wall behind the hearth and the plush furniture that sat before it. The walls were the height of three men. Zeus waved me to an anteroom where there was yet another space set-aside for dressing. Jewel encrusted brushes and pins were set out, cleanly polished, atop the mirrored dressing table as if I'd been expected. I turned to Zeus questioningly.

"They are very old things, Hera. They belonged to my great-grandmother and were passed down. Poseidon's mother had them when she stayed here, before—" He stopped abruptly. "She didn't like the place," he finished.

"It's too much," I said, "I am but a guest, and our people will be sleeping three families to a hut."

"You are a queen and High Priestess," Zeus countered. "The people will want you to have it."

"But my burden is no more than theirs, Zeus," I said, shaking my head.

He moved closer to me and laid his hands on my shoulders. His eyes had deep circles beneath them, and I could see the fatigue etched on his brow.

"Your burden is much more," he said seriously. "And if you don't believe that now, I fear you will come to know it in the days to come."

"What do you mean?"

"You know perfectly well what I mean!" He dropped his hands roughly and turned away from me. "Hera, you know it's impossible to evacuate everyone from Atlantis before the time is upon us! Lives will be lost, and it will be because we, because I—"

He didn't finish. I understood then that Zeus finally had comprehended that we were too late. Even if we began to build the boats we needed to bring our people to safety, the council would still not allow us to leave in time. He'd been serving their selfish design, and now he struggled against it.

"I will not be their instrument anymore," he said as if finishing my thoughts. He turned back to me. "I've allied with Hades," he said.

In response to my apparent tension, he shook his head. "No, wait before you judge. Hades would not tell me exactly what happened that day in the tomb with you, but I can well imagine, being buried alive and facing death. He and our father have laid down their derision of the Emerald Temple and the priestesses' power. You can see this proved by this generous act to serve the people."

He spread his arms about him emphatically. I could see he believed everything that he said, and that he was pleased with this new alliance. Still, the chill of deception clung to my skin. Zeus talked on of Hades's remarkable change in attitude and what a reliable ally the Lucifer would be in supporting Zeus's new vision. After sailing to Kart Hadst and delivering those nobles that were fleeing to their new home, Zeus intended to go on to the peninsula in the north where Poseidon had described fertile farming lands and peaceful tribes. Zeus would see for himself if he could settle people in this land that was outside of the council's control. He hoped Poseidon would join him the following year. With Poseidon's ships and Zeus's men, the council would not be able to stand against them.

"When we return, we'll have a new place to bring our people, and begin the exodus from Atlantis," he finished.

I remained silent as I tried to uncover the flaw in his stratagem, for what he said didn't land well. Something was wrong, but I couldn't point out what. I would have to go along with this new plan, even with artifice, until the truth revealed itself.

"Take the room, Hera," Zeus said. "If for no other reason than to appease my father. He'll never stand for you accepting less." He paused for a moment staring at me intently. I was exhausted and in no mood to argue. I sighed and nodded my agreement. "Good," he continued, smiling. "When I leave, announce that you'll build a city here and send throngs of woodcutters into these hills to start bringing down lumber. Don't use it to build much; just enough so that people will think this is truly your plan."

"You want me to store wood to build boats?"

He nodded, relaxing a bit as I showed my understanding, if not support.

"It will take two full turns of the seasons for all my work to be done. Appease the council, build your city, and store wood. I will return for you and together, we'll fulfill the obligation of the *Heiros Gamos*."

Zeus's eyes softened as he said the words. I felt his need for my approval.

"It's the best plan I've heard in a long while, Zeus," I said.

He beamed at me, thrusting a fist into his open palm with delight.

"I will come back for you," he said again. "Two years is not so long when such important work is at hand."

"No, it's not that long," I repeated and forced a smile.

A bell sounded from the valley below us, and I turned to the window. The sky grew dark, and shadows fell throughout the room. A woman appeared in the door with a fresh bucket of kindling wood and flint. She dropped her head slightly and kept her eyes on the floor as she skirted Zeus and went to the hearth to light the logs. Zeus went to the door and waved for more attendants who had been waiting for his signal. They brought in my trunk and the clothes we'd salvaged from the estate. They laid my rugs on the cold stone floor and set the tapestry of the dragons entwined on the wall opposite the big wooden bed. I moved to the window watching as Zeus directed everything, pleased with himself. I was awed at the planning that had gone into such a display. How had he found the time for such a thing, and why was this so important to him? A tight knot formed in my stomach and for the first time, I felt oddly wary of Zeus's feelings for me.

Food was laid out on a table along with two goblets and a jug of wine. I was hungry and tired, and the smell of the warm broth and greens made my mouth water, but I held my place by the window, watching. There were large oil lamps set about the room, and each was lit with a warm, enigmatic light. Bowls of water and cloth were turned out on the table for washing, but Zeus sent the attendant away before she could call to me. He lifted the cloth in his own hands and dipped it in the water. Steam rose from it. He signaled me to my seat. I hesitated.

"Come, Hera," he said. "Let me wash away the hardship of the day. We will eat together," he hesitated, searching my eyes, but I had kept my look cool, feeling cautious. "And then I'll go," he finished.

I took a step forward, tentatively, pushing my wariness aside. We had spent so much time together in the last month, that if old feelings surfaced, I should not be surprised. The moment he set sails and caught sight of a new woman…

I sat down and let him wipe my hands, dipping them lightly in the water. He took the cloth and filled it with the warmth, squeezing out the excess water and handed it to me. I washed my face with it, drawing it down my neck, wiping away the day's travel. I felt his eyes on me as I slid the cloth across my chest. Glancing up at him, I stopped. He smiled.

"You're more beautiful than ever," he said, sitting down beside me.

"Zeus—"

"You've aged with such grace," he continued, reaching out a hand and brushing away a wisp of hair that had fallen into my eyes. "Your skin is still smooth and soft and young, Hera, and your eyes are, as always, cool and exotic."

"Zeus!"

He laughed loudly, and the warmth of his humor made me smile. He said no more, but reached for a bowl and served me soup and bread, unwrapping a soft hunk of cheese I recognized from home.

"I know it's your favorite," he said, looking pleased. "It was a trick to find it in all that confusion, but here it is."

He cut a large slice and laid it on my plate. I stared at him. How had he managed such a thing? He handed me a goblet of wine, and I sipped it lightly sinking back in my chair. The pillows were soft beneath me, and my body began to relax. Lifting the cup to my lips I took another sip, and then a deep draught. It was sweet and warm, filling my chest with a sensation of leisure. Again, I realized Zeus was watching me carefully, but this time, I didn't mind. I held my goblet out, and he filled it to the brim.

We began to chat easily then, the old familiarity between us. I was tired and lulled by the wine and forgot to be wary or to keep close my secrets. As Zeus spoke again of his plans, I leaned forward, adding ideas, beginning to grow excited by the possibilities that spread out before us without the hindrance of the council.

"Without the council, a king will really be a king!" Zeus affirmed as he sat back in his chair. "We'll finally be free of the dynasties, Hera." He looked at me warmly and leaned forward again. "I'll build you a castle on a mountaintop!" he said. "I'll fill the rooms with people that you love so you'll never grow lonely!"

I laughed, letting him refill my goblet.

"And I want a temple!" I demanded playfully. "A place where people can take refuge and renew themselves."

"Of course!" he cried out merrily. "You shall have it, Hera! I'll have temples built across the land in honor of my queen!"

"Oh, Zeus," I said shaking my head, but my tone was light. He lifted his wine and declared a toast to our success. Our glasses touched, and I swallowed more of the vivid, red nectar.

We finished the meal, and Zeus rose, pulling my chair out from the table. We moved to the couch by the fire, sipping the wine. The slow warmth was languid in my limbs, and my cheeks were flushed. I was exhilarated by our discussion and the freedom of our dreams.

"And what shall we name it, Zeus?" I asked swirling my wine in the cup and letting the aroma fill my head. "This mountain that overlooks your new land?"

"Olympus," he said decidedly, having obviously given this thought. "We shall honor the mountain that looks over us now. It will be the Titan throne from which we will look out upon the new land, and design our cities."

I raised my cup and toasted Olympus. We laughed again, and his eyes sparkled. The light in the room had grown dim as the fire died down. I yawned.

Zeus rose and reached for another log, and as the flames leaped, he turned and dropped to his knees before me. He pressed his palms gently against my thighs, spreading my legs apart, moving his torso between them. He leaned forward, a sly look on his face.

"Hera," he murmured.

"Zeus, what are you doing?" I pushed him lightly on the chest, but I was still smiling.

"You know what I'm doing," he said, catching my flailing hand in his, and pulling me closer so that I could feel his breath on my cheek. He moved forward brushing my lips, while his other hand on my waist moved slowly toward my breast.

Desire flared across my skin, but I felt disoriented.

My body still remembered his touch, his big hands on the soft places that spoke with passion, but my heart was cold. I pushed harder on his chest and pulled away. Reluctantly, he let me go and rocked back on his heels.

I looked up into his eyes, pale blue, but flashing with life.

"I'm sorry, Zeus," I said shaking my head, "it's not right. We've had too much wine, and the journey's been long."

"But you love me," he stated. "All these years you've still loved me. You told Ares so."

I sat back on the couch, startled, trying to clear my head of the wine's influence.

"And I've always loved you, Hera, you know that. You're the only one who has ever had my heart. You're my queen, and I'll make that mean something at Olympus, I swear it!"

He was earnest and kind, showing me his heart. I reached out and took his face in my hands. He was so dear, so well-meaning, but Poseidon's face flashed before me.

"Zeus," I began, "There are many ways to love a person," but he shook his head and wouldn't let me finish, pressing close to me once again.

"I know you've had others," he said quickly, "I don't begrudge you that. I know of your lovers at the temple and that you spent last year with the magistrate's son."

My look must have given away my astonishment, but he continued.

"But you put him aside when I arrived. Neither of us is impinged or promised. Now is the time to reconcile, to come together—"

"No." My voice was steady, and my senses came clear about me. I couldn't let him go on. He'd said too much already. I knew the battle that raged within him between his genuine love and caring, and his outright lust for power and prestige.

"But why not, Hera, you have no one else!"

I looked away.

"I've seen no one at your side," he said with more force then I think he'd intended, for he let me go, and stood up.

I continued to look away, trying to calm my breathing.

He started to pace.

"Who?" he demanded, "Who have you been seeing?"

I shook my head.

"It isn't a matter of another person, Zeus, you and I are not right—"

"Who is it?" his voice was as harsh and compelling as a command.

I struggled to my feet to face him. I stammered some reply, but it made no difference for his eyes had narrowed, and he was defended.

I tried to turn away from him, but he reached out and took hold of my arm, turning me about to face him.

"Why won't you tell me?"

I tried to pull free. "Let me go, Zeus!"

I took a step back, and he took a step forward, his grip tightening. I stared up into his face, which was now visibly filled with anger.

"There are rumors," he said, harshly, "but they can't be true."

I stopped struggling and looked him in the eye. I could see the pain inscribed beneath the growing fury. My silence was all the answer he needed.

"No," he said shaking his head, "No! He's my *brother*," he hissed.

"I know," my voice was low.

"My older brother!"

"Yes," I said.

He gripped me harder.

"But you're mine," he avowed, his voice deep and brutal. "You belong to me!"

"In name only, Zeus," I tried to reason. "I can't force my heart to feel something it doesn't. I didn't plan to feel this way about Poseidon. It just…happened."

"Poseidon," he growled as if I hadn't spoken. "All my life, I've lived in the shadow of the hero, Poseidon. *Poseidon!*"

His face screwed tight with pain and something else, ugly and bitter. I felt a wave of fear move through my body, but I tried to calm myself. Zeus shook his head as if trying to regain control.

"But he has nothing, Hera!" he said with exasperation. "He has no land and no estate of his own. Where is his ambition? Why look at what he's done all these years, all the places he's been, the lands he could have claimed. Has he ever taken anything for himself? He brings back strange food and birds and collects people's stories, but where is his wealth? What can he give you?"

I bit hard on my lip willing myself not to speak, or defend. I could see Zeus's wild look. The memory of the day he'd struck our son in front of me sprang sharply in my memory. He stared at me hard, his teeth clenched, his breath coming in short, quick bursts.

"He's nothing compared to me," he jeered. "You'll tire of him," he said more to himself than to me. "I am a king in my own right, and you," he shook me hard and pressed his strong fingers to my skin. "You are my queen. I'll have you in the end!"

"Stop it, Zeus!"

He seemed not to hear or was fueled by my resistance. He pushed me hard against the wall. I repeated his name, louder, the heat in my bones rising toward the surface. I hadn't used the fire on another person since the day at the Emerald Temple, and I could see by the fierce look on Zeus's face that he'd forgotten I even had the ability.

"Please!" I called out sharply. Then, struggling to control my voice, to touch his heart, I said, "You're hurting me, Zeus."

His eyes seemed to clear, and he lessened his grip but

didn't let me go. Confusion. Consternation. Contempt. The emotions played on his face like thunderclouds in the sky.

Finally, he stepped back and released me.

"I will come for you," he said again. "I will give you what Poseidon cannot, and your heart will turn away from him Hera."

I knew better than to speak against him, now. He turned from me, sweeping up his cloak in his hands and strode to the door. He flung it open, and stood in the frame, his hand on the hilt of his sword.

"I *will* come back for you, Hera. You will *always* be my queen," he said in a threatening tone.

He turned away and strode into the darkness. The door banged closed behind him.

I stood very still for a long time trying to regain my composure. My head swam with too much wine and fear. Slowly, I made my way to the door and bolted it shut. I exhaled, leaning heavily against the rough wood as if it could protect me. What would Zeus do now? I tried to think of what action I should take, but the weight of the day bore down on me so that I turned to the bed and lay myself down. I reached for the pillow, and buried my face in it and wept.

Zeus had left Tintangore before I rose from my restless bed the next day. I received a short message from my son. Ares had gone with his father. I closed my eyes as difficult feelings rose within me. I tried to conjure Ares's form and project my love to him, but our relationship was still too new. And now he'd only have his father's version of me to hold onto. In despair, I turned back to my room, pacing the floor.

I was grateful when my attendant appeared in the doorway with food helping me focus my mind and my heart elsewhere. When I'd eaten, she led me to the council room where I let myself be swept up in a fury of activity, managing and directing the building plan of the expanding town. I met with engineers and carpenters and woodsmen who laid out their plans before me. We sectioned off the design of new roads, and I thought to organize parks and grass-ways between their even rows of houses. I chose a temple site, though that would have to wait until all our people had homes. By summer they promised they would break ground on a building for the women.

"Is there already one here for the men?" I asked Tintangore's magistrate. He nodded and pointed on the map at the building below the fort and the baths built beside it.

"I would like to open it," I said, turning to Kronos. "I'd like to make it accessible for both men and women, at least until another temple can be built."

There was a general commotion about the room, but Kronos only smiled and bobbed his head.

"As Your Reverence wishes," he said cordially.

The magistrate stood with an open jaw.

"See to it," I told the man and moved on to other matters before a discussion could arise.

The craft guilds each sent representatives throughout the afternoon, and long past dusk. At some point, lunch was brought to me and then later, supper with wine. It was very dark, and late before I had seen to the last of my duties. I moved down the hall, aware that my feminine guard had resumed their place beside me, at some point in the day. Athena had been busy on the field, and we hadn't yet spoken, but I could see she was already making her feelings known about the Titan's ability to keep me safe. I had to admit that I was relieved as my female guard trailed me through the courtyard and up the stairs to my rooms. They stopped outside as I went in.

A fire was already blazing in the hearth. I'd have to meet the women that attended me, I thought, for I hadn't even had time to find out their names. The room was empty now, and I was glad for it. I pulled at the throng about my waist and loosened my gown. I let it slide to the floor and moved toward the bowl of water, still warm, that someone had left on the table. I washed my body with the soft rag and then stood in front of the fire to let myself dry. It felt good to be out of my clothes. The windows were shut, and the long, crimson drapes covered them to keep out the cold. The room was delightfully warm. I reached for my oils, sweet orange and chamomile. I breathed in the sweet, seductive scents as I placed them on my skin, dabbing my inner eye on my forehead with the holy oil, which I carried about my neck. Colors jumped and came alive for a moment as the oil awakened my senses in a more profound way.

I moved to the dressing room where my things had been put away. Rummaging about in my clothes I pulled out a simple gray under-gown made of rare silk and slid it over my head. The sleeves were long and soft, draping low at my wrists, and the hem brushed the ground. I'd been traveling and working in practical clothes, but now, as I let the feminine curve of my body kiss the silk, I smiled to myself.

There was a rap at the door, and I reached for a robe, pulling it about my shoulders. I stepped into the main room.

"Come in," I said.

Athena opened the door. She stood there for a moment surveying the room with her warrior's eye, then let her eyes rest on my garment. She stepped inside and shut the door behind her. She was still dressed in her riding tunic and breeches, and I could see the weariness of long days in the carriage of her shoulders. For a moment, I felt foolish for taking my simple pleasure. I wrapped the cloak more closely about me, pinning it at my shoulder.

"We must speak," she said simply.

I nodded toward a chair at the table, but she waved me away.

"I can't stay long," she began. "I must ride back to Caledocean at dawn. A messenger arrived saying that there has been another ship come in from Kart Hadst. Aphrodite's on it."

"What?"

This was very strange news. Aphrodite was our representative, our eyes, and ears in the new city. Being a priestess of high rank, she was essential to keeping our foothold in the city.

"As you're needed here for decisions, I thought you'd want me to go back and find out what's afoot. I'll send word as soon as I can."

I nodded my assent and put my hands to my head, shutting my eyes. I took a long, deep breath.

"There's one more thing," Athena said.

I dropped my hands to my side and looked at her.

"Poseidon," she said.

"Poseidon?"

She held my gaze but didn't smile.

"Be careful, Hera."

I didn't pretend not to understand. Holding out my hand to her in the warrior's way, I reached out and took hold of her wrist.

"I have given my will to the divine," I said in a low tone.

"It has led me here and to him. Would you deny that?"

She shook her head, and I saw understanding in her eyes. Squeezing my wrist with her palm, she bowed her head slightly.

"I will stand by you, Reverence, whatever may come," she said.

Relief swept over me. I looked deep into my friend's eyes.

"My heart to your heart," she said as she let me go and stepped toward the door. "Whatever may come."

# PART TWO
## THE AWAKENED HEART

# CHAPTER TEN

IT SNOWED ON THE PEAKS of Atlantis's volcano, all winter long. Her slopes were covered with white farther down the mountain than anyone could ever remember. Even the fields above Tintangore was powdered with snow.

I looked down on them from the woods that stretched over the hills behind the castle. The town below was burgeoning. Smoke spiraled steadily from the long, wood beamed halls we'd finished constructing just before the snow came. I could see the outlined figures of townsfolk, wrapped in cloaks and shawls, carrying in wood for their morning fires.

I let my eyes settle on the small store of timber that I'd been able to lay aside to be sent to Caledocean in the spring. It was not enough to build the fleet we'd need. I knew that now for I'd watched the building crews push themselves just to make these simple shelters for the winter. We had four or five families sharing most of these buildings and they'd all been helping alongside the construction crews. I couldn't imagine how many people or how long it would take to make seaworthy ships.

There had been no word from Zeus since he had left. With the weather being so bad, I hadn't expected it, but I couldn't help hoping that with the time and distance between us he'd be able to let me go and focus solely on our plans. As I looked down at the growing town, I smiled with pleasure. It had been an adventurous undertaking, and I hadn't forgotten Zeus's vision of creating a new city, separate from the Atlantean council. I smiled at the thought.

My breath was thick in the dawn air before me, and steam rose from the ground as the sun warmed it. I pulled my plain cloak closer to me and turned to continue up the path. The hill was steep, and the track wound into a denser mass of trees. It was dark again in the forest, but I knew my way. I snagged in and out of the thick trunks and ducked beneath the familiar branches until the passage opened before me and I came to the meadow and the sharp, gray rock face of the cave.

A small fire crackled loudly from its mouth. Poseidon sat beside it. Warmth spread through my chest at the sight of him, and I felt my face crease with pleasure.

He stood when he saw me, reached out his hand, and closed the space between us in a few quick strides. His arms wrapped around me and I laid my head on his chest, letting him pull away my hood so that my hair was set free. The soft weight of his lips kissed the crown of my head, and then he held me away from him as he looked down into my face. His hands were warm as he cupped my cheeks, and his lips were like the petals of a rose brushing against my mouth.

"Come," he said, taking my hand and pulled me toward the cave.

The space was small inside. He'd found it just before the first snowfall, and had claimed it as our den. He'd covered the earth with thick carpets and laid a bed of furs in the dark niche that was sequestered from the outside. Oil lamps burned on the rock facing inside and a skin of spiced wine hung beside the bed. The womb-like sensation of the earth reminded me of my years in Hecate's cave, which made the place all the more beautiful to me. Though we'd been meeting here for months now, I still felt a sense of awe and gratitude each time I crossed the threshold and looked into my lover's eyes.

The wind shook the branches of the trees outside and whistled through the cave. As I stepped into the alcove, I dropped the thick *tapa* cloth behind me, sealing our room, shutting out the constrictions of our lives.

Poseidon reached for me. I dropped my pack at the foot of the bed, and he pulled me down upon it. I removed his cloak and blade in a well-practiced rhythm. The sensation of his touch sent pleasure across my skin, and he kissed me again, pulling my gown off my shoulder. He ran his fingers, rough, against my flesh.

There were no words.

Our sounds filled the little chamber, and my voice echoed into the world beyond, but I didn't care. This was our sacred place free from disapproving or questioning eyes. When we lay together here, there was no pretense to our love. I pulled him inside of me and coveted the pleasure.

Later, when the lamps had burned low, I nestled in the crook of his arm, and we listened to the budding sounds of the forest, now awake, outside. Birds sang in rich tones, and the wind had stopped shaking the trees. A small animal rustled outside by the fire that had burned down long ago.

I laid my hand gently over my womb and let it rest there as I listened to his breathing, trying to decide if I should tell him now about the child I carried. I hadn't trusted the first signs of the pregnancy, as I was older than most that conceived, but as the full moons passed and my body changed, I became certain. Now each morning I brewed the herbs for the stomach sickness and swelling and soothed my body with my healing touch. I'd wanted to tell Poseidon, but I wasn't sure how he'd take the news. He was more cautious than I and insisted we keep our intimacy away from Zeus's undoubted spies. This news would change everything.

I felt a small wave of nausea rise and then retreat as I thought of how to broach the subject. Poseidon stroked my hair in long, slow movements. A small gust of wind pushed at the *tapa* cloth door, and the air that brushed over us was crisp. One of the oil lamps sputtered and then went out.

"Spring will be here soon, Hera," Poseidon murmured.

I buried my head beneath his chin. The sweet scent of him eased the anxiety that rose at the thought. I knew he'd have to return to Caledocean when the weather turned. Our time together grew short. I searched my mind for something to say, some way to tell him about the baby, but his hand caressed me slowly, and I was lulled in the comfort of our closeness. After some time, I moved my hand from my womb and slid it around his waist.

"I don't want you to go," I said.

"I know."

He rolled over and kissed me, slowly. "You know I want to stay with you as well," he whispered in my ear.

"Yes," I murmured back.

He stroked my face lightly, tracing the outline of my nose, mouth, and chin, brushing his lips against my ear. The slow sound of his breathing began to soften my senses. I let my mind drift toward sleep, my child soft and safe in my womb.

I dreamt.

A ship rode low in the water, and Zeus stood on its prow. He looked at me as if he could see the child within my womb. Lightning flashed in strong, silver streaks against my bones and there was an intense, singular pain inside my womb. I reached out protectively, but as I moved, I heard laughter rise from behind him. Hades's voice resounded about me, a cold, victorious sound.

"*Hera!*" he said.

I woke suddenly hearing Poseidon's soft voice saying my name over and over. He shook me gently and caressed my cheek to soothe me. My body was shaking. He held me for a long time.

"You had another nightmare," he said.

I shook my head.

"It's just a dream," I asserted, but I was surprised at the fear I could hear in my voice.

"When is a dream 'just' a dream, Hera?" Poseidon said. "What was it you saw?"

I hesitated, uncertain.

"Tell me," he said gently, leaning up on his elbow and looking down at me. My body still trembled. "Was it Zeus?"

I nodded. "And Hades," I said.

He wasn't surprised. I'd been insisting that Hades and Kronos had changed their opinion of me, and the Emerald Temple ever since the earthquake, and our confinement in the labyrinth chamber, but Poseidon had denied it.

"You can't trust Hades," he said emphatically. "A man doesn't say such things about his own brother easily, Hera, so mind your dream." He kissed me again. "It's getting late, my love."

I nodded as he pushed the blankets back and reached for his tunic and leggings. He handed me my silken under-gown and then turned toward the *tapa* door and pushed it aside. A warm beam of sunlight fell thick across the bed.

I slid from the blankets and slipped on my clothes. Poseidon watched me as I dressed, his eyes quiet, but intense. When I was done, he blew out the lamps and covered the bed with a thick skin and led me outside where the fire had died to ash. He pulled out his wineskin from his pack and handed it to me. I recoiled from the scent and reached for my pack where my herbs were already brewed into a mellow tea. He didn't seem to notice. We ate the barley bread and figs I'd brought and then reached for our cloaks. The sun was still high enough in the sky that it was warm enough to make our way without them, but he bade me put mine on.

"Take no chances, my love," he said firmly, pulling the hood up about my head. "Until we know Zeus's mind our love must remain only a possibility."

I sighed heavily, shrugging. My hand reached out instinctively toward my stomach, but I checked the movement midway and rested my hand on his waist. Standing up on my toes, I leaned my lips toward him, demanding. He laughed, kissing me again.

We walked together to the edge of the wood. Our fingers brushed against each other lightly. I would have to wait a fortnight, until the full moon, to see him alone again and that seemed an impossible task, but there was no way to avoid it.

He glanced toward the sun, which had now moved beyond us to the west.

"Take care when you reach the road," he said, brushing his lips lightly against my forehead and releasing me.

I stepped onto the path and walked a short way, stopping just before the bend. I turned and looked back. He stood there as still as the oak beside him, his body like the mast of a ship that has put down its sail. My chest filled with emotion. I had to will myself to turn and continue on my way back to Tintangore.

Hades came to Tintangore with the full moon.

I was in the cookhouse when he arrived, stealing fruit and figs for my rendezvous with Poseidon on the following morning.

"Reverence," a guard bobbed his head in the doorway. "The Lucifer is here."

Surprised, I dropped several persimmons, and they rolled to the man's feet. He leaned down to retrieve them.

"Thank you," I said, holding out my basket.

He glanced inside at the makings of a meal for two but said nothing. I straightened with pride and frustration; I shouldn't have to explain myself to anyone. I tossed the basket aside and followed him to the main hall to meet my guests.

There was already a large group gathered, and Hades was at its center. To my irritation, Aphrodite was at his side. I'd known they were having an affair for several months, for Athena sent me word from Caledocean at each new moon. But I hadn't given Aphrodite leave to join me here, and I was confident Athena hadn't either.

As I made my way to the center of the circle, I saw that Hades had also brought a handful of fighting men. I recognized most of them from Zeus's personal guard and to my dismay, Ajax was their leader. He took a step back and smiled coldly as I passed, but I pretended not to notice. Still, a cold chill swept up my spine.

*Why would Zeus's man be traveling with Hades?* Before I could finish the thought, Hades was before me, bowing with extended, exaggerated gestures. His lips were cold as they brushed the back of my hand. I wished I could trust him, could accept this show of honor, but I shivered at the gesture and wanted to retract my hand. Still, I steadied myself and smiled. When he got to his feet, he motioned toward a young man in the group.

"My protégé," he announced, "Mel'ak."

His protégé was no more than a boy, tall and thin, but very young to be standing so close at the Lucifer's side. His face was still smooth and slightly round, his lips full and pursed in a serious manner. His dark brows furrowed slightly as he stepped forward and bowed.

"It's an honor, Reverence," he said solemnly, and I believed, for him, it was.

Without thinking, I reached out my ring for him to kiss. It was an odd thing to do for the custom was very old, and this young man had probably never encountered it. He hesitated for a moment, then the look on his face changed. He dipped low and reached out with his palm lifting my fingers to his lips. I felt Hades's gaze bearing down on us as the young man's fingers grazed my skin. A sharp sensation moved over my flesh, and then a gentle warmth rose from the boy toward me. He kissed the ring quickly and retracted his hand, but the strength of his gift was clear to me.

He was a seer.

Mel'ak kept his eyes downcast as he backed away and took up his place at Hades's side. Before I could call him back, Aphrodite stepped forward in her flurry of theatrics, drawing all eyes to her as she made her obeisance to me. I tried to smile, and keep my composure, but my mind was racing.

*What did Hades need with a seer?*

When Aphrodite rose to her feet before me, Mel'ak had disappeared.

That night at the welcoming dinner for our guests, Poseidon kept his distance. I tried to console myself with the fact that tomorrow I'd have Poseidon all to myself, but now that Hades was here I knew that would be cut short, too.

Hades came to the meal bedecked as a king and was the center of attention. I was relieved by the distraction. Ajax and the boy didn't accompany him. As soon as it was permissible, I excused myself and headed up the long stairs to my room. There were guards posted at every entrance, as was Kronos's custom, which had given me the excuse to dismiss my own, thus the freedom to slip away at will. I'd sent my honor guard to set up camp outside the gates of Tintangore, charging them to accompany me in my duties in town. This made it much easier for me to escape the castle unnoticed through other routes, and in a serving woman's disguise.

As I walked through the long corridors now, the guards nodded to me in recognition as I passed, but this made me feel even more apprehensive as I realized that I was now surrounded by men.

When I reached my room, I pulled off my jewels and finery and slipped into a simple tunic. I pulled a warm green cloak about me and stepped out onto the generous verandah welcoming the cold crisp air as it sharpened my senses.

Moving to the marble railing, I looked out over the vast expanse of green beyond the castle walls. A few dim lights from campfires flickered near the town below, but most people, I imagined, were already sleeping. I tried to relax and feel into the night and the unknown, intent on prayer, but as I did I sensed a presence on the other side of the long veran-dah. As if alert to my sudden awareness, a figure moved in the dark, and a young voice spoke, "Forgive me, Reverence."

It was Mel'ak.

"I'm staying in the alcove of my master's room," he said, stepping out of the darkness and into the soft light of the torch set into the wall of my apartment. "And the rooms share this verandah."

I was surprised that Hades had taken the room so close to mine. It was the only one, other than mine, on this side of the hall, and the rooms were connected by this porch. If Kronos would've sent anyone there I'd have thought it would be a priestess, Aphrodite perhaps, but then, she was probably staying with Hades anyway.

The boy looked at me intently, and I realized he was wait-ing for my permission to be excused.

"I hadn't known the room was occupied," I started, but regretted revealing it. "What are you doing out here?"

He looked out past me and toward the black horizon.

"I, too, was seeking answers from the night."

It was a bold thing to say, but I liked the honesty of it. He could sense my gift and was letting me know it. I felt certain it was not out of arrogance, but instead, a humble act of disclosure.

"You've seen things in the night before?" I asked.

"I've seen many things, Reverence," the boy said. His tone was low and touched my sense of foreboding. I felt that he wanted to say more and urged him on, but he shook his head.

"Lady, I mean nothing by it. I wish only to serve honorably—"

He spoke softly, but there was a note of urgency in his

voice, and I stepped toward him feeling the full measure of his height. I looked up into his eyes.

"But you serve the Temple of Light," I said.

"It would not have been my first choice if other roads had been open to me."

There was a message here, and I reached out with all of my senses to find it.

"If you'd been born a girl you could've sworn your oath to the Emerald Temple," I said.

"I would have done so gladly."

Another long pause and then he took a step back, glancing over his shoulder as if he'd heard something. I realized that the celebration would be over soon, and the others would come to their rooms, but I'd heard nothing. Then it occurred to me that he was not listening with his ears, but with another sense and that he could read something I could not. A chill ran over my skin with the force of the realization. He turned back to me.

"The Lucifer will require me when he returns to his room," he said quickly.

This time I understood the urgency in his voice. I nodded and touched his shoulder.

"Go then, Mel'ak," I said gently. "And may you use your gifts with honor and for a purpose that will benefit the whole."

The prayer was an old one, and time-honored between priestesses. It slipped from my mouth before I could think and the effect was immediate and telling. The boy stepped back as if I'd struck him, his face tight and his brow furrowed. His eyes looked hurt.

"I'm doing my best, Lady," he stammered into space between us as he backed into the darkness toward his door.

I waited there a few minutes after he left until I heard the sounds of others inside his room and an orange light moved steadily beneath the wooden doorframe. Someone pulled a curtain tighter around it, and I heard the soft, but distinct sound of a woman's laughter.

When I returned to my room, I bolted the outside door and pulled the thick cloth over it. I lit a small torch in the hearth and paced the room quickly looking for any trace that I'd had an intruder, for it was clear to me now that something was amiss. I searched the room, but everything was in its place. Anxiety moved through me as I doused the light and retreated to my bed filled with uneasiness. I thought I might leave my room and look for Poseidon, but I knew he'd already left the castle. It was his habit to spend the night in the cave before I came, making it habitable. At first, I'd insisted it wasn't necessary, but then I'd realized it was a precious time for him, sleeping in the arms of the elements as he'd done for so many years. I knew he missed his ships and the sea.

I thought of calling on my honor guard, but that would alert the castle to my concern. Then there would be questions and no way to get to Poseidon in the morning. I wouldn't bear that.

I lay back on the pillows, my temples pulsing and a strong pulling sensation in my womb caught my attention. Reaching out with my mind I sent calming images to the child. The impression eased, but the strong sense of the baby welled up inside me.

*It's a boy.*

The thought was prominent and clear. I smiled despite my worry, reaching out with my mind again.

*I am Hephaestus.*

A beautiful name! I glimpsed the deep blue that would be his soulful eyes and my body relaxed, utterly captivated by the warmth of his presence.

*There's time to uncover their intentions;* I thought as I began to turn my focus completely to my baby. *I'll meet Poseidon at the cave and tell him everything. Together, we'll know what to do.*

The child's true nature reached out to me again, and I pulled the blanket warm about myself and lay my hand on my womb, mesmerized.

This is how I missed the one opportunity I'd had for escape.

# CHAPTER ELEVEN

THE SUN WAS WARM ON MY FACE as I made my way up the road. When I reached the path beside it, I took off my cloak; my forehead wet with sweat. I walked fast, pressing myself hard as I mounted the hill, stopping to catch my breath at the top. The anxiety of the night before had not left me, and I hurried to reach Poseidon. I knew I had to tell him about the baby and the peculiar interaction I'd had with Hades's new seer. Something was brewing, and Poseidon would help me to face it.

I turned and looked about me, the day bright. Signs of spring were everywhere. The field was green and red, and yellow flowers opened in bright patches. Small animals scurried about the trees before me, which were covered with glossy green leaves. The forest felt alive in a way I'd not experienced before, and I hesitated on the path as I ducked beneath the canopy of green. I was acutely aware of my child, and the need to protect him, which meant that I couldn't call upon the fire. I hadn't realized just how much I'd come to rely on this ability to safeguard myself. Though I'd rarely used the skill, everyone knew I had it, and that knowledge had been protection in itself. Now, as I made my way through the trees, I felt vulnerable.

I moved more quickly on the familiar path until I saw the clearing ahead. Then I began to run. When I reached the open green, I stopped to catch my breath, calling out Poseidon's name, but only silence met me. I stood there, panting. There was no fire kindled before the cave and no sound from within. My skin prickled.

My eyes searched for signs of him, his pack, his boots, food laid upon the stone he used as a table, but there was nothing. The baby seemed to throb inside me, and the dim sense that I should turn and run welled up inside my breast, but I stood frozen in place. I couldn't leave. He was here, I could feel him.

I took a step forward, tentatively. A path was already trodden in the grass, crossing the small clearing, and as I glanced down, I drew in my breath. I could see where patches had been tramped away, and fresh, red blood marked the trail.

I stepped back, but it was too late.

"Reverence," a familiar voice came from the cave, and I looked up to see Hades appear at its opening.

There was a flurry of sound then, and the bushes parted above the jagged, gray face of the hill. Half a dozen armed men moved quickly to the field about me. I heard a familiar voice behind me, and then Ajax took me firmly by the arm. I drew myself up and made to shake him off, but he only tightened his grip. An amused smile curled his lips as he pulled me forward. I tried to stand my ground, resisting his strength, but he only laughed out loud, raised he hand and struck me. I reeled backward, stumbling, my hand moving to my cheek.

The indignity of it hurt more than the blow as the men stood by watching. One sniggered. Their hardened intent was apparent in their eyes as I scanned them frantically for a sign of hope. Ajax reached for me again, and half dragged me across the green before I could collect myself and understand the full weight of the danger I'd walked into. These men were not afraid of me. They knew of my power but were not concerned.

Hades stood on the wide ledge before the cave and called to someone inside. There was movement and struggle from within, and then the *tapa* parted, and two big men stepped forward, Poseidon, bound and gagged, hung limply between them. I gasped and moved toward him, but Ajax pushed me back roughly. Two of the other men appeared at either side of me, and one took firm hold of the collar of my cloak.

Ajax moved toward Poseidon, and Hades stepped down beside me, calm and poised. He smiled at me as if he were holding court and I was his guest. Then he turned and reached out a hand to Ajax in the way a master gives leave to his musicians to entertain him.

"What are you doing?" I cried. "What do you want?"

Hades didn't answer but nodded toward Ajax who'd picked up one of several pails of water and threw it on Poseidon's face. Poseidon spluttered awake, his eyes blinking in the sun. The two men beside him hoisted him back to a standing position. I was glad to see that one man was bloodied, and the other had a deep cut in one arm that still oozed—Poseidon had defended himself. The older man held his blade to Poseidon's throat. I stifled a cry.

Poseidon looked around. His eye was severely bruised, and blood was spattered across his lips. They'd stripped his chest bare. Swollen purple marks bore evidence that he'd been beaten. His side had been gouged by a blade and roughly sewn closed. Tears sprang to my eyes, but I fought them back.

"Why?" I asked again, pleadingly. "Hades, how can you do this to your own brother?"

"I can't," Hades answered easily. "That's why Ajax is here."

Ajax struck Poseidon hard in the ribs, but Poseidon made no sound, his eyes closing tight. He had been staring at me, hard, his blue eyes dim, but now his head sank. I realized suddenly that he must be waiting for me to act, to call the fire forth upon them all, but I could only stand there helplessly.

"You can't use your power, Priestess," Hades said as if he could read my thoughts. There was delight clear in his voice. "The child will be maimed if you do."

I put my hand on my womb instinctively. Poseidon's head snapped up, and his eyes met mine.

"What, you didn't know, brother?"

I had never seen anyone take such pleasure in another person's suffering.

"I was going to tell you today," I said desperately, but Poseidon shook his head, his jaw clenched on the gag.

Rage set itself like a tempest across his face. He struggled in the soldier's grip, but Ajax brought his fist down hard on his cheek once again. I screamed, despite myself, as blood ran from his lip. Already his eye was swelling closed.

My mind raced looking for something I could do, but there was nothing. They beat Poseidon until he fell unconscious at their feet then revived him again with smelling oils and water. One man began to build up a fire as he did this, another pulled out a brand.

I fell to my knees before Hades, humbling myself completely. I begged for Poseidon's life.

"Oh, we're not going to kill him," he assured me. "We'll just keep him… uncomfortable. These men are skilled at such things. They belong to your husband, after all."

Zeus. He wouldn't plan such a thing. No matter how angry he might be, he wouldn't put me in danger or use his men to exact his revenge on his brother.

"I don't believe you," I said. "This is your doing, Hades. What do you want?"

He didn't respond, just watched me intently for a moment as if gauging my pulse. Then he signaled to Ajax who reached for the brand, now red with heat. I shook my head, but his action was swift, and I heard the harsh hiss of the metal against my beloved's chest before I could make a sound. Poseidon cried out through the gag and fell to his knees.

My hand reached out before I could think, or falter. I drew the fire easily from the hearth and heard it crackle through the air as it burst out toward Ajax, but as soon as I did it, a sharp spasm seized me. I doubled over clutching my womb. A soldier threw another bucket at Ajax, and as I looked up, I saw that I'd only singed his hair and tunic, which he now shook the water from.

My eyes met Poseidon's. Tears were streaming down his cheeks.

Hades set a pail of water down beside me, and I plunged my hands into it. My body was shaking. I could feel the child clenching in pain, and I knew that I'd maimed him. I bit my lip hard to stop my tears and quell my hatred and heat that continued to kindle the fire inside of me.

*Pain. Burning. Mother!* Hephaestus's consciousness called out to me.

I'd hurt my baby. My lover was in ruin before me, because of me. All my training, my years of practice at control and acceptance failed me now as I witnessed the ruin of my life and it's purpose. I saw Hades's intent clearly now. He would provoke me until I either gave him what he wanted or until I used the fire gift and killed my child and most likely, myself with him. Either way, he'd get what he wanted in the end.

I was broken.

I withdrew my hands from the water and struggled to my feet. I shut my eyes.

"What do you want?" my voice was small and weak.

When I opened my eyes, he stood very close to me, smiling.

"Hera," he began, "you took the oath of the *Heiros Gamos*. Surely, you didn't think that those in power would let you relinquish it, with their new city and their new order at stake? The old ways are dying, *priestess*. You can't discard the king and take his brother as your consort. You're a wife and mother, an example to all that will come after you."

His voice was low, but I could feel the contempt in the men that surrounded me as he spoke. He stepped away from me then and turned to Poseidon. The men pulled him to attention and removed the rag from his mouth.

"This is very simple," Hades went on to us both. "Your husband requires that you each pay the price for your disloyalty. Hera, you will stay here, sequestered in these hills until you give birth to your son."

Fear flooded through me. How could he know?

"The Emerald Temple is not the only place that has seers," Hades said. "Mel'ak has served us well."

Mel'ak, of course! This was what the young man had been trying to tell me. He was being used by Hades to vision my secret.

"Yes, the boy is gifted," I said bleakly. "But he serves you, Hades, not Zeus."

I said this last so the other men could hear, hoping one might see this was all a ruse. I had no doubt now that Zeus was the sword in this action, but Hades wielded it.

Ajax was smirking. I suddenly recalled the day, long ago, when he'd come with Kronos and Hades to accompany me to my first high council, and I realized that he'd been Hades's man all along. Zeus was being used. We all were.

"When you give birth, the child will be given to a family in Kart Hadst, never to be acknowledged by Zeus. As far as he's concerned, you've been a faithful wife."

I wanted to wretch. My body shook and grew cold. Poseidon breathed heavily, his hands, shackled in front of him, holding tight to his side.

"She can't stay here alone," he managed to say, his voice hoarse. "She can't give birth surrounded by soldiers."

Ajax waved away the two men holding Poseidon up, letting him stand on his own. I could see his legs trembling as he tried to step forward. Ajax caught him, as he was about to fall, pulling him upright again. Poseidon winced in pain, but righted himself and looked at Hades insistently.

"She won't be alone," Hades assured him. "Aphrodite will stay with her."

I felt faint. A wave of nausea moved through me, and I fell to the ground and vomited into the pail. Poseidon dropped to his knees beside me, his hands reaching out, but Ajax pulled him away, drawing out a small thin blade that he held to his throat.

I retched again.

When nothing else spilled from me, Hades let me pull out the flask slung around my side and drink the herbs to settle myself. Everyone was silent, watching. When I was done, I stood slowly and looked to Poseidon, the knife so sharp at his throat that the blade pierced his skin with each breath.

"I will give you the child," I said.

Poseidon closed his eyes.

"Very good," Hades said. "We'll return to Tintangore and spread the word that you've decided to go into retreat. Aphrodite will come daily to assist you as she might if you had truly chosen to do such a thing. Word will be sent to the Emerald Temple, through her. When the child is born, you will remove Demeter from her place in Caledocean and give her proxy vote in the council to Aphrodite." He paused here until I nodded. "After the child is born you'll return to Tintangore and await Zeus's return in the summer that follows. You will not revoke Aphrodite's position as your liaison, or her power to vote for you in the council. You will swear your oath to uphold these things on the High Priestesses' ring that you wear."

Tears fell quietly from my eyes, but I didn't care. A part of me was splitting, wandering beyond the bounds of my body and its emotional need to care.

"Done," I said.

I stared at the emerald ring on my hand, the sign of my position, lineage, and power, and began to lift it to my lips, but Hades reached out a hand to stop me.

"There is one more thing," he said. "When the child is delivered you'll have free access to your power. You must swear that you will not use it against us."

At this last, I lifted my eyes again to his. I felt nothing for him. There was no hatred, no distaste or dislike. For a brief moment, I wondered with a distracted interest what a horror it would be to have to live as Hades did, but I pushed the thought from my mind. As I felt no hatred, I would feel no compassion either. Nothing. That was all I wished to be.

"I swear on the dragon," I said softly, and then again, my

voice stronger and clearer, "I swear as the High Priestess of the Emerald Temple."

He released my hand, and I pressed the green stone to my lips. It was done.

Ajax removed his blade from Poseidon's throat, and I reached out to him, knowing I could still soothe his wounds, but Ajax switched position, stepping in front of me. I stepped back a few paces as he approached, but two of the men behind me closed in. Hades had turned to his brother to speak, and I looked on confused. What more could Hades want?

"Your men," Hades said simply.

A jagged smile broke across Poseidon's face, and he began to laugh. The sound rose up around us all, hysterical and beyond fear, filling the little grove in an eerie way.

"They'd never follow you, or Zeus," Poseidon said.

His legs began to tremble and his knees buckled beneath him, but he continued his strange laughter until Ajax reached for another pail of water and doused Poseidon again. The laughter stopped. Poseidon fell to his knees, the sun bright in his eyes so that he had to squint to see us. "They'll never follow you, or Zeus."

The men shuffled uncomfortably beside me. I could sense their indignation. These men had stood as Zeus's own honor guard. Their loyalty would never come into question. Hades didn't seem to mind the statement. He moved toward his brother, his body casting a shadow across Poseidon's form.

"No," he said directly, "I don't imagine they would."

He stood there silently, staring down at his brother until Poseidon shook his head, understanding spreading across his face. He held up his hands before him and stared at the ring on his finger.

"You want my position?" he said slowly, "You want me to abdicate as the heir to the Titan dynasty. You want the ring."

It was a statement. All humor and derision had gone from his face. He was deathly still. Then he shook his head again.

"You must take my life, Hades. You must spill my blood here and now to have this ring, and in doing such a thing my men will know there has been treachery. They still will not follow you."

Hades had been expecting this, and so had Ajax, who moved toward the fire that still smoldered behind them. He stirred it until the flame caught and leaped, and reached for the branding iron. I cried out and tried to move to Poseidon, shaking my head and pleading, but Ajax pulled the brand out of the fire and strode directly toward me. It took a moment for me to realize what was going to happen, but my body moved backwards instinctively until the heavy hands of the soldiers caught and held me. Ajax moved quickly to my side and reached out for my cloak pulling it away.

"Her chest?" he asked Hades over his shoulder. "Or her face?"

I felt the world around me grow thin and transparent. Someone shouted, and Poseidon staggered to his feet, but the horror overcame me. I saw Ajax raise the orange brand, and then heard Poseidon's voice, but the scene slipped away as I swooned into darkness.

# CHAPTER TWELVE

I WALKED THROUGH THE NEXT YEAR as a dreamer might move through a terrible night. My mind cracked and faltered, my spirit lifting up and away from my body, as I faced each thing that must be done. Time passed slowly, a dark, wretched night in which I came to know real fear, and finally apathy. My lover lost, my child… *lost*! My role as High Priestess usurped.

I lost track of the seasons, sinking into the abyss of loneliness and the sweet oblivion of potent herbs and strong wine. I awoke late in the day, and barely ate, or dressed, or went out at all. I kept to my apartment and the vast verandah, sinking into the lounge, weary and broken.

All the days lulled into one, until a distinct change of season fell upon Tintangore. I was on the porch, letting the sun warm my cheek. I had turned my face toward the golden beam, shutting my eyes. The sound of the bees that clung to the jasmine vines, which crawled up the columns to my verandah, drew me in, and out of my dreamy state. That is when it came, a cool, sharp breeze, which sent a chill over my skin. My eyes flew open, and I wondered at what time of year it was. For a moment, I saw beyond my prison, looking out on the green fields below seeing the gold and purple flowers in magnificent bloom.

A woman who now attended me crept to the table beside me and reached out to adjust the shawl about my legs. I searched my wandering mind for her name, but could only grasp the outline of her pale, thin face.

I opened my eyes.

"Get away," I hissed at her, my voice swollen with wine.

I pulled the cloth back up toward myself, my hand clumsily snagging it on the armrest. I struggled with it for a moment then gave way to the effort, letting myself slip back in the chair. The woman said nothing, just moved again for the wrap, and pulled it free from its captivity. She laid it gently on me as the breeze stirred. I said something under my breath, but even I didn't know what it was.

I shut my eyes again, listening to the sounds of her movement about me as she lifted the uneaten plate of fruit from the table and refilled my empty goblet with a fresh cup of wine. I smelled the strong, lavender blend mixed with the grapes. It was Hades's wine from his vineyards in the west. He'd made a point to tell me so before he left for Caledocean. I didn't care. I would drink his wine, anybody's wine for that matter if it would dull the raging pain inside me.

I let my mind wander with the colored patterns the sunlight burned into the back of my eyelids. Red and gold spiraled before me, and I tried to focus on them to push away the image that preoccupied me whether awake or asleep: *Hephaestus*. Two full seasons had passed since they'd taken him from me, but not a moment of that time had, in peace. The memory of the few minutes they'd let me hold my son in my arms haunted me. My mind and my heart were consumed by it. His eyes had been so round and clear--too clear for an infant. Those eyes had stared at me intently as if he knew I'd given him away, traded him for my life and his father's. I'd tried to reach out to him with my inner sense and touch his essence, as I had when he was in my womb, to tell him I loved him and wanted him and had no choice.

But one always had a choice.

His tiny hand had clenched my finger, and for a moment he stopped crying. In that stillness, I sensed only resignation. He had fought against his birth, struggled to stay with me, inside me, for as long as he could, but I'd pushed him out, his body twisted and misshapen from the misuse of my fire gift. He would suffer. My boy would know pain from this deformity, and the horror of it would never leave me.

As a cloud passed before the sun's rays, the image of Hephaestus's leg, too short and too thin, flashed before me and I shook my head roughly to chase the image away. I'd done that. I'd given him that leg and the pain it would cause him all his life. Opening my eyes, I reached for the goblet, but the chill wind rose again, and I sank back down into my seat, pulling the shawl around me.

Looking back out over the fields I realized it was still early in the summer, and suddenly I remembered hearing that harvest would go well, but I hadn't been outside the castle in a full turn of the moon. I could see everything I needed to from my plush seat outside on the verandah, my view of the courtyard, fields, and village beyond had become my world. Here I spent my days, one after the other, watching and waiting. Watching and listening for the messenger that would signal Zeus's arrival. Waiting for some unknown mercy to save me from having to face him, to take him to my bed and call him my husband.

At the thought of Zeus, I wrenched the shawl off and flung it on the ground, pulling myself out of the chair to stand on my unstable feet. The world swooned. I realized it was from the wine, and that I shouldn't drink more until I could navigate my body more clearly, but that would mean letting this dull haze of apathy diminish, and that I couldn't do.

I moved toward the balcony, letting the breeze lift my hair and sharpen my senses. It was an odd chill for this time of year, but it felt strangely comforting. I held on to the railing, taking a deep breath as I looked out at the horizon. Something moved in my vision a long way off, and I stared at it as my mind began to slowly clear. It was a figure on horseback, and then two and three—no there was a dozen of them coming round the bend in the road, a cloud of dust rising behind them. They were riding fast. The leader was hunched down over the head of the horse, and the others were in tight formation behind it. My pulse quickened, and my head grew light. It was still too early in the season for it to be Zeus, and Hades was with Poseidon in the west. Hades wouldn't return before the fall and Poseidon... I closed my eyes as my chest constricted. It had been a year since I'd seen my lover. He'd been taken to Hades's estate while his men were put to work building ships at Caledocean's docks.

Opening my eyes, I steadied myself and watched as the figures drew nearer. I heard shouts from the lookouts in the tower, and horses were saddled at the stable. Ajax shouted an order from the gate, which was followed by a commotion in the courtyard as armed men took their places. So, they hadn't been expecting riders either. Something about that pleased me. The men scrambled into position as the riders approached.

I squinted and held my hand up to block the sun, which let me make out the first form. A woman. Then the next came into view, and I saw another and another, all females, charging up the hill with apparent purpose.

Women, *my* women, warrior priestesses coming for me.

I gripped tighter to the railing trying now to clear my head, the very real sense of danger upon me. *Fools,* I thought. *I haven't called on you for your own protection!* Yet here they were, and now I recognized Athena at the lead.

The cold wind lifted itself about me again as if propelling me forward.

I cursed, calling for the woman attendant who took her time in answering me.

"We have visitors from the Emerald Temple," I said with annoyance. "Get me my robe and jewels!"

She stood there for a long moment staring, as if deciding whether my words were true, but then the commotion in the courtyard below grew louder and the distinct sound of horses' hooves brought her round. She rushed to the railing beside me, and we both looked down at the scene. Ajax, who'd been my jailor for this long year and more, now drew his sword against Athena who slid from her horse to face him, her hand on the hilt of her own blade. There was a deep growl in the man's voice as he dismissed her, but she shook him off, raising her voice so loud that we could hear its echo even at this distance.

"We've come to see the High Priestess," she cried, "and we will not be deterred from our purpose!"

An argument arose, and the men began to circle the priestesses, but the women stayed their horses in perfect formation, hands on the hilts of their swords, ready to clash. Ajax spoke again, but I didn't wait to hear what he said. Turning to the woman beside me I searched my mind for her name trying to sober myself. *Lia.* I caught hold of the name and snapped my order again, and for the first time in the long months she'd served me, her eyes displayed deference. She disappeared into my wardrobe as I moved toward the brass mirror to survey my reflection, something I had not done since the day....

I was shocked by what I saw. Stepping closer it took me a moment to recognize myself. My face was drawn and thin, my once shapely breasts and hips now flat and straight beneath the pale green dress that hung loosely about my form. Age and pain showed around my eyes, and my hair, once as lustrous and black as wet obsidian, hung in wild, gray ringlets that covered my breasts.

The woman stepped toward me with the emerald green robe in her hands and slid it over my shoulders, then fastened the medallion into place about my neck. Voices were now carrying into the room and footsteps were echoing in the great hall below us. The wine still ran warm in my limbs giving me enough courage to turn away from the ghostly sight of myself. I headed out of my rooms. The woman followed close behind as I clung to the rail of the long staircase that circled down to the main hall and the courtyard beyond.

As I reached the bottom of the stairs, I was panting for breath. The woman stared at me hard but didn't reach out her hand to help. I was grateful for that at least, though annoyed by my weakness. More shouts came from outside and then the distinct clash of swords, and I pushed myself forward out into the light.

Ajax held his sword poised to strike and Athena had her blade drawn. I called out as steadily as I could.

"Put up your weapons! Peace!"

I wasn't sure where the words had come from, some last vestige of my pride and authority that swilled with the drink, but I was glad for it as the women put up their swords and the men hesitated in frank surprise. I snapped the order again, sharply, moving unsteadily toward Zeus's honor guard. They looked to Ajax who threw me a sour stare and pursed his lips.

"You're in no condition to see guests, Reverence," he said. "I was only explaining to them that it's Aphrodite they should give their news to and she's in Caledocean where you sent her."

No one had used the title Reverence in so long that the sound of it sent my spine tingling. He still hadn't put up his sword and stepped toward me menacingly so that I instinctually stepped back.

"How dare you!" It was Athena, and in a moment she'd brushed by him and was standing between us, her sword drawn again. "No one speaks to the High Priestess of the Emerald Temple that way," she said in a low and dangerous tone.

The women slid off their horses in an instant and took up their positions around her before I could think what to do. I hadn't felt safe for so long I didn't recognize it for what it was. All I could think was that my women were in danger. Danger, because of me. Yet I couldn't react fast enough to try and save them.

In moments the scene unraveled and fighting broke out. There were shouts from behind us as more men ran out of the guardhouses and the horses scattered. I cried out for them to stop, but was pushed aside by a heavy hand and then Athena struck out in front of me, slicing through the flesh that had touched me. I heard a woman scream in pain from across the courtyard and then her sisters surrounded her and a man went down and then another. Again I was pushed, but this time I fell to the ground, my thin palms scraping the graveled ground. To my surprise my dear friend Apollo was suddenly beside me, his warm hands lifting me easily to my feet. He must have come with the women. I watched in a haze of shock as he whirled around to fight again, but stopped as Ajax stood in front of him with a captive in his arms and a knife to her throat. Apollo stood frozen beside me and dropped his sword arm. I stared at the woman before me until a dim sense of recognition passed through my confusion.

"Tell them to stop," Ajax shouted at me, pressing the blade hard against her skin. The image returned of him holding the same blade to Poseidon's neck, and I struggled to find my voice and obey him, but the woman spoke.

"Hera," she said simply. "It's me, Artemis."

There was a calm certainty in her voice that reached out through the haze and confusion.

"Artemis?" I said, and then stronger, "Artemis!"

The heat stirred in my bones.

"Let her go!" I commanded, stepping toward Ajax.

The fighting had stopped around us as Athena called the women to attention. They still had their swords in hand and faced the men, but now they circled Ajax. All eyes were on me as I took another step forward, the heat visibly darkening my skin. I felt a moment of terror as it welled up, familiar and horrible, the cause of so much pain and loss, yet I didn't quell it. This was Artemis, MY Artemis.

"Let her go," I said again, my voice high and half-hysterical, "let her go!"

Ajax's face tightened, his brows arching, but for the first time, I saw him hesitate. His eyes dropped to my hands that were shaking, but hot. He dropped the knife, letting Artemis go.

"Remember your vow, Priestess," he snarled with disdain.

My priestesses gasped.

"Stand down, Ajax, and see to the wounded," I commanded, ignoring him. Then to them all, "Stand down!" To my relief, the men put up their swords without looking to their captain. I turned to the priestesses and their leader. "It's over now, Athena," I said. "Put up your swords."

She took a step back to stand beside me but didn't put away her blade. Neither did her women.

"All of you!" I cried out almost pleadingly, "Stand down on my order, and on my *life*!"

At this Athena snapped around, shock clear on her face. She slid her blade into her sheath and the women followed suit. Before there could be further argument or confrontation I motioned her to follow me and bade the guard see to her women's needs. To my relief they obeyed.

I struggled to take control of my mind and shake off the strength of the drink. All eyes were upon me. I turned unsteadily and walked into the large meeting hall with its tall, arching ceilings. Athena, Artemis, and Apollo followed me. My voice carried as I bade my attendant to bring us food and drink. This time she didn't hesitate, curtseying nicely before she left the room. I wondered suddenly when the last time I'd seen such a thing was.

I slid gratefully into the heavy backed chair that was on the raised platform at the head of the room where Kronos, or Hades usually sat. It was the place I used to take when giving council, or planning the village expansion. It had been a very long time since I'd felt the weight of its size and grandeur lending me strength, but I needed it now. I let my hands rest on the wolves' heads carved at the base of its armrests as if they too could lend me power.

The others took their seats across from me and sat quietly as if waiting for me to speak. I sat there dumbly, unsure what I should say for now that the immediate danger had passed, and the fire had seeped from my blood, I felt as fragile as before and worse, afraid. The realization that I'd confronted Ajax unnerved me. I had shown my power, but couldn't use it, and he knew it. I'd sworn an oath and would keep it. That is what was required of me. Because of my station and my vow.

Lia returned with a tray and set it down on the table in front of our guests. She poured them wine and then took a separate cask and set it beside me, filling my goblet and handing it to me. I reached out an unsteady hand and began to drink in a practiced movement before I realized how this must look to the others. Putting the cup down beside me, I sucked at my lips to remove the hasty swish of the wine. None of the others had reached for their cups. Anxiety gripped me.

"He said you have sworn an oath," Athena said finally, breaking the silence.

"It's none of your concern," I said dryly, "What're you doing here, Athena? And why have you disobeyed my specific directions to stay away?"

She stared at me in obvious frustration. The deeply defined lines on her forehead creased, and her tan cheeks flushed. Age had hardened her looks and sharpened the edges of her body. When she spoke her words were as precise as her features.

"You've been absent from the high council for over a year," she began, "and two winter solstices have passed without your blessing at the Emerald Temple. Demeter acts on your behalf there, and all of her communications have come back with Aphrodite's seal on them."

I scowled and reached again for the wine. "You give me accusations, not answers!" I said too loud.

I finished the cup and leaned back in the chair, letting the dark warmth sweep over me. Closing my eyes for a moment, I felt my mind soften toward its familiar complacency. I took in a soft breath of pleasure. When I opened my eyes all three of them were staring at me intently.

Artemis rose to her feet.

"We've brought you a message from your daughter," she said.

The sound of her voice moved through me like a familiar song. I blinked hard to keep her in focus. As she moved toward me, my body leaned forward, and I felt my hand longing to reach for her.

"Ilithyia has need of her mother," she finished.

I sat straighter in my chair. "Illi," I said vaguely. "Illi needs me?"

Artemis nodded. "She has sent you a message."

"What is it? What does she need?" I snapped.

Artemis shook her head. "I can't deliver the message when you're like this."

"What?"

She held out her hand and signaled Apollo who got to his feet and strode to the table beside me. He reached for the wine cask and put it to his nose taking a long, slow whiff.

"Poppy," he said, "and something else, I'm not certain."

I stared at him icily. What was he implying? Was I being drugged?

Athena stood and joined them.

"Reverence," she began, "Hera, please, come with us now. We can fight our way out of here if we must. Whatever has happened is my fault. I should never have left your side. Come away now and let their wrath fall upon me—"

I shook my head, rushing to my feet so that my head swam. Apollo reached out a hand to steady me, but I threw it away.

"Don't say such a thing!" I shouted stepping toward Athena. I gripped tight to her tunic and shook her with all my strength, but she stood her ground. "Never say such a thing again! You must never face their wrath, never!" I started to cry hard, bewildered tears. "I can't go with you. I've given my word, an oath sworn as High Priestess. Zeus will return soon, and I'll stay with him, I'll be his wife. Now go, please go!"

"You heard her!" Ajax's voice carried through the room and my body stiffened.

I felt Artemis's hands on my shoulders, guiding me back to my seat, and then Lia was there. She poured me more wine. My hand reached out as if in preservation, but when I had the goblet in my hand, I hesitated to remember Apollo's words, *Poppy, and something else.*

I threw the cup across the room.

"Go!" I shouted, "Go, and don't come back!"

Athena's face was frozen in a genuine grimace of pain. Apollo backed away from me and stood by her side. Ajax remained at a distance across the room, and the serving woman fled. Only Artemis still stood beside me. She reached out for my hand and squeezed it.

"Ili needs her mother," she said quietly.

I looked up into her face and glistening eyes.

"Go," I whispered.

She dropped my hand, and turned away, joining the others.

"Go!" I said again to them all, my voice filled with sorrow. "And don't come back."

# CHAPTER THIRTEEN

THAT NIGHT, I refused my sleeping draught and slept badly, my dreams mired in fear and images of Ilithyia. What message could Artemis have meant to give about my daughter? Why hadn't I insisted she deliver it? When I woke, my bed-gown clung to my clammy skin. When Lia appeared to attend me, the haze that I'd come to rely on to shield me from my life had dimmed.

Lia pulled out a clean gown. I let her help me dress, and when she brought me food, I forced myself to eat. She poured me a strong cup of tea, but when I lifted it to my mouth, I hesitated. I did not doubt that Apollo had been right; the wine was drugged, and I hadn't cared. Now, I thought beyond the wine to my tea, my food, and certainly the sleeping draughts that Lia brought each night. I took a long whiff of the tea, steam flushing my cheeks. I could make out the strong hint of mint and chamomile beneath it but there *was* something else. When I opened my eyes, Lia was staring at me.

"Is something wrong?" she asked.

I shook my head and forced a smile and raised the cup to my lips taking a small sip.

"It's just too hot still," I said.

She stared as if waiting for me to take another swallow. I hadn't noticed her watching me this way before, but then, I hadn't noticed anything since they'd taken my son away from me.

I sent her to fetch my cloak and shoes. She looked surprised.

"Why?" she asked.

It was an impertinent query, and I was about to say so when I realized that I'd allowed her to speak to me this way for as long as she'd been with me. Just how long, I wasn't sure anymore. I clenched my hands together but held my tongue.

"I'm going to the bath house," I said.

She shook her head. "That's not necessary. I'll have a bath drawn for you in here."

"No," I said.

She shifted heavily on her feet and looked down at me. "You should drink your tea first."

"No," I said again. "I don't want tea this morning. I'll take some fruit with me to the bathhouse, and then I'll go to the healer's den. My body aches."

At this, she began to gnaw on her lip and wringing her hands, and I saw past her hard, black eyes and the severe knot in her hair. She was younger than I'd thought, and not so bold. I stood and took a step toward her, raising my hand and pointing toward my dressing room.

"Go get my cloak and shoes," I said roughly and then turned away, hoping my bravado would win the moment.

I heard her movement behind me as she fetched my things. Gripping the back of the chair tightly for support I let out a long, tight breath and swallowed hard. My head throbbed. I was certain that whatever was in that tea could

soothe it, but something had changed within me. The sound
Artemis's voice rang in my mind, "Ili needs her mother," she
had said. The thought of my daughter in need had moved
me. Fleeting images from my dreams rose before my eyes.
I'd abandoned my daughter. If I was going to find out what
Ilithyia needed from me, I was going to have to face my loss.
I couldn't do so in this state.

There was a sound behind me, and when I turned, expecting to see Lia with my things, I was surprised by the
figure of Ajax filling the doorframe. Lia stood a few paces
behind him, her eyes cast to the ground. So, she'd fetched the
master rather heed my command. My resolved floundered.

"You can't go out alone," Ajax said. "I'll escort you."

He signaled Lia to get my cloak, and I put it over my
shoulders. I let my hair hang down. Slipping my feet into my
sandals I began to step past Ajax, but he reached out his hand
and took firm hold of my arm.

"You should drink your tea."

I glanced back at the pot still steaming on the table, and
then nodded to Lia. "Bring it to the bathhouse," I said as
casually as possible.

I took another step forward as if I could take for granted
that she'd do my bidding. Ajax let go of my arm and nodded
at the woman as we entered the hall. I walked as steadily
as I could, surprised at how badly my legs shook beneath
me. With great regret, I gripped tightly to Ajax's arm as we
descended the stairs. Twice I had to stop to catch my breath
on the way to the bathhouse, and when we were there, I had
to sit on a bench while Ajax had it cleared of other people.
The place was built stone, a replica of the public baths in
the town below, but this one had been constructed for the
women of Tintangore. I'd hoped to find strength here among

them, or even an ally, but when I entered the room I found it empty, except for Lia who'd set my tea on a platter beside the tub.

I consoled myself with the thought that at least Ajax hadn't followed her inside. I dropped my clothes on the floor and eased into the warm water. It was a wonderful shock and soothing to my aching limbs. I let my head dip beneath the surface and called to Lia to bring me the Awa plant and sponges to wash my hair and body. She turned to the cabinet across the room and as she did I reached for the cup of tea and poured it into the water. When she approached me, I pressed the rim to my lips as if I'd just finished it. I handed her the empty mug and watched her refill it from the pot. Again I dipped beneath the water. When I stepped out of the tub, she pressed the red plant into the pumice stone, creating lather, then helped wash my body and hair, pulling her fingers through the thick knotted strands. She lifted a bucket of warm water to rinse me, and then I stepped back into the pool.

My head still throbbed, and I could feel the pull within me to drink the tea, but as Lia bent to clean away the suds, I spilled the drink in the water. I moved about hastily to disperse the colored tincture. She looked at me abruptly but smiled as I held the empty cup out to her.

"You'll be feeling better soon," she said.

I nodded, resting back into the water, lingering lazily in the warmth, trying to still my nerves. Already my mind was coming back to itself, beginning to wander over obvious ways to leave this place. I dipped my head beneath the water again trying to wash away such thoughts. They had Poseidon, didn't they? And they knew where my son was. I knew he would only be safe as long as I cooperated.

I breached the water and gasped for a breath. Signaling for more hot water, I moved to the stone vent that funneled it into the pool and let the steam fill my lungs.

*Ilithyia needs you.*

The thought rose sharply in my mind and my stomach tightened. How could I help her? I'd taken the oath that I'd stay on here as Zeus's wife. I'd taken the oath on the ring, as High Priestess of the Emerald Temple, and no matter what personal danger I might face, I couldn't go back on that. I had to clear my mind and regain enough strength to face Zeus. He might allow me to see Ilithyia.

I rose from the water and let Lia dry me, as was the custom, then wrapped my hair in ribbons, scenting it with rose. I hadn't tended to myself in such a way since before the baby was born and now I felt guilty doing it, but something pressed me forward. I pulled a clean, white linen wrap from the shelves as the novices did, and then wrapped my heavy cloak about me and stepped back outside. Ajax stood by the door, disgruntled, but alert. He looked me up and down, his eyebrows reflecting his surprise.

"I must begin to prepare myself for my husband's return," I said softly, not quite sure where the words had come from.

"It's about time you did," he said roughly. "You're not a bad looking woman, even at your age. He should be pleased."

I gritted my teeth and turned quickly to avoid his eyes. I began to walk, more heartily this time, toward the healer's den, but Ajax stopped me. He insisted he would have a healer sent to my rooms, but I shook my head.

"Thank you, Ajax," I said gently, "but I've always been in command of the healer's den, and it must look strange all these months that I've not attended my duties. The arrival of Athena yesterday proves that. I must return to some of my duties, and this is one that will not conflict with your interests."

I watched him closely, and could see he didn't believe me. "I can't have my priestesses at the Emerald temple returning here like they did yesterday. Surely, you can see that as well. I must start to be seen as an active member of this community. The healer's den is the obvious place for me. I'll make it a routine so that word will spread."

Ajax turned to Lia who thankfully seemed to like the idea. I realized she was bored with my self-pity and me.

She nodded to Ajax. "I'll be with her," she said quickly.

"Alright," he said slowly. "I'll assign you a guard. You can call them your protectors but we both know why they'll be there."

He turned his back to me and led the way through the courtyard and out the main gate. I enjoyed the feel of the earth against my bare soles. It had been a long time. Even with the dim ache in my head and soreness in my joints, I could feel the gentle pulse of the earth pulling me down just a little closer each time I set my heel upon it. My skin prickled with a delight I'd forgotten I could feel.

When we reached the long, stone building, I felt my resolve waver as throngs of people moved to greet me, many asking for my blessing. I smiled as best I could and pressed my hand to their foreheads, but shame welled up within me. Who was I to give a blessing? I was a betrayer, and I'd failed them all to protect myself and the ones I loved.

Quickly, I pulled the cloak about my head and ducked inside the building where a tall woman in a simple black shift approached me. I recognized her from the temple training at Caledocean. Glancing about me I saw no other familiar faces and was surprised at how young all these women were.

"Reverence," the tall woman said. "I'm Mira. It's an honor to have you," she said.

I nodded in respect, but again, a wave of shame moved over me. The room leaned with short beds separated by soft flowing fabrics. The healers sat at the bedsides, their hands placed lightly on their patients. Some dipped their fingers into thin bowls of scented oils then anointed the forehead or palm of the one they worked with. The scents swam together as if they were alive, opening my senses to a state of calm and understanding.

I turned easily to Ajax.

"I'll spend the afternoon here," I said evenly. Then to Lia, "I'll take my lunch with the others. If you stay, you must help at the grinding stones outside where the herbal teas are being prepared."

I didn't wait for either of them to answer, but moved forward and took up Mira's hand.

"It would be an honor to have you treat me," I said.

The woman smiled warmly and beckoned me to one of the empty beds. She pushed aside the long silk strands that surrounded it, and I lay down. Glancing at the door as I did, I could see that Ajax had left. Lia had moved to the far corner of the room toward a wall of herbs and gourd jars. I could smell teas brewing just outside. I watched as a woman approached her easily and held out her hands in a familiar way. Lia embraced her and beckoned toward me over her shoulder. *Of course*, I thought, I should have known that Lia must know how to brew herbs. Who else would have been able to drug my wine and brew my morning tea? So, even here there were people I couldn't trust. Any thought of sending a message to Ilithyia through one of these women died in my mind.

Mira's touch was soothing, and I drifted into a long and pleasant sleep. When I awoke, I joined the others outside and ate a full meal, carefully avoiding any drinks that Lia brought to me, pouring water from the jug the others drank from. Afterwards, we returned to my room, where I slept again.

Days went by in this manner. I accepted my evening wine but was careful not to ingest it, finding creative means of making the liquid disappear. I brewed my own teas each day at the healer's den and strengthened my mind, trying to soothe my dreams in the old way, with meditation and prayer. But the images broke through, the sadness and horror of what had happened to me and the ones I'd tried to protect. The words of power couldn't keep the visions away, but they leant me strength in facing them on my own.

In the late afternoons, I took up walking through the fields behind the healer's den to look for herbs. Ajax or a small troop of his men appeared at my side whenever I'd achieved some distance. I ignored them, as I used the time and effort to rebuild my body's strength. Soon, my legs were not so weak, and my mind stopped racing to the terrors of my past. The sun warmed me with courage, gracing my sallow skin with a healthier glow. When I caught my reflection again in the mirror, I didn't look so drawn and I was able to hold my own gaze evenly. It was true, I realized, that Zeus would find me more pleasing this way, and though I recoiled at the thought, I knew it was the only way I'd be able to manipulate him. For a moment I relished the idea of using Zeus, but then the obstacle occurred to me. Did he still want me?

I shook my head. It was an impossible thought. How could he?

My years of training had taught me to separate my caring for a person from their behavior or actions. In this way, I had always been able to have compassion for his eternal nature, or essence, even though I would pass judgment and make my decisions based on his actions.

That ability had gone from me now.

Feeling the ugly desire to exploit, or control Zeus rising within me, I realized how hard my feelings had become. I might be able to reclaim my body, but my heart was badly bruised and locked away. The only thing I could contemplate was the hostile urge to fulfill my vow. Somehow, I'd find a way to support my daughter *and* keep my word. Because my sacred honor was the only thing, I had left.

# CHAPTER FOURTEEN

SUMMER PASSED SLOWLY. The women at the healer's temple came to expect my daily visits and their company helped me find my sense of leadership once again. I began treating people from the village. The act of opening myself to the great current, and using my hands to heal, helped me to reclaim my intuitive gifts. As my body became a channel for the universal healing force, it was also healed.

As I regained physical control, my mental clarity returned as well. The long, hot days of autumn filled with camaraderie and service gave me the strength to face my nightmares. While I pretended to drink my spiced wine each night and morning, and maintained a beleaguered nature in front of watchful eyes, I had in fact regained my ability to restore myself.

In the early afternoon of one unusually hot day, I stepped out of the healer's den and looked across the valley, where the hills had turned to gold. My eyes moved instinctively to the horizon and the thin stretch of road that would soon bring Zeus's messenger with news of his arrival.

I clenched my teeth and shook my head as hatred welled up inside of me.

Though my body had healed, the bitterness of my loss still festered within me. My thoughts were resentful, and my emotions were driven by a desire for retribution. I had to watch my temper carefully for I was quick to flare.

Stretching, I closed my eyes and let the distant sound of the woodcutter's axes beat its erratic rhythm into my mind, hoping tit would soothe me. I opened my eyes to find Lia standing before me; a pack slung over her shoulder and a water flask tied to her side. She held out my herb basket. I smiled, realizing Lia had become accustomed to our new routine, and I could see she was beginning to enjoy it.

"The weather's so nice," she said. "I thought we might forage for herbs."

I nodded and took the basket, slinging it over my shoulder.

Four armed men stood behind her at a short distance, but they wore only leather tunics and open sandals, having abandoned their breastplates and armor some time ago. They leaned on their spears as if they were walking sticks. A thought of my honor guard passed through my mind. They would never have been seen in such a pose. Well, it didn't matter to me. I had no intentions of running off, for that would be a breach of my vow and bring certain punishment to those I cared for.

I stepped past Lia, and she fell in behind me as I headed to the woods. A familiarity was growing between us, but I never forgot that she was the eyes and ears of my jailor. We walked in silence. When I came to the trailhead I stopped for a moment, a strange sense pulling at my mind. I'd noticed sensitivity to the natural currents returning to me as I worked in the healer's den, but I still hadn't regained control of my emotions and intuitions. I took a deep breath, and turned away from the trail.

"What is it?" Lia asked.

I ignored her, opened my hands, and turned the palms toward the sun instinctively. A current moved through them, pulling at me. My heart pounded harder in my chest.

"Well?"

I turned to Lia, grimacing. How could the woman not sense this?

"This is the way," she said with annoyance, pointing to the path.

Her voice irritated me. The desire to shut her out was strong. I turned away.

"I sense what we're looking for is elsewhere," I said as evenly as I could.

Not waiting for her response I turned away from the trail and headed down the hill. I didn't look back, but was aware of the crunching trudge of Ajax's men behind me amidst Lia's disgruntled sighs. I kept my palms open before me and let the thin pulsing direct me. I had no idea if what we looked for was indeed in this direction, but I was a priestess, and I would follow where the invisible current led me.

We walked for a long while and dipped down behind Tintangore, finding goat trails that led us through the dry fields to the far edge of the forest. When we stopped for water, Lia complained to plan that we'd never come this way before. I could see by the smiles on the men's faces that they were relieved to have a new landscape to explore and so I used their enthusiasm to take us further. I pointed to the sun.

"We'll have plenty of time to return," I said.

I pressed toward the trees as the path snaked down the

hill, no longer needing the pulse in my open palms to guide me. A deep pounding in my chest gave way to a familiar knowing: something waited for me ahead. As we entered the tree line, I shivered. A thin mist rose around us. I hesitated for a moment, looking again to the sun, but thick, gray clouds covered it, and a shadow fell across us. The others didn't seem to notice. My pulse quickened.

"Look," Lia said suddenly, pointing to the ground where a large outcropping of mushrooms flowered before us. "You were right," she moved forward to pick them.

I shook my head.

"No, there's more. We're close now," I snapped, the old tone of command in my voice.

She protested, but I pushed past her and headed down through the variegated green, slowing my pace, as the fog thickened about us. A man stumbled behind me and cursed, but I didn't stop, or look back. The leader called out to me to wait, but I pointed to a thin opening in the green and pushed forward. He moved up behind me quickly, but I was already standing in the open meadow.

"The fog's thick," he grunted. "It'll make finding our way back difficult. We should go."

The white mist swirled all about us now, and I shivered from it. I could still make out our surroundings though, and pointed to the old oak tree that stood on a squat, gnarled base. I recognized it immediately.

"I know where we are," I said calmly. "My mother brought me here once on our way to the Emerald Temple."

Lia stepped to my side; her arms wrapped tightly about herself. She glanced about herself furtively and I could see by the expression of awe that crossed her face that she could feel the power in this place.

"We should go back," she echoed the leader, her eyes fixed on the tree.

My body pulsed with strength and a desire to approach the tree.

"It will only take me a few minutes to gather the herbs," I said, my voice still steady and reassuring. "We've come all this way. We shouldn't go back empty-handed."

I didn't wait for consent, but moved toward the tree. A cold gust rose about me and the ancient limbs that stretched out before me shuddered. When I was only a few paces away, I stopped, narrowing my eyes. The mist billowed and dissipated making forms appear beside the tree. There was a sharp cry from behind me and then another. I spun around to see Lia swatting at her neck, and then falling to he knees. She looked up at me with hard eyes and opened her mouth to speak, but before a sound could issue forth she fell forward, unconscious. The men lay about her in similar crumpled states. I looked about frantically, but the gray had risen thick, shrouding them in a wall of mist.

"Hera."

I turned around to the tree, and this time the two figures on either side moved toward me.

"Athena," I gasped. "What are you...Why have you..." I couldn't find the words. My body shook too hard. "I told you not to come!" I shouted finally.

She and the other woman said nothing, but moved toward me in long, graceful strides until I could make them out clearly.

"We've come for *you*," Demeter said.

"You shouldn't have, I won't go with you!"

"You don't have a choice," Athena said.

She signaled to someone behind me, and I turned to see Artemis at my back, a small reed in her right hand and a sharp-tipped dart in her left. They were the tools she had used to sedate animals when we were young. I stared past her at the five bodies that lay limp on the ground, and then back to her unwavering eyes.

"The dreamers won't be able to hold the mist much longer," Athena said as I snapped back around to her in disbelief. "You can come with us of your own accord, or not. The choice is yours."

"I'm still the High Priestess!" I cried. "And I've sworn an oath I will not break, I command you—" but there was a sharp sting at the back of my neck, and I swooned.

Gentle hands caught me. Demeter's familiar touch was through on my brow as I blinked, unable to move or speak. They carried me to a wagon, and laid me on soft hay and covered me lightly. I heard their voices and the sound of horses taking up the line as the cart began its steady rocking that lulled me against my will, to sleep.

# CHAPTER FIFTEEN

I awoke to the sound of a crackling fire. I lay with my eyes open for a long time before I realized I was awake. The night sky stretched out above me, and its silver sea of stars seemed to be holding me in place. My head ached.

"I have some tea for you that will make things easier," said Artemis.

I felt her hand slip around my neck and lift me up gently. The earth seemed to move beneath me. She pushed the cup toward me, but I knocked it away angrily. The tea spilled all over her tunic. I opened my mouth to speak, but the words came out slow.

"You... drugged... *me*!"

"I did what had to be done."

Athena came up behind us and propped up the hay I laid on. Artemis eased me back with the same care with which she'd lifted me. She picked up the cup on the ground and took it back to the fire, then ladled it full once more. She moved back to my side.

"This will help the pain," she said in a voice that suggested she would not let me rile her. She held it out again.

I clenched my teeth but reached out for the mug. My hand was unsteady, and she helped me lift it to my lips. I had trouble swallowing, and when I spilled it down my chin, she reached out with her sleeve to dry my skin. When I'd finished, they laid me back down.

"Ilithyia?" I asked despite my frustration. "You said you had a message."

"She's chosen a mate," Artemis answered. "She seeks your blessing."

I exhaled with relief. My mouth seemed to soften, and I could feel sensation returning to my limbs.

Athena came to my other side and lay down beside me as if she was going to sleep.

"What's this?" I asked. "You're going to let me lie here beside you unbound? No cords to tether me to the spot?"

Neither one answered. Artemis reached for the blanket and laid it over me, while Athena took up her long knife and laid it across her chest. I could've reached out and taken it, or at least tried, but she didn't appear concerned. Somehow this infuriated me further.

"And I suppose the rest of your army is standing guard?" I continued, my tone hard and cold.

"There's no army, Reverence," Athena said staring up at the sky. "I've sent them down the main road as a decoy. I'm sure they are making quite a display of themselves as they head back to the Emerald Temple. Demeter plays your part at the center of their group. No one will follow us. No one knows where we are."

The pounding in my head was already beginning to ease, and I could feel my hands more firmly now. My legs still tingled, but I thought I'd be able to walk. I tried to sit up and look around, but we were in the trees and the night was dark.

The fire cast a low light over our bodies and nothing more. A small stack of branches and logs lay beside it. As it was a warm night, I realized it was lit to keep away animals that might stalk us. Turing back to the stars I found the bright light in the north and the sisters that lay above us.

I shut my eyes angrily. Escape would not be possible tonight. They had forced me into an impossible situation. Hades would undoubtedly think I'd been a part of this scheme and there was no telling what he would do. He still had Poseidon, and with Zeus returning with his men, I was afraid that they might try to overpower the Emerald Temple.

"Sleep, Hera," Artemis said. "Just rest and let the medicine leave your body."

I tried pulling at the blanket but fumbled, and Artemis turned on her side to fix it.

"Sleep," she said again, stroking my forehead. "Sleep."

I awoke to the sound of birds rustling in the trees about us, and the thin splash of color in the sky. I lay on my side in the crook of Artemis's shoulder; my arm draped comfortably around her waist. I lay still for a moment enjoying the rise and fall of my head with the even pace of her breath, and the wonderful sense of safety she emanated.

Then I remembered my anger.

I sat up sharply and pulled back my hand. Her eyes were open, and alert, staring, but she didn't move. I rose and steadied myself, surveying the landscape.

We were camped in a small thicket surrounded by high trees with thin branches. The fire still burned and Athena was already up, stirring something in the pot. I felt my stomach lurch at the scent of the food. I put my hand to my mouth. Athena looked up and pointed toward a clump of trees.

"The privy's over there," she said.

I nodded and headed around the brush. On my way back I looked about for a trail but saw nothing but thick trees. There wasn't even a horse tethered nearby. Back at camp, Artemis began to fill our packs, and Athena handed me a bowl of thick oats. I ate and drank in silence, my stomach soon soothed. The sun was now up, but beneath the trees, it was still cold and somewhat dark. I wrapped myself in a simple cloak Artemis had given me.

When we were finished with our food, Athena put their things into packs and handed me one.

"We're on foot from here," she said.

I lay a hand on my pack and stared at her.

"Athena," I said as calmly as I could. "You can't possibly expect me to come with you of my own accord. I have to go back. I have to be there when Zeus returns." I paused, and when neither woman looked perturbed, I pointed to the ring on my finger.

"I've taken an oath!" I cried out with exasperation.

"We know," Athena said. "That's why we've come."

She looked at Artemis who stared back, saying nothing. Athena shook her head sadly and laid down her pack.

"We know everything," she said. "Mel'ak came to us."

"Mel'ak!"

She held up her hands.

"Just listen," she said. I could hear the exhaustion in her voice. "Mel'ak was used. You know that if you feel into it. He told us about the child, Hera; we know what you've lost. Poseidon has sent us messages as well."

At this, I sat down. Pain streaked through my chest at the

sound of his name. Artemis moved to my side.

"He sent a message through Apollo," she said. "Poseidon wants you to escape, Hera. He wants you to live free."

I shook my head sternly. "No, he'd never say that. He knows what they'll do to him if he's no longer needed to keep me in my place. I can't bear the weight of it!" I put my head in my hands for a moment and closed my eyes. "He would never ask me to break my word, and he was there; he knows I made the vow!"

"On the ring," Artemis said.

"As High Priestess," Athena finished.

They both stared at me. Slowly, Artemis reached out and took my hand, brushing the finger the emerald ring blazed upon.

"The ring binds you to the vow," she said, "as does your position as High Priestess of the Emerald Temple. Without the ring, and your position you would be free."

I withdrew my hand. "Are you suggesting that I step down as High Priestess?"

The thought had never occurred to me. It was a coward's way out. I was injured that they thought I'd do such a thing.

"The word of the High Priestess is a reflection of the temple as a whole," I said curtly. "If I step down—"

"Ilithyia can take over," Athena said. "She's grown, Hera, she's changed. Ilithyia can do it with Demeter's help. This will free you of your obligation, and you can retire to the Elysian mysteries, as you've not had the chance to do. Your whole life has been spent in service. Now you could look to your own peace."

I glared at her and clenched my fists at my sides. Couldn't they understand? I had traded my own child! I would never know peace.

"Just let the idea find its way into your heart," Athena said, breaking my reverie. "We have several days' travel on foot. Come with us, and you can decide what to do when we reach our camp."

I had no choice. I didn't know where we were or where we were going. I couldn't get back by myself. I reached for my pack and slung it over my shoulders. Artemis took up the lead, heading into the trees.

We traveled in silence. They often rested, which I knew was for my benefit, but this only fueled my resentment toward them. As I walked, I found myself fingering the ring.

After two full days, I recognized the constellations in the night sky and realized that we were heading for the Emerald Temple, skirting the road and villages by staying in the forests of the eastern hills. Artemis guided us, and we moved at a good pace, but it was not until the end of the fourth day that we came out of the trees and descended to the lip of a stream that led to the river just above the lake. We were very close to the temple now, only a day or so of travel, and despite my anger, I could feel my desire to set foot on the sacred shores. Artemis led us to a small, round, house with a thatched roof and mud brick walls. Smoke already rose from the center hole, and horses grazed in the field beyond. Two women, I recognized from Athena's guard sat outside by makeshift tents. Both women leaped to their feet, waving we approached. When we neared the entrance I saw a familiar banner flying by the *tapa* door—it bore the symbol of the deer, with a white stag painted beside it. This was Ilithyia's work. They'd brought me to Artemis's hunting lodge where she and my daughter had spent many seasons.

The women came to take my pack, but I brushed past them and set it down myself. One woman bowed slightly, and I could see she was concerned that she'd made an offense. I waved her away irritably, unconcerned with her feelings. Athena called them to her and began to give instructions. Artemis signaled me toward the entrance of the roundhouse, and I went inside.

The space was ample with two small alcoves built into the walls where beds were laid out. There were two goblets and a wine flask set at the ready on a table carved from fragrant wood. A simple cooking area made of long, stone slabs was set on one side of the fire, which crackled, and glowed, filling the room with warmth. Plush carpets covered the floor, and colorful pillows were spread about. Between the bed alcoves, a small altar was set into a carved niche of wood. On the far wall hung bows of various sizes and several quivers full of arrows. Ilithyia's small loom sat in the far corner.

Artemis handed me a cup, and I sipped the mint water as I moved toward the loom. A massive bolt of almost finished tapestry hung there. I could make out the image of the dragon in green, its counterpart in red still in the making. I felt tears rise.

"She'll make a good High Priestess," Artemis said as she stepped up behind me.

"She's so young," I replied, rubbing at my cheek with the back of my hand.

"You were young, too, when you came to power."

I turned on her. "And look what it's done to me!"

She said nothing. I stared into the calm, black pools of her eyes as my anger rallied inside of me.

"She'll have to face them, Artemis!" I said with fury. "If I give her this ring she'll be forced to deal with those terrible people!"

There was a commotion outside, and the *tapa* door was pulled aside. Athena stood in the doorway. She moved toward me, but I thrust my finger at her accusingly.

"I know what you want from my daughter," I continued, "you want to use her the way you used me!"

Athena stopped in mid-stride, her face stricken. I paced back and forth in my rage, my voice rising to a hysterical pitch.

"You'll send her to deal with Hades and Ajax," I said, "They can't be trusted. They're ugly and mean. The only thing they care about is power. Nothing can redeem them!"

I stopped at the altar. A small bowl of cedar was set at its center, and I knocked it to the floor in my rage. Athena stepped back in shock.

"I tried to protect you." Her voice choked as she spoke.

"Well, you failed!" I said turning on her.

Artemis stepped to Athena's side, placing a hand on her shoulder to steady her. I'd never witnessed such kinship between them, and a wave of jealousy washed over me.

"I thought I could trust you two," I continued indignantly. "I thought you cared about me, about my children, about Ilithyia—"

Artemis took a strong step toward me then; her eyes were suddenly fierce. The words died on my tongue. She drew a long, slow breath, and then took another step toward me and I stepped back, despite myself.

"You're in great danger, Hera," she said, her voice very low.

I straightened in front of her and shook my head.

"No, they won't kill me," I said. "Zeus will make sure of that."

"Death is never a danger," Artemis answered. "It's the loss of kindness and compassion of which I speak."

I opened my mouth to respond, but no sound came forth. I stood there, frozen, panic taking hold of my senses. All my years of training in touching the invisible divine seemed wasted at this moment, for I knew she was right—all I could feel was hatred. A sharp painful rage.

"They've hurt you," Artemis went on. "It's wrong, and we'll do what we can to stop them, but Hera, none of this means they aren't part of the great creation. None of this gives you leave to turn away from love."

I glared at her backing away. "Go, leave me alone!" I shouted, lifting my arms toward them both. "My hands already ache with the fire gift!"

Athena's body recoiled toward the door and her brows furrowed, but she steadied herself. She looked from me to Artemis, who stood tall and quiet, unmoving. I felt myself caught in Artemis's presence, like a deer in a thicket.

"Leave us, Athena," Artemis said without taking her eyes off my own. "Hera won't use the fire on me."

I stared in a fury at her presumption, yet I took another step backward, my shoulders brushing up against the wall. Athena seemed to notice this and looked again from me to Artemis. I saw some form of understanding appear in her eyes. She bowed slightly, then turned and left the house.

I looked toward the fire, glancing at Artemis sideways. My jaw closed tightly, and I crossed my arms in front of me. Artemis held her place, but her leg muscles were taut and firm, ready for motion. Her look gripped my body, and the possibility of my attempted escape, in its scope. I'd seen this steady gaze before, watched her size up her prey to will it into submission. A cold sensation of dread spread through my chest.

"You can't make me do this. I won't break my oath, or sacrifice my daughter!"

She didn't answer but stepped toward me.

"I won't do it, Artemis, I've made my choice already," I lied.

She took another step, but this time toward the fire so that her body was in full view. I tried to ignore her, to stare at the flames.

"Hera," she said. "Hera, my love."

It was a statement and her voice held an unmistakable tenderness I hadn't heard in a long while. The candor of her words moved through me, and I looked into her eyes despite myself.

"When we were young, and you killed the boar," she continued, "You came to me, you asked me to take you in as a lover, but I turned you away. I thought it would ruin our friendship. I didn't have faith that our love could endure time, could endure other loves and desires. I was afraid."

Images of that day, long ago, rose up before me, and a hint of that longing, that young, cherished need to be held, and wanted, and loved by her, touched the borders of my hard defense.

"I made a vow to you that day, do you remember?"

I shook my head, defiantly, but I did remember.

"I told you that you'd saved my life, and one day, I'd do the same for you," she continued patiently.

I stared at her, shaken by the memory. My arms fell loose at my sides. She took another step forward so that she stood right in front of me.

"I remember the first time I took you out tracking," she said. "You were so eager, do you remember?"

I nodded.

"It was your first night away from home, away from the village, and I thought you would be apprehensive, but no—"

Her wide lips softened with pleasure. "That first night together beneath the stars, the scent of the wild ginger and the sound of the fire were our companions."

I took a breath in and caught the familiar scent rising off of her skin, laying itself like a wreath about my heart.

"That was a long time ago and doesn't mean anything to me now," I said.

Something stirred softly inside me.

Artemis only smiled broader.

"Hera," she said taking the last step and closing the distance between us. She reached out and touched my cheek tenderly, then brushed back a thick strand of hair.

In a slow, natural movement she slid her hand behind my neck, pushing it gently, but firmly into the tresses of my hair. I felt her grip tighten before I realized how close she was, and then I felt her breath on my lips as she kissed me long and soft, a shadow of love brushing past my defense, touching my heart. My body stiffened, prepared to struggle, but as her lips moved over my flesh, as I felt the keen defiance drain from me.

I kissed her back.

My hands unclenched, my shoulders dropped and she tilted my head, delicately, and moved her mouth to my neck and ear.

"I'll help you let your hatred go," she whispered. "It's the only way to save your life, Hera. Let me repay my debt."

I let out a long, tense breath, and my eyes closed lightly, then my arms wrapped themselves about her neck. I tucked my forehead under her chin, and all the fight emptied from my body.

She held me, rocking lightly back and forth. The fire sputtered and sparked dropping to a warm, orange glow. She put her hands on my shoulders and drew me away from her gently, then took my hand and led me to her bed.

I did not resist.

She pulled at the corner of her tunic and let it fall away. Her body was weathered and lean. I looked down at her leg where the long, thin trace of the scar from the boar's tusk was still visible all these years later. Following my gaze, she brushed it lightly with the tips of her fingers then smiled.

"It changed both our lives," she said.

I couldn't speak.

"Now we have Ilithyia," she said. "And you have Ares and Poseidon, and they both still need you. They love you."

I stared at her, trying to feel.

"And we'll help you find your baby, Hera. We'll call the dreamers together and find him in the night when he sleeps."

*Oh, Artemis!* I thought. *If only this could be true.*

"And you have me," she said, pulling me close again. "And I love you, Hera. I've always loved you."

I shuddered in her arms, my skin alive with sensation. I felt something wonderful and familiar as she moved her hands down my spine with the softness of smoke. Wanting. Caring. Love.

She laid me down on the bed and pulled away the top of my shift. Her hands were precise and firm, bringing my body to her. She slid her thigh, warm, against my own and laid her mouth to my breast.

"Artemis—"

"Yes."

She parted my legs as her lips brushed the hollow of my neck, her fingers pressing deep. I clutched helplessly to her waist.

"I'm here, I have you, Hera. I love you; I love you…"

I shivered. Somewhere outside hounds howled in the distance, and a raven cawed. Feelings began to flood the numb places in my body. Artemis led me to my tender sorrows and held me. Her strong, repeated movement and sound became a rush of wind upon my senses. Her scent rose up around me; my hands found her breasts, her hips and the smooth curve of her back as she pressed herself inside me, pulling my heart beyond the reach of hatred. I fell into the pool of her desire and caring.

The fire burned low. I pressed my lips to hers, grasping her body as it moved above me, her hands and mouth finding sacred places of pleasure.

When it was done, I had touched something eternal, beyond my loss. I lay in her arms and wept.

In the morning, I rose before the sun and reached for another log to stir the fire back to flame. I slipped on my tunic and wrapped myself in Artemis's cloak, putting on my sandals and stealing outside while she slept. I made my way toward the low, burning pit of coals, which lay beside the tents where a cloaked figure already stood. Athena turned at my approach, and when she faced me, I got down on my knees before her and reached for the hem of her cloak, pressing it to my lips. Then I pulled the emerald ring off my finger and placed it in my open palm.

"Forgive me," I said handing her the ring.

She slipped the band into the pouch at her side, and then her strong hand encircled my palm, pulling me to my feet. Her eyes glistened with tears.

"I'm no longer a priestess," I said.

"I will stand by you," Athena replied, her voice quivering with feeling. "From my heart to your heart, Hera."

She looked deep into my eyes, putting a hand on my cheek. "And you will *always* be a priestess," she said.

# CHAPTER SIXTEEN

THE WIND SHOOK THE DARK BRANCHES that we slept beneath and sent leaves cascading lightly about my head. I pulled the blanket closer about me and pressed my body into the warm curve of Artemis's skin. Her arm enfolded me.

"You're awake?" I whispered.

She squeezed me slightly, and her hand moved to my forehead. "You haven't slept well," she answered.

I rolled over on my back, restless. The wind swept over us, making more leaves scatter. I strained to hear the first sound of morning's approach, but the night was still upon us. We had waited at this site for three days with no word from the temple rider we'd been expecting; my senses told me something was wrong. The last time we'd been here was just weeks ago at the autumn equinox, and the rider had been waiting for us with the very good news. I let my mind recount it now to ease my nerves.

The rider had told us that Ilithyia had been initiated in Caledocean in full view of her father and the Titan dynasty. Zeus had returned from Kart Hadst but had shown her no sign of ill intent. In fact, he'd begun talks with her and

Demeter, trying to ally with the Emerald Temple as if he intended to fulfill our plan. Ares had been given his own command and was actively enrolled in the temple's plight to secure more ships for the next crossing. Poseidon's men had rebuilt his fleet, and Hades had let him join them.

The old sorrow welled up as I recalled this last, but I took a deep breath and steadied my mind. I wouldn't allow such emotions to overwhelm me anymore. There was work to be done and love at my side. That is what I would give myself to.

Artemis encircled me once again, lending me her strength as she'd done all summer long. My body softened as I let the distress go.

"You sense something," Artemis asked.

"Yes. Something's wrong. I feel it."

A small animal rustled somewhere above us in the thick branches. I reached out to it with my inner knowing wondering if it could tell me how long this night would be.

"Things have been going better than we'd expected, Hera," Artemis said after some time. "Even Ajax's stopped his patrols for you. By fall we'll be on a ship to the new city. We'll be with Poseidon at some point soon, and we'll find your son."

She'd been confident of this plan for some time, and up until now it had soothed me. I looked at her gratefully, settling my head beneath her chin.

"I love you," I said softly.

Her arm tightened around me.

"Artemis…"

"Yes."

"If we do see Poseidon…"

She stroked my hair with her hand and kissed my forehead softly.

"All is well, Hera. I told you," she whispered. "Poseidon and I are friends. We both love you. Let that worry go, now."

I closed my eyes relaxing, intent on letting go of the search for my anxiety. I felt Artemis's hand on my forehead and listened to the sound of her breath until I drifted back to sleep.

My dreams were scattered and sharp. Scenes of the Emerald Temple rose in my vision, and then clouded over. There was Zeus's face, smiling, and then Ilithyia with a sword in her hand.

I awoke to the sounds of a fire snapping, and the smell of cinnamon and apples was wafting in the air about me. I opened my eyes and blinked hard, the sun sharp and bright as it cut through the open spaces in the canopy of leaves above me. Rubbing my eyes as I sat up, I tried to collect myself.

"It's good you slept," Artemis said as she turned the apples over in the small flame.

I looked over at her and smiled. Her hair was tied back as usual, but a long wisp had already pulled free and hung softly about her shoulder.

"I adore you," I said suddenly.

She turned her head and flashed a wide grin. "I know."

I lay back down staring at the flecked montage of green, taking in the goodness of the moment, its stark simplicity and caring. I thought of Poseidon; Artemis had told me that he had sent her an urgent plea to free me, and the generosity of the act filled me with love. Poseidon and Artemis. I said their names silently, like a prayer. They had been my strength this season, but now I could feel my own courage returning.

I rose and stretched, then splashed cold water from the bucket onto my face. I dried myself quickly, threw on my robe and moved to the fire. Dry leaves crunched beneath my sandals as I walked. Artemis handed me my tea. The aroma of mint rose with the steam as I put the cup to my lips.

We ate in silence, and afterward, I poured the water from the bucket onto the dry earth and headed down to the stream to refill it. Artemis sat in the golden grass honing an arrow. She was still there when I returned, and I realized she wasn't going to hunt as she'd done each morning before. I stood there staring at her, trying to sense her intention.

"You may not be the High Priestess anymore," she said without looking up from the soft, white feather she fixed into the shaft. "But your intuitive abilities are clearer than ever, Hera. We must trust your—"

A low whinny broke the stillness below us, and we both cocked our ears in its direction. In a moment Artemis was on her feet, her bow and quiver slung over her shoulder. I picked up the pail of water dousing the fire as she heaped dirt on top of it. My body was tense as we waited, the unmistakable sound of horses' hooves coming from the field below.

"There's more than one horse," Artemis said, alarm evident in her voice.

She handed me my cloak, and I covered my head to hide my face, though the day was far too hot already for such a thing. Then I stepped back behind the thick trunk of the tree. Artemis set an arrow into the bow.

I closed my eyes again and tried to sense the intent of the riders, but my anxiety was too high. Suddenly, Artemis called my name, and I stepped around the tree to see Athena charging through the dry grass, two rider-less horses in tow behind her. She called out my name.

Dread returned to my limbs.

Athena pulled the mounts up sharply and slid from her horse, handing the reins to Artemis, but turned toward me.

She opened her mouth to speak, but her voice was choked. Her legs shook beneath her, and from the look of the horses, I gathered she'd been riding them hard for a long while. She looked as though she might faint.

I pulled my water bag from beside the fire pit and made her drink. She gulped the water down, and drew a long breath.

"Calm yourself," I said, taking firm hold of her wrist to find her pulse. I moved my palm over the erratic pounding I found there.

She took several more gasps of air before she found her voice.

"Your grandmother," she began, her voice cracking with emotion.

My grandmother was very old now; I'd expected news of her death would come and I had prepared myself, but I hadn't expected a reaction as strong as this from Athena. Again, I tried to calm her, to quiet her pulse so that she could get the words out. I pulled the vial of oil from my pouch and made her breath in its sweet, calming note.

"Your grandmother," she said again, but her look was stricken. "They've taken her."

"What?" I pulled back, staring.

"She's been...taken," Athena finished.

Artemis had tethered the horses in the shade and given them the other pail of water. They slurped at it noisily. Bees hummed low in the grass, and my head hurt from the sound.

Artemis took hold of Athena's other arm and guided us both to a log and bade us sit down.

"What happened?" she demanded.

Athena shook her head wearily. She was a priestess that would never give in to age, but her body was old now, and very thin. She shouldn't have been riding this hard or far. She was fragile and shaken.

"Rhea's been preparing to join Hecate in the caves," she began.

Hecate was even older than my grandmother, but she was still the most powerful priestess I knew. Hecate had sent word that her own time was coming, and was preparing the death ritual for them both. It would be a beautiful celebration to honor their transition out of their bodies. It was to be a blessed event.

"Rhea had moved into the actual temple, spending her nights in prayer. Your serpent was agitated the evening before, coiling beside your grandmother as she slept. We thought it a sign of Rhea's imminent passing, nothing more. But now I know—" she shook her head, stricken. I sat patiently while she collected herself and managed to go on. "Someone breached the mist and landed in the protected cove. I found clear markings of a boat in the sand. The footsteps that were left are big. It was a small group of men. They killed the sentries I'd stationed around the temple. The dreamers didn't feel their presence until it was too late. Somehow they cloaked themselves from all our intuitive natures. I don't know how they could have done such a thing! I don't know how this could happen."

Her body shook as she spoke and tears spilled down her cheeks. I'd never seen her look so much her age. I put my arms around her, urging her to go on.

"They entered the Emerald Temple? They took my grandmother from the island?"

Athena nodded.

"But you said Medusa was protecting her."

Athena's eyes grew wide at this. She stood then and moved toward the horses, reaching for the thick leather bag that lay across the rump of her stallion. She pulled it down and brought it back to where I stood. My skin prickled.

"When I reached the temple I saw that your serpent, Medusa was cut in half," she said. "But she wasn't dead. Something happened, something, remarkable—" she hesitated as if she didn't know how to say it.

She laid the bag on the ground away from the horses and untied the knots. Medusa sprang toward me from the rumpled folds, and I staggered back in surprise and relief. Hot tears moved down my cheek as I steadied myself and knelt down, reaching out a hand. The snake moved steadily toward me and wrapped herself about my arm. I could sense the cool fury in her body as she slithered across my skin and took her place about my shoulders. But, before I stood, another snake emerged from the bag, one identical to Medusa. It also slithered toward me, but stopped at my feet as if waiting, unsure.

"The two halves reshaped themselves, Hera. Right before my eyes, the one snake became two!" Athena's voice was unsteady. She moved a step closer to me, and I looked up into her eyes. "I know Medusa's been anointed with the Dragon's Blood, and that the holy oil has blessed her with longevity, but how can she be made into two whole and separate beings?"

I dropped my hand again to the ground in amazement. The snake moved as Medusa had, and when it touched my skin, I felt a warmth and kinship move over me as if it already knew me. Her body was lighter than Medusa's and not as long, but clearly, both had an innate knowledge that reached far beyond the age of my own body. The newborn snake, Medusa's twin, wound itself over Medusa's form and both serpents settled on my shoulders as if one.

"It must be part of the oil's power, Athena. The oil is a mystery even to my grandmother. But she certainly knows more about it than anyone else. We must find her, we must—" I stopped suddenly realizing why someone would take my grandmother.

I got to my feet.

"The oil," I said in a low voice. "No one knows more about the oil then Rhea. That's why they took her. And they took the oil as well, didn't they?"

"I don't know," Athena answered. "Rhea hadn't initiated Ilithyia into the mystery yet, and none of us know where it's hidden. I can't imagine anyone could find it with the old magic in place."

I put a hand to my stomach, which now turned over to the truth that was dawning on me. Only a powerful visionary could've broken through the web of spells and deceptions that we'd woven to protect the oil. Foolishly, we'd thought no such seer existed. But now I knew there was one that could see through all our illusions; one that had seen through my very own.

"Mel'ak," I said. "The Lucifer's tool. The Titan's have the holy oil, I'm sure of it! The only reason they took Rhea is that they intend to use it."

I turned sharply to Athena, taking control. "Where did Hades take her?"

My tone seemed to bring her around. She looked at me as she used to, her eyes alert and with a desire to serve.

She shook her head. "No, it wasn't Hades, but Kronos, his father. The old man sent us word, admitting he's holding Rhea at Tintangore. It was an honorable thing to do for it clears his sons of the crime. Now, Zeus leads his brothers to lay siege to the palace. Ilithyia has already called our women to arms. They ride to Tintangore as we speak."

This didn't make sense. How could Kronos have breached our defenses? I remembered the old man's fear of death the day of the earthquake, and how I'd overheard him speaking to Hades. It was clear he believed the legend of the holy oil of immortality and wanted it, but I couldn't believe he had the resources to attain such a thing.

"No, something's wrong. It was not just Kronos. Zeus is not to be trusted," I said to them both. "But no matter who's to blame, we can't stay here. We've got to stand by Ili. We've got to warn her that the Titan's are planning something."

They nodded agreement. I turned to Athena.

"Can you ride?"

"Even if you have to tie me to the horse," she said. "I will ride."

Artemis pulled up camp, while Athena rested.

I searched my little pack for the dragon blade that my father had given me so many years ago. I'd been using it to collect herbs since the days of my captivity, but now I tied it to my calf as I used to do, ready to use it for the true purpose for which it was intended.

We rode as hard as the horses could manage until we reached a small village on the outskirts of the forestlands. Even there, the people were buzzing with the tale of my grandmother's kidnapping and the warriors gathering at Tintangore. Blood hadn't been spilled on Atlantean soil in generations, and the idea of it set everyone on edge.

"It's a sign," a woman told us as she ladled food from her cooking pot into our bowls. "It's been prophesied well enough, you know. The end times are near!"

Her son came in from tending the horses and pulled up a chair.

"The priestesses will protect us, Mother," he said simply. "Word is they gather at Tintangore, and the new High Priestess will lead them. They'll get the matriarch back, don't you worry."

Athena looked at me sideways but said nothing. We slept there most of the night as it was too dark to ride and the roads too rough, but we were back on our horses at dawn. By midday, we'd reached the Titan territory. Hills thick with trees and tall forests now made up the landscape. We changed our horses at the first town we came to and got the news—the infantry had passed through from Caledocean on their way to the fight. Young men from all over Atlantis were thronging to Zeus's call and joining his swelling army. Poseidon had brought his sailors to stand at their side. The full force of the Emerald Temple guard had taken their place on the field before the gates of Tintangore itself. Fighting was inevitable.

We didn't stop to sleep, but pushed on, riding late into the night. We held our torches high to make our way as the air grew cold around us and the road narrowed before the valley of Tintangore. Artemis found us a path that would lead to water. I was too weary to notice precisely where we'd left the road, but I knew we were close.

We dismounted and walked our steeds to a small, open field with the sound of water running nearby. Artemis took the horses, and I laid out our bedding beneath a tree. Athena handed me some bread, and I ate a few small pieces, but exhaustion overcame me, and I fell to sleep in a vast expanse of darkness.

When I awoke, the others had already saddled the horses. I rose quickly and readied myself, eating quickly. I moved to their sides. Artemis's face was grim.

"I've scouted the valley from atop the hill," she said pointing. "There are thousands gathered."

"And Ili?" I asked.

Artemis's jaw was set. I knew the thought of Ilithyia in battle disturbed her as much as it did me.

"She's clear on the field. Her tent is marked with the emerald dragon. The temple's taken the front position. They'll take the brunt of the fighting. Kronos has manned his walls. There are hundreds there, but I don't see how they can face a force such as this. Perhaps there is still a way to negotiate?"

Athena shook her head. "Not if Zeus has anything to do with it. He already sent me a message before I came for you. He's prepared to fight to the last man. It was clear from the tone that he wants to fight."

"What does he benefit?" I asked.

"Kronos's wealth and title," Artemis said quietly. "If Tintangore falls, so will Kronos, and the Titan dynasty will need a new leader. Poseidon has given up his claim, and Hades is a priest and has no right."

We all stood in silence as the truth of it settled in.

I moved toward my horse, burdened by the terrible feeling that I'd caused all of this. I should have taken the oil into hiding with me. I was the one with the gift of fire; it had been my duty to protect it. As Artemis and Athena mounted beside me, I turned my steed around in the field and for the first time saw where we were.

The sacred grove.

The old oak was unmistakable. I turned my horse around again and looked to the trail that led down to the water.

"I've been here before," I said suddenly.

They were both quiet and I felt the tension pass between them.

"No, I mean *before*. I know this is where you came with the dreamers to—" I paused. "*Rescue* me. But I was here once, before, with my mother."

I slide off my horse's back and let him go. Athena protested, calling me back, but I kept walking toward the path to the water. I waved them forward.

"Yes, this is it. This is the place. There's a cave at the base of the hill, and it leads to a cavern below Tintangore. It's been years since I've been here but I can sense the way."

I pointed to the narrow path and reached for the pack that held Medusa and her twin. I opened it hurriedly and let the two serpents entwine themselves lightly about my arms.

"There is something here for me," I said. "I may be able to get into the castle this way."

Athena's eyes widened. She made as if to get down from her horse, but I put up my hand.

"No," I said, "Listen. Zeus and Hades would like nothing better than to see me arrive here. For all, we know another reason for this fight is to flush me into the open. They know I'll have to come, if only for Ilithyia."

Athena remained on her horse, but her face was doubtful. "But what will you do?"

"I'm not sure," I said honestly. "But there is power here, and I have access to it. And if I can get into the castle, I may be able to get to Rhea before the fighting starts. If there's this hidden way in then, perhaps I can get her out. You try to slow things down. Get to Ilithyia and help her negotiate rather than fight. Pull the priestesses off the front line! If I can't get

Rhea out, I'll send you a sign. I'll make a fire. Then there will be no need for an attack."

Athena shook her head.

"Its too dangerous, Hera. And I tell you, Zeus will attack whether you send your sign, or not."

"Many will die this day, Athena. I must do what I can to stop this, to protect our people and the priestesses. I can do more good if I get to Rhea and at least keep her safe until you come. I have to try, my friend."

Athena's horse paced, but she kept my gaze.

"If you can't get her out send us a sign," she said. "If we see the fire, we'll try to stop the fight!"

I turned to Artemis then. Her eyes were soft as they took me in.

"Protect Ili," I said.

"With my life," she answered.

She looked in my eyes for a moment more. "I'll find Poseidon," she said. "He'll help us keep her safe."

"Thank you," I said, my voicing breaking.

She nodded. "My heart to your heart, Hera, always."

Somewhere in the distance a raven cawed.

They turned their horses around to go trotting out of the grove. I watched them disappear through the trees before I turned to face my destiny, alone.

# CHAPTER SEVENTEEN

I FOLLOWED THE STREAM DOWNHILL. The water led me to the sharp rock face that hid the cave's entrance. I followed its sound behind the rocks until I came to the black opening where I searched for signs of nesting animals, but only the feathers of birds lay in patches about the place. Stepping inside warily, I cast out a wide net of protection. My senses were alert and my eyes keen, as I let them adjust to the darkness before moving forward. I remembered that there had been torches on the walls, but they hadn't appeared until I was well along the path, and so I used my gift of fire to create my own out of a cast-off remnant. I held it high over my head and made sounds, hoping to scare out any predators that might be lurking. My voice echoed about me, but nothing moved inside. I took a few more steps and repeated the ritual, but still, nothing moved toward me. My old fear of the darkness nagged at me as I walked further into the round opening and faced the black immensity, my limbs shivering slightly, but not with cold. I moved as quickly as I dared, passing the old chests and clothing that had long ago enchanted me deeper into the tunnel. They were all disintegrating now into the staleness of the space.

When I came upon a decent torch, I touched my withering flame to it and filled the passage with light. I moved more quickly now for a long way, snaking upwards, through the earth, until finally stepping into an ominous cavern. I looked up but couldn't see the top. A steep set of stairs was hewn into the rock before me, and I moved quickly toward them, holding the torch high above my head. I put my foot gingerly on the first step and then gave it more weight, finding it was cut firmly into the rock face. I began to climb the stairs. Rats scurried from their places ahead of me and my snakes, which remained alert around my shoulders, raised their heads as I ascended. More torches hung on the wall to my right, and I lit each one as I passed.

I climbed steadily upward as if walking into the great belly of a mountain, the air stale, but breathable. When finally I reached the top I stopped and looked back at the outposts of red glowing along the wall behind. A sense of hope filled me. The fire was my friend.

At the top of the stairs was a long, thin walkway and to my relief, a door. It was made of wood with large, metal chains tethered to an ancient lock. I put down my torch and found a rock, and with all my strength I bore down on the lock. It cracked in two, and the chain fell to the stone floor. The door itself was rotting away. I could see a stone slab on the other side. Now, a new fear rose up inside me. What if I'd come this close but couldn't actually enter the place beyond, for I was sure I was in the bowels of Tintangore itself.

I pulled the door open and lifted what was left of my torch. A stone wall lay before me. I slid to the ground before it and closed my eyes with frustration. My snakes hissed and moved as I did. When I opened my eyes, the torch shaking in my hand, both snakes moved toward the stone.

"No," I said aloud into the darkness. "Don't leave me Medusa!" but the serpents didn't stop.

They slithered easily over the stone and began to climb it, each disappearing into a hole. When I peered closer at the rock and its sharp face I noticed many holes of different sizes carved into its face.

This was a snake priestess's stone!

It hadn't been set here by men or warriors, but by women to protect a sacred place. I knew of no such place in Tintangore, but then the memory of the labyrinth beneath our temple at Caledocean rose in my mind's eye—a place of feminine power, of magic, that kings had built over.

I stood again, excitedly, knowing that if a priestess had laid this stone, there was something on the other side I could access. My inner voice was growing louder, my pulse beating so hard I could feel it jumping at my throat. I intoned the words of power, calling out to Medusa and her twin, asking them to find the way. I opened myself to my intuitive sense and felt an internal pull toward the stone. I placed my hands where they felt drawn to go. Power surged through me, and my seer's eye began to burn on my forehead. As the urge welled up in me, I plunged my right hand into a dark hole at the center of the stone. My fingers grasped something cold, and hard and I instinctually pulled.

The stone moved. It creaked and moaned as it swayed slightly, but as it did my body moved with it. The torch wavered in my hand, but I continued to hold it above me. To my right, there was now a thin opening I could squeeze through.

Medusa and her twin slid out of the holes on either side of me and wrapped themselves firmly around my arms as I withdrew from the stone. I turned sideways and slipped through the space into a large chamber on the other side. I didn't have to look down to know what was etched on the stone floor. The power of the labyrinth filled me before I saw its entrance. I began to walk its intricate pattern, moving from the outside to the center, knowing I'd been led by the invisible current to this place, and this moment.

My own death ritual had begun.

The labyrinth held the secret of immortality for those who knew the way and chaos for those who lost it. I welcomed the test. I shed my fear with each step. I wasn't alone. The wisdom that was always with me came into focus. When I'd finished walking the pattern, my fear had subsided, and peace stood in its place.

At the center of the labyrinth, I raised my head to see the dragon, symbol of immortality, carved on the wall across from me. A door was sealed in its frame. I moved quickly to the handle and pulled it open. The sound stretched out down a long, stone hallway, but there were no voices on the other side or warriors set in place for defense. This place was abandoned.

Following the corridor a long way, I came to a thin, tattered wooden wall, one that had been hastily constructed. Sound rose vaguely on the other side, and I pressed my eye to a sliver of space between the boards. There was a large room on the other side, filled with food supplies and sealed urns. An open window looked down on the courtyard outside, and sun flooded the space.

I doused the torch and laid it in the dark hall behind me, then broke through one of the thin planks into the storeroom. Covering the hole I'd made with an urn, I stole to the window and peered out. Men and women moved about quickly, and soldiers filled the yard, but I could sense the tension between them and a certain lack of strength. Their attention was elsewhere. That was good.

I sent the snakes slithering beneath my tunic and pulled a black tablecloth from a shelf, draping it about my shoulders and head. Then I lifted several wine jugs and went to the door. Keeping my head down I passed through the courtyard as an attendant might, slipping behind the cookhouse and into the passage that led to the back stairs. It would bring me to the second floor behind my old rooms. This was the logical place for them to keep my grandmother. She was so old now, and frail; they wouldn't have locked her away. Not even Kronos would be that cruel.

No one stopped me. I moved quickly through the castle and went up the stairs. When the guard at the top questioned me, I held up a jug of wine and mumbled something unintelligible under my breath, and he let me pass. When I came to the double door with the dragon still set above its entrance, I hesitated for a moment. Four guards paced restlessly outside of it. I continued to walk slowly, taking note with relief that none of them were from Zeus's guard. These were Kronos's men, and they might not recognize me. I kept my eyes down and let the head-shawl fall across my face, and was thus able to walk right by them and to the next door. One of the men approached me, and I froze, but he only reached down and opened the door for me. I curtsied and smiled up at him.

"I'll be cleaning up in here," I said.

"Aye," the big man replied stepping away. "Hades will want things done up, sure enough."

I tried not to startle as he spoke the name. I backed into the room and closed the door behind me, breathing hard.

Hades.

How could the man say such a thing openly? Hades was behind this somehow even though he now stood on the other side of the fight. I shuddered at the thought but didn't let myself linger. I set down the wine, then moved immediately toward the doors of the verandah, which would give me access to my old room. Pushing them open I stepped outside.

The scene that caught my eyes made me stand stock-still. Before me, stretching across the great expanse of the valley was a sea of people, their swords, and shields flashing in the sun. I looked out at their colorful banners in awe. Moving slowly toward the edge of the balcony I dared to look over the side at Kronos's soldiers who sharpened their swords on the practice field below. They couldn't see what waited for them beyond the gates, but I was sure they'd heard enough about it. They were outnumbered ten to one. There was no way that they would hold this castle. Suddenly, it occurred to me that they were not even going to try.

*It's a ruse,* I thought.

I stepped away from the edge and slowly turned toward my room. As I neared the doors of my old apartment, I could sense Rhea's essence already free of her body, and the placid chill of death laid itself upon my skin.

I pushed open the doors and went inside. No fire was lit, and the food on the table was untouched. I turned toward the bed. There lay my grandmother's body, perfectly still. I moved toward her in a rush. Grief arched in my throat, but I swallowed it down. She wouldn't want tears.

I took her limp hand in my own, but her skin was already cold. I pressed my lips to her forehead and stared for a long moment at the peaceful look on her face. Her eyes were closed, and though her body was already growing stiff, her cheeks looked as though they were filled with flame. She was even smiling.

"Oh, Grandmother," I whispered. "I've failed you."

A small vial sat open beside the bed, and I recognized

her personal oil, the scent strong and high, trying to lift me from my sorrow. I poured the oil into my palm and anointed her forehead and the palms of her hands and the soles of her feet, as was our tradition. I blessed my grandmother's body and thanked her for all she'd given and who she'd been.

When I was done, I turned away and moved back to the sitting room. Drums now beat in the distance. War drums. My skin prickled. Clearly Titans were not going to announce my grandmother's death—that would put an end to the blood bath that was soon to ensue. This brought me to the truth behind this battle: the Titans must have the holy oil. Why else would they have broken into the temple? They must have used my grandmother to find the oil's secret place. The Lucifer's apprentice, Mel'ak, was their pawn in this play for the ultimate power, and they'd masked it by kidnapping Rhea, hoping to weaken the Emerald Temple's warriors with this ludicrous charade.

I sat down quietly at the table, fury rising in my heart. The thought that Rhea had served all these years but met death here, alone, and like this, sent anger and heat through my breast, which the oil could not temper.

A large, copper bowl sat before me. Water inside it shimmered in the light. I recognized that my grandmother must have been trying to scry an answer before she'd died. Scrying was a mystical art; some of our seers used the water bowl as a tool to access their inner sight. I'd never used the water bowl before, but I knew my grandmother had seen many things on its surface and been guided by its tremulous light.

I stared into its mirror-like surface hoping the energy of the labyrinth beneath this fort and my training as a priestess might let me find a way to save us.

I reached for a candle and pulled the flame close, letting its light skip across the face of the water. Blue moved beneath my gaze and then green ran through the copper bottom. Gold light splashed in the water and filled my eyes. I stared harder, not blinking, letting my headache, and my senses merge into a wet mire of vision.

"Where is the holy oil? Show me the dragon's blood."

There was a sudden flash and color overwhelmed my sight. I felt as though I was falling, but then I steadied my gaze, and a scene rose up before me.

The large, round tent was set atop a sloping hill that looked down at the battlefield. A lightning bolt flashed on the banner that flew outside the door. A full guard stood at attention just below the hill. Ajax led them. He stood in full battle dress like a gate, guarding the entrance of a palace. Athena and Artemis strode up to him and said something I couldn't hear. He smirked but stood aside waving them past with a royal gesture. As he did so, he rang a bell as if announcing their arrival.

"He's waiting for you inside," Ajax said loudly. "Everyone is."

I felt a dull pulse in my body as he spoke, the sound of their voices becoming clear.

"Who's everyone?" Artemis asked.

"Go in and see," he said, turning his back on them.

Athena looked at Artemis and then back to her small troop of women that stood just behind the men.

"Only the leaders gather inside," Ajax said. "Your women can stay here."

*No*, I thought, trying to reach out to Athena through

the water and the vision. *"Bring them with you,"* I said out loud, but Athena only turned with Artemis and continued up the path entering the tent.

The light was dim, but the scene, clear. Zeus stood in the doorway, his arms open and a vial of oil in his hands. Hades stepped up behind Athena and put a knife to her throat as Zeus swooped down on Artemis. He smeared his open palm across her head. I could see oil glistening on his hand, and when it touched Artemis's skin, she cried out and crumpled to the ground at Zeus's feet. He knelt down beside her.

"Easy, easy," he said. "I'm giving you eternal life. From my hand, you will be born again!"

Athena struggled in Hades's grip, and the blade nicked her neck so that blood spilled down onto his hand.

"No!" she moaned, her voice broken as Zeus stood up and faced her, pouring more oil from the open vial into his palm.

He moved toward her quickly, splashing his hand over her forehead as he'd done to Artemis. Athena inhaled sharply, and her body went limp. Hades lifted her easily, as if she weighed no more then a blanket, and set her down on a thick cot beside a row of others near the side of the tent. There lay Persephone and Demeter, Apollo and my son, Ares, all thrashing as if they were dying. The reality of the scene hit me with horror. They *were* dying. Zeus had awakened the Dragon, the holy oil of immortality. He had trapped them for eternity in a mortal form.

Athena's body shuddered hard as Zeus kneeled beside her. I looked at him more intently and saw the smooth, shining marble of his skin. His hair was black and sleek as it had been in our youth, and his bare chest was free of his battle scars. When he smiled down at her, his teeth shone brilliant and white.

"I give you eternal life," he said benevolently. "I welcome you to my family of immortals."

She opened her mouth and moved her lips, but no sound came forth.

"Don't fight against it," a shaky voice came from Athena's other side.

It was Demeter. She'd pushed herself up into a sitting position and placed a hand on her daughter's forehead. Persephone, who'd been whimpering in pain, quieted immediately. I stared longer at Demeter; my friend's face had changed entirely. Not a line shone on her aged skin. Her hair hung in wild curls down her back, and the vibrant earth-red color had returned to it. She reached her other hand out toward Artemis whom Hades had now laid beside her. The fingers that had gnarled with time were now thin wisps of grace. When she spoke, her voice was crisp.

"Don't struggle against it my dears," she said. "It's too late for that. The only way through is to surrender to it." Her tone was tearful as she stroked Persephone's forehead. "The oil is sealing in your light."

I watched as Artemis closed her eyes and went within, a true priestess in her response. Her whole body shuddered hard and then stilled. Her skin grew young, the strong muscles of her arms re-defining themselves. Her hair became black, her deeply lined face turned smooth, and the sun darkened hue of her skin returned to the soft brown of her childhood.

Apollo sat up across from her, shaking his head, holding out his own arms, detecting the differences in himself. A dismayed look crossed his face.

"What have you done to us?" he said in disgust. "Zeus, what have you done?"

Zeus laughed as Apollo climbed unsteadily to his feet. "I've given you immortality, and you complain!"

Apollo shook his head angrily. "You've trapped us in our bodies!"

"I've set you free!" Zeus chided. "Free for all time. I've chosen to let you join us, Apollo, as we free ourselves from death and suffering. Feel your body, sense your new strength. You'll never grow old, never be sick, or weak. You'll never die!" He spoke this last with genuine wonder.

Artemis moaned, and Apollo bent to her side, laying his hands on her head.

"Be careful," Demeter warned. I could see she'd come back to herself more fully now. "I sense our innate gifts are much stronger, as will be our physical strength."

Persephone opened her eyes and sat up with a look of pain and shock on her face. As she stared down at her hands, tears filled her eyes. Hades moved to her side, reaching down to help her to her feet, but Demeter pushed his hand away.

"How dare you!" Demeter hissed. "You've killed her! You've killed us all!"

Hades' face took on a genuine look of surprise. Persephone stared up at him as the tears flowed down her cheeks. She turned to Demeter and leaned into her mother's protective arms.

"No," Hades said, shaking his head. "You don't understand. Persephone, my love, I'm the one who named you for eternal life!"

Persephone sobbed loudly, her head on Demeter's shoulder as Hades raised both hands in a helpless gesture.

"Dearest," Hades said. He slid closer to her, his voice soft and pleading. "I wouldn't go into eternal life without *you*. And to make you happy I've brought your mother with us. I know I haven't always done the right thing. I haven't always followed my heart, but this time…"

Persephone did not let him finish. With tears still flowing, she pulled back from her mother and got to her feet. Hades stood up, reaching out tentatively, but she scowled and pushed him away.

"You've always been selfish," she said. "I told myself it was because you were afraid, or because you had never known *real* love. I thought I could save you Hades, from your fear and insecurity, and terrible need for power. I thought my love would be enough."

She wiped at the tears. Demeter stood up and put a hand on her daughter's shoulder.

"You don't understand," Hades demanded. He looked around the room, holding up his hands. "None of you understand, or appreciate what we've done!"

"You've trapped us in our bodies forever!" Persephone cried. "You've had no care or respect for what has meaning to *me*, while adamantly proclaiming your love. That is not real love, Hades. This is NOT what love looks like. You are a misguided and foolish man."

Hades opened his mouth as if to protest, but then stopped. The aura of true strength and the dignity of a priestess emanated from Persephone as she stared into his eyes. He looked around the room at the stricken faces that regarded him with such mistrust. Nodding, he lowered his head.

"What is the truth?" Persephone continued. "Why have you done this to us?"

Athena stood up, and the others followed. They came to stand together beside Persephone whose body radiated fantastic courage and strength. Hades stepped back, returning to Zeus's side.

"Why?" Persephone demanded again this time turning to Zeus. "Why us?"

Zeus stood before them, radiant, smiling.

"Because *she* loves you all," he said. "She'll want you with her as we move through time."

"She?" Apollo questioned.

There was a long, stunned silence as the truth dawned on them. I could see it in their faces as they looked at each other in dismay.

"Hera," Artemis said. "He means Hera."

As the reality of it sunk in, Apollo stepped forward, his face stricken.

"Hera?" he said. "You transformed us to please Hera?"

Before Zeus could answer, another figure stepped from the shadows at the back of the room. She was tall and fair skinned, and her hair fell in light ringlets about her radiant, unscarred face. It was Aphrodite.

"Hera?" she said moving toward Zeus and Hades. "You never said anything about Hera!"

"Aphrodite," Hades held up his hands. "Not now—"

"No! That wasn't the agreement, Hades! I didn't do this so Hera could have—" but she stopped there as the other priestesses turned to her exhaling sharp sounds.

"It was you," Athena hissed. "You brought the men through the mist!"

Aphrodite stepped back.

Athena clenched her fists and began to move. I thought she would strike Aphrodite, but Demeter put a hand on Athena's shoulder, holding her still.

"No, not now," she commanded seeming to finally take hold of the situation. She lifted herself, a High Priestess in her own right, turning to Aphrodite.

"We'll deal with her later. Now, we've got to warn Hera."

Before Demeter could give another order, the bell clanged loudly outside the tent, signaling another arrival. Everyone turned towards Zeus as he pulled the vial of oil from the cord around his neck, where it hung in the tradition of the priestesses. Opening the vial, he poured the oil into his palm.

Hades stepped to the side of the entrance, expectantly. I felt my own body leaning forward over the scrying bowl as I stared harder at the images in the water, a sharp pain streaking through my veins.

The tent flap moved aside, and my daughter, Ilithyia, stepped inside.

"No!" I screamed the words out loud.

Zeus stepped back as if he'd heard me, and Ili spun around.

"Mother?" she cried. "Mother?"

Then the flap moved again, and another form entered the tent. It was Poseidon.

In a strong, swift move, Hades reached for Ilithyia, but a thin slicing sound pierced the air, and an arrow thudded into his chest. He cried out and stumbled backward, steadying himself against the wooden table. Everyone turned toward Artemis, who was nocking another arrow and deftly let it fly. It struck Zeus just as hard as the first had hit his brother.

Ilithyia screamed.

Zeus stumbled backward, his hands open, flailing in the air. Poseidon instinctively reached out, catching Zeus by the hand, steadying him, but as the brother's locked palms, Poseidon gasped. Zeus's palm was slick with the holy oil, and Poseidon slid helplessly to the ground.

"No!" shouted Zeus, even as he clutched his chest.

Poseidon's body arched tensely while the oil began its transformation.

Blood burst from Zeus's breast, but he shook his head staring down at his older brother who writhed on the ground.

"No, not you Poseidon. This isn't meant for *you*!"

"Father!" Ilithyia's voice shook as she stared at the arrow in his flesh.

Zeus's head snapped toward her.

"It's nothing," he said. "I can feel the pain, but there's no danger. Look!" He took hold of the long shaft, wincing, and pulled it from his chest.

The bloodied wound began to close immediately, the flesh binding itself together. Ilithyia gasped. Zeus looked at her and smiled. He held up the vial of oil.

"Run Ili!" I cried out again. "*Run!*"

In a moment, the scene blurred with motion. Ilithyia moved, but Hades reached out to catch her. Then Athena's form sliced through the men with a long, sharp blade. Red streaked across my vision as my daughter pushed through the flap of the tent with Athena and Artemis close beside her.

"Run Ilithyia!" I cried out again. "*Run!*"

# CHAPTER EIGHTEEN

WHEN I OPENED MY EYES, I lay on the floor. There was a dull ache in my head, but I waved it away. Pain couldn't matter now. The oil had transformed ten people. I knew who the eleventh would be. My fate was sealed.

I realized that no one would be safe as long as the oil was in Zeus's possession. I understood, finally, the meaning of the prophecy my grandmother had shared so long ago.

*A woman of flame and the holy blood shall rise from the common folk, and she will come to carry the dragon's blood into the world in safety. She will become the living temple, and upon her neck, it will rest, protected from the greedy, ignorant hands of those that would use it for power.*

Those words came back to me as if she were in the room speaking them.

I was the woman that would fulfill the prophecy. I was the only one that could protect the oil, for although Zeus was now immortal, he could still feel pain. Around my neck, the Dragon's Blood must hang safeguarded by my skill with fire. No one would stand against me and risk burning for eternity! What greater fear could there be than that?

My destiny was now clear to me. I knew what I must do.

I wrapped my grandmother's body in an emerald green robe from my old wardrobe and took her into my arms. Whispering words of blessing and love, I carried her body onto the balcony and set it down on a wooden bench. From this place I could see that the courtyard was now full of Kronos's warriors and the fields in front of the castle were filled with Zeus's troops. I could not stop what was to come. I knew that now.

I set to work creating a sacred circle around what would be my grandmother's pyre, pulling herbs from the gourds on the tables and spreading them thickly around us. Opening my old priestess chest, which they'd left in the room, I brought out my favorite things. There was Mother's plain, woolen cloak, and the dried rose petals Ili had once given me as a child. There was a string of pearls Ares had given me, and the soft doeskin boots Father had fitted to my feet and sewn so long ago. I laid them all on my grandmother's body. Then I stepped back to the door and lifted my hands gently, calling forth the fire. It rippled lightly, a joyful thing, and set the little wooden seat to flame. As the glow of crimson leaped from the base to the emerald robe, I called on the inferno within myself to set it blazing. The funeral pyre for the High Priestess, of the Emerald Temple, would be the sign I promised; a victory flame that would signal Rhea's release.

*Rhea would like that*, I thought.

Looking out over the battlefield I could see the Emerald Temple's warriors had been pulled back to the rear. Athena would see the fire and recognize it as a sign. She'd know there was no need to attack now and could keep our women from the fray. There was some consolation in that.

When the fire burned steadily, and the smoke rose in a charcoal streak above me, I heard the battle horn sound. Riders thundered down the hill on horseback, and the foot soldiers rushed in. Kronos's men, who stood before the walls of Tintangore, dispelled the first onslaught. Archers on the walls and ramparts let loose their arrows, and dozens of soldiers fell. Wave after wave of warriors attacked the castle, the clang of swords and the shouts of desperate men filled the afternoon.

I watched it all from high up on the balcony of the castle, as my grandmother's body turned to ash beside me. I stood calmly in the center of the circle, holding empty presence, as the dead escaped their bones, and the living claimed the castle.

When finally the gates of Tintangore were breached and Zeus's men flooded inside, I called to Medusa and her twin, guiding each serpent to coil tight against a forearm. My physical senses were muted, and my intuitive awareness fully engaged. I moved very close to my grandmother's ashes as they began to lift lightly with the breeze. The wind was cool on my face, pushing the silver curls from my cheeks. Soft, gray ashes floated around me as formidable in their transformed state as my grandmother had ever been in the form of a body. The rush of her power and the delight of her freedom washed over me. Turning my back on the madness of the warriors below I faced the balcony doors, waiting for Zeus's approach.

It was not long before I heard the sharp sound of metal on the stair, as the warriors took the castle. Yet no one approached my rooms or entered the verandah. When I finally heard Zeus's voice in the corridor the last of my grandmother's ashes rose through the air above me in a spiral dance, and I heard the distinct sound of laughter on the wind.

The doors to the room beyond opened and I felt Zeus's presence sweep toward me. Standing in the doorway to the verandah his body was a mass of light. I stepped forward holding out my hand to him. My muscles were taut, but I faced him with confidence. My flesh and bone were singing him love songs, drawing him close to me. I could feel the heat emanating from his body and the relief that swept through him as he laid his eyes on me.

"Come," I said, my voice even, my tone direct.

He smiled broadly.

"So, you understand?" he said.

"I understand."

"I knew you would. I've come for you as I said. I've done this all for you, Hera, my love."

His eyes were full of feeling. He looked young, almost innocent, and for a moment I could feel the old caring, the love even, that had drawn me to him. I let it emanate from my chest, a wave of kindness, knowing that in the end—*in the very end*—this love must win.

But today was not that day.

"Come to me," I said again. "Anoint me."

Zeus laid down his sword and stepped into the sacred circle. I watched as my grandmother's ashes settled lightly atop his shining black hair like a crown, and I knew his fate was sealed. With a swift movement I threw the fire about us, a circle of flame that licked at the sky.

Zeus only laughed as though he thought this a fittingly dramatic gesture.

The noise in the courtyard below began to dim as the fire rose higher, and the crackling wall of red heat surrounded us. Zeus and I were sealed in the circle of flame.

"You are magnificent," Zeus said as he stood before me.

"The most beautiful and powerful of all women."

He reached for the alabaster jar at his neck and pulled it free. Oil still glistened on its rim. I could smell its distinct aroma, an ancient earthen fragrance that was alive with longing. A brilliant red streak of light flashed before my eyes as he pulled off the lid.

The fire leaped higher.

"Anoint me!" I commanded. "Do what you have come to do!"

Zeus was swift. The oil swept across my skin like warm water spilled across an altar and I caught my breath. There was a sharp pain and a burning in my limbs, but I was prepared as the others had not been, my inner sight strong and clear, guiding me through the transformation. I heard my grandmother's voice as light pierced my vision and fused me forever inside my flesh.

"Give yourself up to the origin of your being," she said. "Priestess, *rise!*"

I began to burn with light. I fell to my knees as my body transformed itself. I opened my eyes to see my skin tighten and grow young, the fullness of my breasts returned, and the marks of my children's births disappeared from my skin. A wave of sickness moved through me, but I held myself erect, breathing deep and pushing out a sacred sound that kept my mind focused and clear. Sensation swept over my scalp as my hair returned to the long, dark and thick tresses of my youth. I focused on the waves of light rising inside of me. Sound filled my body as if my bones were singing. Time seemed to shimmer before me as my body trembled and transformed. A final wave of grief washed over me as I was sealed into my flesh forever.

When it was done my chest heaved a great sigh. My body relaxed and was my own again. I opened my eyes, staring at

Zeus who had kneeled before me. He still held the holy oil in his palm. He reached out with the other hand and took hold of mine.

"You are my queen," he said. "Forever."

"Yes," I said. "I am your queen."

With that, Medusa and her twin slithered out from beneath the cuffs of my robe binding our hands together.

Zeus startled, but smiled.

"A fitting symbol," he said. "Handfasted as we once were."

"Yes, a fitting symbol," I replied as the two snakes continued to coil and bind us, their immortal bodies stronger than any cord.

I reached out my other hand.

"Now, give me the oil Zeus," I said.

The smile faded from his face.

"No," he said, "The oil is mine."

"No," I replied calmly, the fire steady, and hot all around us. "The oil is not yours. It was never yours. Give it to me. I will keep it safe."

He shook his head, struggling to his feet, pulling me up with him, but as he tried to retract his arm, the snakes tightened their coil, keeping him close.

"Hera," he began, but I had already reached out to the fire and brought the circle of flame dangerously close.

"Hera!" Zeus commanded, but I only laughed.

"There is nowhere you can go that my flames cannot reach you," I said.

Zeus looked about us as if realizing for the first time the extent of the fire. He tried again to pull away and this time I let him, signaling the snakes to withdraw. They slithered to their places on each forearm. I pulled the circle of fire even tighter around Zeus.

"Give me the oil," I cried out over the crackling flames.

There were sounds in the outer chambers of my rooms as men and women spilled onto the balcony, some crying out for help, others batting at the flames, but the intensity of the heat drove them all back.

Zeus was looking about frantically, as sharp orange sparks bit at his skin and singed his hair.

"Give me the oil," I said again.

"You wouldn't," Zeus cried out. "Hera, you—"

With that I let the flame take Zeus' arm. He screamed and dropped the oil. As soon as it left his hand, I had it in my own. The vial holding the Dragon's Blood was mine.

In that moment I released the flames, and they responded to my command with ease, as if they were a part of me. I had full control of the fire, feeling it ebb and flow with the temper of my mind. As I called back the fire from Zeus, it leaped, like a living thing, into the air, and disappeared. He gasped and grit his teeth as the blackened skin on his arm rippled with a soft light and began to heal.

I lifted my arms again, and the flames that had caught and spread to the beams of the castle were drawn up into the air, transforming into smoke. In a few short breathes, the fire was gone. The space around us was blackened and charred, with thin wisps of smoke rising.

Zeus was on his knees clutching his arm close to his body. He looked up at me with a hard, bitter face.

"But why?" he said. "My love for you is real! Doesn't all of this prove that by now?"

"You still don't know what love is, Zeus," I said in a low and furious voice. "And until you, and men like you, understand what it is to care about another person's well-being as much as your own, there will never be peace in the world."

People had spilled out onto the verandah staring in horror at the charred scene. I could hear voices from the crowd.

"The High Priestess," one said.

"The Draconigena," cried another.

Zeus let go of his arm. The skin was already healed.

I stepped forward reaching for him. He stared into my eyes, brows furrowed, and jaw clenched, but he reached out and took my hand.

"Come," I said. "You are the king of Atlantis. There is much for you to do. You must put things back in order."

"I'm more than a king," he retorted, his voice quivering. "I'm immortal! We are the first immortals, Hera!"

He was filled with wonder at the thought of it; I could see it in his eyes. There was no way to get through to him.

I took the oil and clasped its cord around my neck.

"And by the hand of Grace," I said, "We will be the *last* immortals."

"The last?" He threw up his arms with disgust. "You have no vision, Hera, no idea of what I've planned for us."

Taking hold of my arm, he pulled me toward him. His hand squeezed hard, hurting me. I let my palm fill with heat and grasped his wrist with menace. He tried to pull back, but I was as strong as he was now. I held him close, letting a soft flame lick his skin.

"You will follow my command, Zeus," I said. "I'm done playing your games."

He tried to shake free of the burn, but I let the flame crackle about him on all sides. People were watching, drawing back, with loud gasps and exclamations.

"Alright," he said facing me. "Stop, Hera, that's enough!"

I let the flame go. His face was contorted with anger, and something else, something cold and broken.

"You would make me suffer this way?" he said.

"I would."

He shook his head as I let go of his wrist.

"This isn't you, Hera. You're my wife, my queen. You know I only wanted to bring us together, all of us! Forever…"

"Stop, Zeus," I said stepping toward him again. He stiffened, taking a quick step back. Turning toward the battlefield beyond us, I spread my hands wide. "This is all your doing, Zeus. Every death is on your hands, including our own."

He stood very still then, looking out across the fields as if seeing the death and destruction for the first time. He moved closer to the edge of the balcony surveying the disorder below us. The air was still choked with dust, and a long line of wounded was still being carried to medic tents. The painful cries of fallen warriors rose up across the turf.

I came to stand beside him, gasping at the sight of so many who had fallen.

"You must do what you can to set things right," I said.

He nodded.

We stood there, side by side, for a long while, watching the sad and painful scene before us. My rage subsided while the warm glow of my transformed state began to soften me. Finally, I moved closer to Zeus and slid my hand in his. He turned, looking down into my eyes.

"I wanted to be with you, forever," he said. "I love you, Hera."

I shook my head.

"No, Zeus, this," I waved my hand toward the field, "This is not what love looks like."

Letting go of his hand I turned toward the door, but he stopped me.

"Hera, what will happen now?" he asked.

"I don't know," I answered. "I don't know the way forward yet, but whatever happens, we must all become part of something *good*, Zeus."

I was surprised by the emotion in my tone and reached out to touch his cheek.

"That's what I was trying to do, Hera," he said softly.

"Yes, Zeus, I know."

A bitter regret flooded my body as I dropped my hand and walked away.

# CHAPTER NINETEEN

THE NIGHT WAS CLOSING IN AROUND US as I walked through the castle gates. Fires were lit across the hillside, and the battlefield was being cleared of the fallen. I could see that the captains had withdrawn. The main force and Calvary had fallen back on the township to the west, leaving the Emerald Temple's warriors to hold the field and castle. Medical units were set up atop the hill and priestesses tended the wounded. Burial parties would be hard at work all through the night.

When I reached the Emerald Temple's encampment, I stood in the shadows of the great tent, watching as Ilithyia directed the council of warriors and priestesses that surrounded her. Poseidon and Artemis were still at her side, and so I waited and watched, cherishing the three of them, burning this moment into my memory for all time. I wanted to rush in and take them all in my arms and protect them, but it was too late for that. As the realization swept over me, I stepped back further into the shadows. I did not want my daughter to see me like this, transformed and unnatural. And then it struck me, full force: I would not see my daughter again.

An agony gripped me, but the truth of what I must do was suddenly before me.

*My dearest loves!* I cried out with my inner voice, bereft. *My family!*

Artemis turned her head away from the group staring out into the night, in my direction. Poseidon moved to her side. He leaned down murmuring something in her ear. Her hand flew to her chest, and she shook her head, but he laid a gentle palm on her shoulder.

*This is good*, I thought. *At least they will have each other, and they will watch over my daughter and my daughter's daughters. And life for them will go on…*

I backed further into the darkness, disappearing into the forest.

I traveled back to the Eastern shore of Atlantis. I wanted to go home one last time. Staying away from the roads and villages, I kept to the dense green forests and then the wild jungle shoreline. I journeyed on foot, traveling both day and night. I quickly discovered that in my immortal state I required no food or water and my body needed little rest or sleep. My eyes were keener, and once accustomed to the darkness, I could find my way in the night as well as an owl might. I could control the temperature of my body as readily as I might call to the fire. Those mystical gifts I'd acquired as a mortal woman, were now enhanced one hundred-fold, and I had no trouble finding my way back to the wet jungle village in which I'd grown up.

I arrived just before dawn. The first birds were whistling as I set foot on the path that led up the hill to my parents' house. By the time I reached the top, the sudden cacophony of their early morning chorus had surrounded me.

I stopped for a moment to take it all in. Looking out over the small, green pasture, shimmering in the early morning light, I was filled with emotion. I listened to the steady swoosh of water in the stream and caught the familiar aroma of my mother's jasmine and gardenia as it rose about me. I was flooded with a memory of safety and love, which I had only known in this place.

As my gaze rested on the house, there was movement inside, and light from the fire wavered in the window. I slipped off my boots and dropped my cape, walking barefoot across the field as I'd done when I was just a girl. I came to the blessing bowl at the front step and dipped my hand in the water, anointing myself. Such a simple ritual, yet it flooded with me with an old sense of devotion and grace.

"Hera," it was my father's voice, old and thin.

I looked up, and there he stood in the doorframe, his body slightly stooped, his long white hair pulled back in a braid.

"Hera, my daughter," he said. "Come, we are waiting for you. Your mother has had a dream."

I smiled. *Of course, she has,* I thought. I moved up the stairs and took him gently in my arms, afraid of my newfound strength. He seemed surprised but softened into my embrace. When I let him go, he took up my hand, pulling me toward the hearth in the middle of the room, where my mother sat stirring a boiling pot. She looked up as I reached the light of the flames.

"Is it you?" she said softly. "Hera, dearest, come closer so that I can see you."

Soft tears filled my eyes, and I dropped my head in shame.

"I don't want you to see me like this, mother," I said. "I am transformed by the oil. I have failed you and the temple, and grandmother too."

Mother got to her feet, her body slight, and venerable. Tears spilled down her cheeks as she reached for me, taking my face in her two rough, aged hands, tipping my head back and looking at me in the light.

"My beautiful girl," she said through her tears. "So, it has come to this."

She pulled me to her, stroking my head as if I was a child, and my father stepped close, wrapping his arms around us both. In their arms, I let myself be loved and held for the last time.

When all the tears had passed through us, I kissed my mother on the cheek and put her hand in Fathers'.

"You have come to say goodbye," my father said.

I nodded, taking a step back.

"And I have come to say that I love you."

Father reached his arm around Mother, whose body had started to tremble.

"We will always be with you, Hera," she said. "We will be free of our bodies soon enough, and we will come to you. You will not be alone."

I nodded again, forcing a smile.

"Yes mother," I said.

I slipped through the jungle and came to the crescent shore of the village where the fishermen's outriggers nestled in the heavy sand. I chose one with a large sail, dragging it into the water. Climbing in, I began to paddle toward the bay. There was commotion on the shore behind me, but I did not look back. I put up the small sail, calling to the wind. It arrived in a sudden, great gust, catching me up in it, pushing the outrigger out to sea. I did not need maps or the knowledge of the stars to guide me for the wind knew where I wished to go and provided safe passage.

I sailed for many days and nights, restless and strained with the loss. It was not until I glimpsed the Great Pillars, the familiar landmarks that sailors had described to me in the past, that a sense of ease finally came to me. As I passed through the Great Pillars, entering the Mediterranean Sea, I felt my inner compass pull me forward. I sailed onward past the Iberian Peninsula, and our outpost at Kart Hadst. A robust and steady gust carried me all the way to the coast of Philistia. Each day I called the wind, sensing into the ocean about me, avoiding ships and fishers as I intuited their presence. Each night I lay beneath the stars thinking of my loved ones and the hard days that lay before them.

When finally, I reached Hellas, and the many isles in the Aegean Sea, I knew I was close to the place that was calling to me. Poseidon had told me of the isle Samos, which he had discovered during one of his explorations. He said the people there were rich with philosophy and art, and that they were devoted to the kind and cooperative ways of the Sacred Feminine. It was a place where the Mother was still honored and even revered.

I traveled through a vast litter of islands, past Chios and Patmos, until I found the coast of Anatolia. Soon, I came upon the long, thin island of Samos, a place that once celebrated the old ways. Opening my intuitive senses, I called to the earth and the sacred caves that had long since been forgotten. In the stillness, my body felt their welcoming reply.

"Come, daughter!" The words touched my mind and heart. "Come, rest here in my womb."

Taking a deep breath, I bowed my head. This would be the end of my journey.

I kept my craft at a distance, sailing by the southeast shore where a beautiful city sat benefitting from arable mountain slopes and fertile plains. I traveled past the town until I happened on a deserted bay. Dusk was falling as my craft glided across the crystalline waters toward the shore. Looking over the bow, I could see straight down through the water to the white sand many feet below. I slipped over the side of the boat, letting my body ease into the warm sea. The vessel moved on towards the shore without me as I swam through the bay toward a protected alcove with a small, black sand beach. Stepping out of the water, I caught my breath as the air brushed my wet skin. To feel such a vulnerable, physical sensation in a body that was so clearly altered, unnerved me. Suddenly, weariness overcame me. I climbed up the rocks and into the brush out of sight, lying down at last, on the earth that would soon hold me. I closed my eyes, drifting off to sleep.

When I awoke, the new moon was high above me, and it took some time to adjust to the dark. I stood up, gradually making out the rough terrain of shrubs all about me. A strong desire to move urged me forward, and I traveled through the night until I came upon the sacred place, guarded by a thick set of stones in the side of the hill. I did not need to wait for daylight to find the entrance of the cave. Nor did I care to wait and see the sun for the last time.

A great need, a hunger, drew me in, and then down the narrow passage into the belly of mother earth. The air was thin and cold, but I pressed on until I had dropped down, far beneath the surface. My eyesight began to merge with the blackness, and I had no fear as I walked deeper and farther underground.

When I came to the heart of the place, I called the fire to me. The air about me cracked and hissed. Light suddenly leaped in the center of the space. The cavern was large, and continued, winding downward farther still, but I knew this was the place, my place, for all time to come. The only sound I could hear was that of my breath.

I laid my palms on the cold stone. Medusa and her twin, who'd remained coiled about my body, as if in hibernation, slid easily from my wrists disappearing among the stones.

In the rock face on the far wall, there was an indentation in the black stone, a seat that looked hand-carved as if it was a throne. I walked over to it and sat down. The flames flickered, and with a long, deep breath, I let them go out forever.

In the darkness, I found empty space devoid of any sense of time.

Lifting easily from my body I became pure awareness, everywhere and nowhere.

I drifted into the sea of consciousness from which I could witness all things unfolding. My immortal flesh, and bones, sat far away in the darkness of the cave as the years passed by. Formless, I traveled, over sea and land, witnessing.

At first, I followed my daughter. Artemis stood by Ilithyia's side, as my daughter rose up to become the most powerful High Priestess Atlantis had ever known. She sent thousands across the world to safety before Atlantis fell into the sea. She entrusted her daughters to Artemis's care, and when they were old enough, she sent them to govern the temples she had constructed in Sumer and Minoa, Britannia, and Malta.

When Ilithyia's last days were upon her, I moved in a formless state to rest by her side, reaching out, stroking her head, whispering the soft songs of love I'd sung to her as an infant. I watched helpless as she lifted from her body into a formless state of awareness and then became light. For a moment she saw me, and in the dream-like state between life and death she whispered, "*Mother.*" Then she was gone, and I could not follow.

Soon after Ilithyia passed, Atlantis fell, and the immortals spread themselves across the world.

Zeus took many of them to the Aegean settling at Mt. Olympus. He created the first myths of the Titans and the Gods, and Goddesses of Mycenae. He told people stories about us, half-truths, calling us Gods, promising we would guide and protect the people. Tribes gathered and followed him for generations, holding him up as the supreme father, a true God. He wove fantastical stories naming me as his wife and queen, erecting temples all over the world in my name. I watched in wonder as people thronged to him taking up his stories as truth, giving up their power and surrendering their lives to him.

It did not take long for the other immortals to abandon Zeus, each disappearing into the vast and burgeoning world.

Athena went further east, drawing to her a growing number of displaced and despondent women who had been abused and outcast. She taught them how to defend themselves and their children, and she gave them the tools to live off the land. As her numbers grew, Athena raised a group of warriors, called Amazons, who protected the women for a time. Then, Zeus' men, the Greeks, turned against them, and all were lost.

Demeter went to Britannia helping the ancient mystical people there, the Celts. She shared her wisdom and the mysteries of the Sacred Feminine, founding temples and sacred circles of stones all across the Island.

Persephone went to Mesopotamia, to the people of Sumer and Egypt. They called her Ki, Inanna, Hathor, Isis and Nut. Then she journeyed farther, to the lands of Bharatvarsha, where they called her Lakshmi, Shakti, and Kali. I watched as the centuries passed, with a distant sense of pleasure, as Persephone came to know her power through the gorgeous darkness, and depths, of the Sacred Feminine. Through the mist that I rested in, I was drawn to her courage as she breathed beauty and respect into all of the women she initiated.

And then there was Poseidon, my noble man. I often caught glimpses of him through my hollow darkness. He found our son, Hephaestus, and raised him up to become a great man. He followed Hephaestus's children and watched over them for generations, but all the while, he never stopped looking for me, traveling to every island, every town and city, calling my name. There were some nights I would hear his voice weaving itself amidst the darkness, but by then I had learned the art of retreat and would rise above the sound of even *his* love.

There were times through the ages that I would catch a glimpse of one of the immortals… Ares in the midst of a battle, or Apollo laying his healing hands upon a child, saving a life. Mostly, I drifted, high above it all becoming more and more like light.

Time passed, and I moved farther and farther away, as temples of light, dedicated to the work of the feminine principles of life, were raised up by women and then torn down by men. I could not endure the truth of it, even from my great distance. In every place across the world, men gathered together in groups, making laws and religions that demeaned women. Everywhere, men took away the safety and dignity of women by force.

I watched it all from afar letting the unconscionable actions of human beings and the loss of those I cared for push me farther into empty space. I could not say how long I remained this way. Civilizations rose and fell while my body was enshrined in the cave. My awareness drifted, wide open, and free.

And then something changed. One night, a sound cracked through my formless state and caught me, like a hook, reeling me toward it. Downward I went, through the soft, vapid spaces of my own uncaring, until I could perceive myself again. The sound rose up all around me and I was inexplicably drawn toward it. As I got closer the mist surrounding me lifted and I recognized the sound. It was laughter.

I stared out of the darkness at a small firepit rippling with orange flames. Three women sat close around it, holding hands. Something about them drew me in, closer and closer, until my memory sharpened and I understood what I was seeing.

It was Artemis that I recognized first. She was holding hands with Demeter and Persephone and they were speaking in light voices and laughing. There was movement in the brush beside them and Athena stepped forward.

"I can hear you all half a league away," she scolded, but she was smiling.

The women stood, embracing each other warmly.

"It's been a long time," Demeter said as she wrapped Athena in her arms.

"Too long," Athena answered. "It's been 3 decades, sisters. Since Gaius Octavius defeated Cleopatra!" She shook her head. "Rome's power truly has no end!"

"Yes," Demeter responded, "but that is soon to change!"

The women shifted back to the fire and sat down. Athena

looked up at the night sky and pointed to one bright star that shone above them.

"The men are here too," she said. "They've followed the star. They're close by in Jerusalem."

"All of them?" Demeter asked.

Athena shook her head. "I saw Hades and Zeus, they've come as kings, of course. And Ares is there, but he's never far from his father's side. I did not see Apollo or Poseidon."

Artemis stirred the fire. "They will be here," she said. "Neither will want to miss the birth."

Athena scowled. I could feel the wave of fear in her gut and see the worry on her brow.

Demeter took Athena's hand.

"Quiet your mind, sister," she said. "While the men are in Jerusalem waiting for the boy to be born, we'll be here and will protect the girl."

The others nodded in assent. Persephone reached out for Athena's other hand taking it in her own. She looked long into Athena's eyes.

"I promise you, Athena, the next High Priestess will be born here, tonight. She will be heir to the Temple of the Rose and keeper of the great feminine mysteries. A daughter of Judea and a priestess, called Magdalene, will carry our message of kindness, justice, and love into the world."

Athena's face was still grim. She withdrew her hands, nodding her head.

"Yes, she will be born tonight," Athena said. "And she will learn the ways of the feminine face of the One, and take it forth, but what then? We have seen this before, a hundred times. As the women rise in righteousness and stand for justice, the men rise against them. What will men do to this precious one? What names will they call this cherished being?

How many terrible stories will they make up to diminish her?" In a low, strained voice, she finished, "How brave will this one have to be to stand amongst men, and speak the truth?"

Tears glistened in Athena's eyes and the women sat in silence. The glow of orange flame illuminated their weary faces.

It was Demeter that finally spoke.

"You may be right, Athena," she said. "For it has all happened before, again and again. But we must hold the light, dearest. We must stand together as long it takes and hold the light!"

Her words seemed to rise out of her and move through me. With a sharp sensation and shock, I felt myself and my broken heart. All at once, I was both inside the cave and there, with my sisters, wanting to reach out and be part of this light in the world, unfolding.

The fire crackled, and the flames flared high. The four priestesses shifted, looking in my direction. Artemis rose to her feet.

"Hera," she cried. "Hera!"

But then I was gone. In a sharp, hot flash, I was far away, lost in the distance I had created around myself. The last thing I heard as I lifted up, dissolving into empty space, was the sound of my voice echoing Demeter's words.

"Stand together as long as it takes!" I cried. "And hold the light! Hold the light."

For more information about the author and Sacred Healing, or to receive updates on Julien's NEW books and offerings, sign up for her newsletter at: www.JulienDuBrow.com

# AUTHOR'S NOTES

In writing The Priestess Chronicles, I explored a myth-making process in which I imagined a time before the concept of God existed. I've always wondered what compelled our species to create the concept of an all-powerful being or beings, and I've often pondered how this being became gendered. As a scholar of mythology and mysticism, I've found that the oldest text, songs, hymns and sacred poetry from around the world refer to an experience of unity as the primary and enduring reality. Even the mystics symbolize their experiences through gender and analogy. Thus, in writing my myth, I've represented the primary divine experience as unity and used the Minoan and Mycenaean cultures that lived 2600-1100 B.C. to create an entirely fictional time-period, in a setting that lives somewhere between myth and reality.

While it is a work of fantasy, I've used the storylines of western culture's Greek Pantheon to craft this tale and in so doing, I feel it is important to share a brief description of their creation story and the true origins of their Goddess, Hera. The primary sources of the information below are Edith Hamilton's book, *Mythology*, and Vicki Noble's groundbreaking book, *The Double Goddess*.

## Greek Mythology:

Ancient Greek civilization is generally acknowledged as the foundation of western culture. The Greeks reached a high level of sophistication in their philosophy, art, science, and political life. The aspect of their civilization that intrigues me the most is their mythology, which pervaded their daily lives. Many of their myths date back to the pre-Greek cultures. These people lived in a matriarchal society and worshiped the Great Goddess, or Earth Mother, who represented fertility and the cycle of the seasons and the wondrous mysteries of life and death. This goddess had a consort who was linked with the starry heavens and who became the Sky God, Zeus. The Great Goddess was then Hellenized by the Greeks into the goddess Gaia, and her daughter Rhea.

## The Greek Creation Myth:

In early Greece, the mythology was handed down by a strong oral tradition, until the time of Hesiod's *Theogony* in the eighth century BCE. Hesiod's telling of the Greek creation myth begins with Gaia, the Great Goddess of the earth emanating from Chaos, and thus the world begins. Chaos also births Uranus, the embodiment of the sky, and Gaia and Uranus mate. They have many offspring, two of which are Rhea and Kronos. Uranus devours his offspring until his son, Kronos, outwits him. Kronos mates with Rhea, and also devours his offspring until his son, Zeus, outwits him. Zeus then marries his sister, Hera, and divides the universe into three parts, giving his elder brother, Poseidon the sea, and his brother Hades the underworld, while he becomes the ruler of heaven and earth.

## Hera:

Hera has been portrayed in western culture as Zeus's wife and sister. She was raised by the Titans Oceanus and Tethys, and Ilithyia (or Eileithyia) was her daughter. In Greek mythology, she is presented as the protector of marriage and married women, and most accounts describe her as a jealous wife with a wicked temper and very little compassion.

This is the image that the western world has perpetuated of the queen of the gods, and yet, in my research, I've found that this couldn't be further from the truth. Recent archeological finds now make it clear that Hera *predates* Zeus. She was venerated long before the sky god appeared. It is now thought that the worshipers of Zeus conquered the early Greek tribes that worshiped the goddess, and had their sky god (Zeus) marry the mother goddess (Hera) in order to bring him into the people's new worship. Over time, Greek authors change Hera's role of beloved mother protector to that of a jealous wife.

Before Zeus, Hera was known as the double goddess, the mother, nurturer, and wisdom keeper. Somos was the Greek isle dedicated to her teachings, and her temple still stands there today.

Although the Greeks consistently tell stories of Hera's angry nature, they couldn't hide how deeply venerated she was. We see this primarily in the fact that there are more temples built in her honor throughout Greece than any other god or goddess.

When reading the mythological tales of Hera, and comparing them with the evidence of her superior worship and ancient status, I couldn't help but notice that the Greek men writing their culture's histories had changed and maligned the character and stature of this mother goddess. This led me, and my storyline, to the usurper god, Zeus, and his motives for changing Hera's true story. Their relationship mirrors the fall of matriarchic living and the rise of patriarchy in the western world. Also, it gave me a backdrop to explore the remarkable invention of the God and the Goddess.

## Poseidon:

Zeus's older brother is the ruler of the sea. His wife was Amphitrite, said to be a granddaughter of the Titan Ocean. I found this very interesting as it is said that the Titan, Oceanus, raised Hera. Also, though Zeus is leader of the Greek gods, it is clear that Poseidon is a much older deity, like Hera. It made sense to me, therefore, that the goddess Hera, representing the mother and the earth, would unite with the old god, Poseidon, who represented the water element, and the all-important sea. For to the Greeks, the sea meant life, as fishing was their main repast. Poseidon is as much honored for his gift of the first horse to human beings as he is for being the ruler of the sea. He was called "Earth-shaker" and was always seen carrying his trident, a three-pronged spear. Poseidon was also connected with bulls, which also made me think of uniting them in some way as Hera's most universal image is that of a cow. Both Hera and Poseidon have similar names: Pallas of the horse.

## Zeus:

Zeus is the king of the Greek Gods. He is their supreme ruler, though he is the youngest of the three brothers (Poseidon, Hades, and Zeus). He was Lord of the Sky, the Rain-God, and the Cloud-Gatherer, and his weapon was the thunderbolt. It is said that his power was greater than that of all the other divinities together. In the *Iliad* (Homer's first book chronicling Greek Mythology) Zeus tells the immortals,

I am mightiest of all. Make trial that you may know. Fasten a rope of gold to heaven and lay hold, every god, and goddess. You couldn't drag down Zeus. But if I wished to drag you down, then I would.

Hence, Zeus is mightiest, and he makes sure everyone knows it.

Strength and virility are the two characteristics most associated with Zeus. He is not omnipotent or omniscient, and he could be opposed and deceived. Both Poseidon and Hera dupe him in the stories of the *Iliad*. His bird was the eagle, his tree the oak. He had an oracle in the land of the oak trees. Zeus's will was revealed when the oak leaves rustled and were then interpreted by the priests.

## Hades:

Hades ruled the underworld and ruled over the dead. He was not death itself, but the ruler of the dead. It made sense to me, then, that as a mortal character, Hades must have a deep relationship with death and his fear of it suggests he would embody it in immortality.

## Hephaestus:

The wonderful god of fire is sometimes said to be Zeus's son with Hera, but at others, he is called Hera's son alone. It is said she bore Hephaestus in retaliation for Zeus having brought forth Athena. The story goes that when Hera saw that he was born lame, she cast him out of heaven while in another version Zeus casts him out, angry with him for trying to defend Hera. In Homer's descriptions, he is highly honored in Olympus as the smith god who makes their dwellings and their weapons. His wife is one of the three Graces called Aglaia, but in the Odyssey his wife becomes Aphrodite. Hephaestus is known as a kind and peace-loving god. Along with Athena, he was patron of the handicrafts and supported civilization.

## Ares:

Son of Hera and Zeus, Ares is the God of War. Unlike Athena, who ruled over war as an effort to keep peace, Ares is thought of as hateful and disruptive. Edith Hamilton tells us that Homer calls him, "murderous, bloodstained, the incarnate curse of mortals; and strangely a coward, too, who bellows with pain and runs away when he is wounded." There are no cities where Ares was worshiped. His bird was the vulture.

## Athena:

Called Pallas Athena, she was said to be the daughter of Zeus alone. He bore her full-grown and in full armor, from his head. She is a battle-goddess, but warlike only to defend the state and the home. She is a much-honored goddess of the city, the protector of civilized life. She is said to have invented the bridle and was the first to tame horses for mortals to use. She was the chief of the three virgin goddesses (Athena, Artemis, and Hestia) and was thought of as the Maiden (Maiden, Mother, and Crone). Her city was Athens. Her tree was the olive, which she created, and the bird associated with Athena is the owl.

There is a competing tradition with the Greek version of Athena involving some of her mysterious epithets: Pallas and Tritogeneia. They denote her as also being a very old and honored goddess who most likely pre-dated Zeus. She was often shown with her helmet and shield bearing the Gorgon head, the hallmark of early goddess cults in Greece. A serpent (symbol of the old goddess) is often associated with Athena and is depicted at the base of the staff of her lance. She is seen wearing a breastplate of either goatskin or snakeskin called the Aegis, which is associated with ancient cultural contexts, yet in late Greek myths, it is said that Zeus gave her this magical breastplate.

## Artemis:

Artemis is Apollo's twin sister, daughter of Zeus and Leto. She was one of the three maiden goddesses of Olympus. This idea of the trinity—the maiden, the mother, and the crone—was a revered cycle of maturity shared by women and nature. She was known as the Lady of Wild Things, huntsman-in-chief to the gods. She was thought of as the moon goddess, called Phoebe and Selene (Luna in Latin). In later Greek poetry Artemis is identified with Hecate and is "the goddess with three forms." (Selene in the sky, Artemis on earth, and Hecate in the lower world and the world above when it is wrapped in darkness.) She was the Hellenic goddess of forests, hills, and virginity and was often depicted as a huntress carrying a bow and arrows. She was one of the most venerated goddesses and one of the oldest. She is often portrayed with her hounds, and her female hunting companions, sixty beautiful nymphs. Her symbol was the silver bow and arrow. Her tree was the cypress and all the wild animals, but the most prominent was the deer.

## Apollo:

Apollo was Artemis's twin brother, son of Zeus and Leto, grandson to Coeus. He is thought of as the "most Greek of all the gods." The Greeks portray him as a beautiful figure, the master musician, and archer. He is the god who taught men the healing arts. He is the god of oracles and truth. Delphi under towering Parnassus is the location of Apollo's oracle, and it played an important part in Greek myth. At one time it became known as the center of the world for so many pilgrims came to it. He is known as the god of light for his purely beneficent power. The laurel was his tree, and his most sacred creatures were the dolphin and the crow.

## Aphrodite:

Aphrodite is the Greek goddess of love, beauty, and lust. She was the consort of Hephaestus and was considered the ancestor of the Roman people by way of the founder, Aeneas. She is closely associated with the Myrtle, dove, sparrow, and swan all of which were sacred to her.

## Demeter:

Demeter is the goddess of grain and fertility, the one who nourishes youth and the green earth. She is identified with the earth itself and is the bringer of the seasons. She and her daughter, Persephone, are the central figures of the Eleusinian mysteries that, along with this goddess, predate the Olympian pantheon.

## Persephone:

Daughter of Demeter and wife of Hades, Persephone is associated with the changing of the seasons (she leaves Hades's realm each spring and returns to her mother then goes back to Hades in the winter).

## Hecate:

I mention Hecate last for she is not often thought of as one of the main Greek gods, yet she is an extremely important deity in my story. The Greeks malign this ancient goddess by calling her the goddess of witchcraft and the night as if this is a bad thing. The night has long been the time of women, the blackness a beautiful face of the feminine divine. The moon, also, was a venerated symbol of the female.

In truth, Hecate is the wisdom keeper. She was originally a goddess of childbirth and the wilderness originating among the Carians of Anatolia where Hecate remains a great goddess into historical times. She is a deity-free from the negative ties to the underworld that the classic Greeks paint her as. She was venerated as the mother goddess. She is the protector of entrances (caves being the crossroads,) and is the moon goddess.

# ACKNOWLEDGMENTS

I give thanks to my remarkable family and friends. You have held me through my own journey of healing and awakening. You have been a light in my life, and I am deeply grateful.

To Martin, who has stood by side in the light and dark moments of my life, holding up the torch of love that has so often been my guide... thank you, dearest. With all my heart, thank you.

To my teachers, I bow in gratitude for the gifts you have so generously given. I carry your teachings, your strength, and compassion within me, forever. Thank you.

And to all who will read these chronicles—I thank you for your support and wish you love and kinship on your journey.

My heart is with you.

Julien